I0721272

Gymnopedie

Lauren Wantz

Zeta Publishing

Ocala, FL

Zeta Publishing, Inc
3850 SE 58th Ave
Ocala, FL 34480
www.zetapublishing.com

This is a work of fiction. All of the characters, names, incidents, organizations, and dialogue in this novel are either the products of the author's imagination or are used fictitiously.

Ordering Information:
Quantity sales. Special discounts are available on quantity purchases by corporations, associations, and others. For details, contact the publisher at the address above.
Orders by U.S. trade bookstores and wholesalers. Please contact Zeta Publishing: Tel: (352) 694-2553; Fax: (352) 694-1791 or visit www.zetapublishing.com

ISBN: 978-1-47191-84-6 (sc)

ISBN: 978-1-947191-85-3 (e)

Library of Congress Control Number: 2018939468

Printed in the United States of America

"Ground control to Major Tom,
Your circuit's dead,
There's something wrong."
-David Bowie.

Table of Contents

part 1

Chapter 1

She stared in the mirror and saw a distorted, twisting, aching face that had always hated her and which she had grown to look at as if it were a sin she wanted to absolve. She saw the blue eyes, the blond hair, the Roman nose, and thought to herself that every feature was inherited from the worst barbarians of history, the people who had never lost anything but filched rapaciously, unthinkingly, never once wondering why they always wanted more when they were already much more wealthy than those they stole from. It was a prosaic face, that could not compensate for the Lamarckism of philauty and narcissistic, haughty evil even with the sadness in the eyes, that tried to speak wordlessly the painful regret of themselves, but no one ever looked into her eyes. They were too frightened to, and Laura understood them for this. She was afraid of what could be in them, as well. A shameful history, an incredible debt of violence.

She remembered the Holocaust survivor at the museum. He had not been afraid to look into her WASP eyes, but she supposed after one lived through something like that, one no longer had the luxury to be afraid. He had looked at her kindly, though. He had looked at her as if to say, also mutely, that it was not her fault, that he could sense in her something that was desperately yearning to be good. He was wrong, though, she felt in this moment. It was her fault. She may not have been there in body, but she was in spirit, the heartless Aryan, the one that was always accepted, even worshipped simply, for how "normal" they looked. It seems the only things we ever deem as normal are the things that are truly terrible and gelid inside. And when one thing is determined normal, everything else around it that does not appear similar becomes prey, becomes hunted by the normal as they hold pitchforks and torches in their hands, wanting to burn Joan of Arc, wanting to crucify Hillel, wanting to throw Perillos into the brazen bull, wanting to torture all goodness, and to spit in the face of mercy and drag its holy name through the dirt, while still holding the ridiculous notion in their heads that they were what was right in the world. She thought about the Holocaust survivor. She hated herself even more deeply when she realized she did not remember his name, that she was just like anyone with her eyes, who thought all victims were obscure. She took the mirror off the wall and threw it violently, with a strength she did not know she had, down the stairs.

It shattered brilliantly, a cascade of broken glass stumbling down the stairs like a waterfall of broken vignettes, as the pieces of glass reflected what they could, forming a spiraling collage of absurdity, of variably sized pieces of memory that formed nothing, that were random, scattered, abstruse, like particles in space, the complete chaos that builds the universe with its near total absence of life, except for the human beings, the idols of profanation. Laura felt her head spinning. The friends she had invited over had just left. As soon as they did she had finished off the bottle of vodka they had given her, as well as the entire bottle of Anna's Zoloft. She wanted to vomit but knew she could not, so she continued to swallow it as if it were something she desperately wanted to say, but would not dare to.

She had been thinking about suicide all day. Then Joseph had given her the klonopins and they had made her feel dizzy with boldness, as she had thought all day at work with a great sense of triumph: "This is it. This is finally the night I will do it." And she had felt proud of herself for her courage to at last expiate herself.

Then Anna had come and visited her, telling her she was going to a party that night and wouldn't be home until the next morning. 'Perfect,' Anna thought. 'Then there's nothing in the way.' It had also seen like it was a moment from God, that He, in His infinite mercy and condemnation, was trying to tell her He wanted her to do it, too. It was a strange thought, considering she didn't believe in God, but she took it as a sign.

So she invited Joseph and the others over so she could get just drunk enough for the mixture of the alcohol and the bottle of Zoloft she would eat when they left would effectively kill her. Joseph had given her more klonopins as well, and they made her feel even more strongly the conviction to die. And so she had done it, she had taken the pills and smashed the mirror, hoping she could kill not only herself, but her ego, as well, hoping it would not linger after her.

She laid down in her and Anna's bed, trying not to wonder if she would miss the love and comfort they had shared in it, and she imagined she was in a coffin, as she crossed her arms around her chest, ready for death. A figure came towards her. She briefly panicked, hoping it was not Anna, but she saw the figure was merely a shadow on the wall, but it was not her own, and there was no one else home. Joseph was calling her but she didn't want to answer.

"Death?" she called with longing towards the shadow. It did not answer.

Then it stood over her aspiring death bed and put its cold, insubstantial hands over her eyes.

"Who are you?" she asked. Still the figure did not answer. Then it removed its shadowy hands from her face, and suddenly the hands became flesh. She looked up into a pair of soft, brown, and profound eyes. It was the holocaust survivor, the one whose name she had carelessly forgotten. She clutched at him desperately, gasping for breath. What she did not know, was that the man had already died.

"Forgive me," she begged in a hurried voice. "Forgive me!" But he did not say anything. She screamed.

"Oh God!" she screamed, as she felt the pills eating away at the lining in her stomach. "OH GOD!" And of course He would not answer, either.

Then she passed out, into an incredibly deep slumber she hoped pitiably she would not wake up from.

…But only into a few minutes of this slumber she had vomited unknowingly onto her chest.

Lilith was in the bathroom, staring absently into the combination of rubber and black concrete that took the place of mirrors in all the bathrooms at Gymnopedie State Mental Hospital. It had been so long since she had seen her reflection, she had forgotten what she looked like. This was the most blessed, merciful part of living in an asylum.

She scratched the mock mirror and it made a horrible sound. This sound delighted her, because it was the sound that was always in her head, at last transposed to physical reality. She remembered with the crystal clear clairvoyance of memory the day she had been admitted to Gymnopedie. The man, the psychiatrist, Il medico della peste that had anchored her in, with his long, beaked mask with the round, glass eyes attached to it, how he told her they were going to start her "moral treatment." And then she remembered she stared at him aghast, wondering what the hell had ever been immoral about insanity. Then that terrible, ancient feeling had hit her once again, that feeling that she had to adjust to other people but other people did not have to adjust to her.

They told her she was "emotionally high strung." That is what they always tell you. They tell you not to be emotional, but what they really mean is not to be passionate. People, particularly the sane, are not comfortable with anything but complacency, and complacency was something she had never been able to bear. It was what had driven her to attempt suicide to begin with, feeling a profound disappointment in herself that she had ceased to strive, ceased to believe any longer in her passions, ceased to feel as deeply as she once had. It was not the emotion that had made her do it, it was the lack of it. And what the hell was wrong with emotion, anyway? If not for emotion how does one know they are no longer an ape?

She had wanted to scream this to Il medico della peste, but she knew he would not understand. He had always been granted the comfort of his mask, whereas she had always had to wear her face bare. At least she did not have to see it anymore.

"It's eerie, isn't it?"

Lilith turned around and saw Adam, the janitor, as he, in what was a terrible mixture of both complacency, and just plain abject misfortune from birth that America would not let him fight or overcome, was mopping the bathroom floor.

"What is?"

"The lack of mirrors. Not being able to see yourself."

"I don't mind it."

"I see why they have them like that," he said, pointing to the rubber and concrete wall where the mirrors were supposed to be. "It would be all too easy for a patient to break it and slash their wrists with one of the shards." Lilith thought about this and for a second thought she had seen herself.

"People like me, you mean," she said sharply. "One of the lunatics."

Adam ignored her, but continued speaking. "It's a good thing," he reiterated, "that there are no mirrors. They break so easily, and you know, it's seven years bad luck if you break a mirror."

…It's seven years in Gymnopedie State Mental Hospital.

Chapter 11

Laura stayed in bed for almost a week, pulling the covers over her face and clutching her hands over her ears, trying to block out all the noise both inside and outside of her head, as the boundaries between her private world and the world around her became indistinguishable, making both of them unbearable. As she lay in bed she did not sleep, but she did dream, being unable to extricate herself from the oneiric, yet nightmarish qualities of the imagination, the *einbildungskraft*, that was, after having been ignored too long, retaliating with its most powerful darkness.

Laura was terrified. She saw on her ceiling, written in blood, the words of one of her own poems. She tried to scream again, but could not. Then, the poem written in blood on the ceiling was suddenly being read aloud, in a derisive, sneering voice. It was Anna's cousin Riley, which was strange, considering she had only ever had about two conversations with Riley.

"'I am so tired, death is the only sleep that can alleviate it,'" he proclaimed cruelly. "Jesus, how melodramatic, Laura." He guffawed, and continued his heartless criticism of her work. "Why do you take yourself so seriously?" And he laughed a cold, loud laugh. "Why the hell do you take yourself so seriously? The rest of us think you're a fucking joke. You'll never be a writer. You're not creative. In fact, you're the vacuum that sucks up all creative energy. You're ruining Anna's life. Please just kill yourself, you stupid bitch, it would make the rest of us feel a lot happier."

Laura pulled the blankets over her head tightly, hoping they would block out his diatribe. Of course, Riley wasn't really there. He didn't even know Laura wrote poetry, or was aspiring to be a writer. And he liked Laura. He thought she was a little odd, "not all there," as everyone said about her, but he liked her. He would have never actually done something like this to her.

Laura stared up at the ceiling once more and saw that the writing in blood was gone. She sighed with great relief, but then she looked at the door to the bathroom and saw it was torn in ribbons, as if someone had drawn a knife along it.

"D…Did I do that?"

Anna, who had been sleeping, grunted. "Do what?" she asked, but then Laura looked at the bathroom door again and saw the long scratches it had adorned only a moment ago were now gone.

"Nothing," she said. "Nevermind." She put an arm around Anna. Anna shuddered.

"Sorry," she said to Laura unkindly, "but I thought you were going to suck my blood."

Laura whimpered pitifully and withdrew her arm. Of course, Anna hadn't really said this, she had merely said, "try to get some sleep," but there was no reality to Laura right now. There was not even a world outside of her, the only thing that existed right now was the inside of her head. She tried to cry, but couldn't do that either, as she thought lugubriously how she had told Anna that taking all of her Zoloft was an accident, that she was merely drunk.

She was telling the truth when she said she hadn't remembered taking the pills, though. She hadn't. Nor did she remember smashing the mirror, or vomiting onto her chest. Sadly, and this was a fact it would take many years for her to even admit to herself, she had been planning to take those pills the entire day, though. It was not an accident. It was strange. Laura had never been one prone to self- deception, but she did manage to convince herself, and even more amazingly, everyone else, that she hadn't tried to kill herself with the alcohol and Zoloft that night. She said she was "just trying to feel a little happier, so I took some anti- depressants." And no one argued with her. No one said, "but you took an entire bottle of them." They didn't want to believe it. Neither did she, and she looked at it as a weakness she would not own up to, but she would walk around for years with the secret shame only she knew, in spite of how often she would try to deny it, that she actually was hoping to die that night.

Still, Anna, not out of a lack of caring, but from panic and confusion, did not take her to the hospital the morning she had found her naked, covered in her own vomit. Laura did not need to have her stomach pumped, because she had already vomited, and Anna, who chose to believe naively that this was an accident, did not realize that Laura was having her first,(in what would be a long series, spanning years,) psychotic break.

But Laura was unable to sleep for several days, as her unconscious wanted to keep her up with all the terror in it she had too long been ignoring and refusing to assuage. It was taking it's revenge upon her, by robbing of her reason, by at once no longer blessing her with the gift of consciousness, but still keeping her up for many days- she had no longer her quiet, peaceful consciousness, only the strident roar, the death cry of the unconscious, and it drowned out every other noise, until everything she heard was another facet of this cruel imagination, another gambit of the darkest hinterlands of her mind that now could no longer stand not to be seen, which were, in many ways, like Laura, whose agony could no longer be ignored, as well. In many ways, the hallucinations, though frightening and inconvenient, would at last let others, who really had always found that she was just melodramatic, know there actually was something wrong with her, that she truly did need the help most people were unwilling to give, as they refused to register its necessity due to its inconvenience.

She could not sleep, and as she lay awake curled next to nothing but Anna, who herself had become another one of the many sided faces of her delirium, and as she lay, staring at the ceiling, hoping there would be no blood on it, she felt like many months had passed. Many months were she was drugged and helpless. She felt as if she had betrayed Anna and her family, that everyone who had grown, if not fond, at least *adjusted* to her, now hated her. And still she felt the only way she could expiate herself was to die, but she remembered the blind panic in Anna's eyes when she had found her half dead in her own vomit and feces in their bed. That look in Anna's eyes. It was as if she was helplessly watching her entire world burning, unable to do anything to hinder its destruction. And besides that, Laura was not rational enough even to attempt suicide.

Anna had hidden all the knives, all the pills, and she herself was dangling on the chasm like precipice of her own nervous breakdown, as she was now out of Zoloft. She had caught Laura trying to stab herself with one of her butterfly knives the other day, and just reached her in time to take it away from her.

"What are you doing?!" Anna had screamed, shaking and bewildered, afraid to even leave Laura alone, and she was right in this.

"But, didn't you want me to?" Laura had asked with genuine confusion on her face.

"No!" Anna had cried, and held Laura through shaking sobs. "Why would you think that?' Laura had just shrugged.

Currently she was hallucinating the sounds of sex. The sex did not sound consensual.

Everywhere she went these days, (which was mostly just to the bed, amassing sores on her neck and not even showering,) she could hear the sounds of rape- the violence, the begging, and then the awful silence sometimes punctuated by the briefest sobs. But she never called the police, because she knew in her heart that it wasn't real, at least not to anyone else but her. And also, of course, because she was a coward.

Then she heard more knives dragging across the walls of their apartment, and bitter laughing, the sounds of broken glass, and the most horrible screaming.

"You think you have problems!" a voice called to her angrily. "Well why don't you hear for a second what it's like in my head!" And then the knives continued dragging… the screaming…the laughing…the sounds of broken glass.

"I'm sorry," she whimpered. "I'm sorry, I won't do it again," but what she had done, she didn't even know, but still she felt that, whatever it was, she was ineluctably guilty. Then the sounds of rape continued loudly next door, the soft, pleading, "stop. Stop," repeating over and over again. Laura put her hands over her ears once more, beginning to cry as silently as she could.

From a few inches next to her that currently felt like whole galaxies away, she thought she heard Anna laughing at her. Perhaps she even did.

Laura went downstairs to look for the knives, but found there weren't any, and what was even more jarring, the fact that in spite of this voice she heard castigating her, there was no one there. She sat under the kitchen table and read a book. She looked at the time. It was 4:15 in the morning. She wondered how old she was now.

She read the book, Nabokov's "Bend Sinister," but her mind twisted all of the words until they somehow related to her hallucinations, and she felt the at once grand and terrifying illusion that this book, which had been written sixty years before she was even born, was documenting her madness as it was happening. But the book was already finished, so she read it to reach the end, for she thought it would tell her what would happen to her. She was looking for either death or sanity, or even better than those things, absolution, but she still felt strongly that the only way she could absolve herself was through self- destruction. It was a religious madness, one that had paradoxically struck the mind of an atheist, as a form of punishment. But punishment was all she felt she deserved right now, as she would not protect whoever it was she thought was getting raped next door, as she had failed at everything, even what she thought would be her final ambition (as her other ambitions felt too impossible) to die.

She realized pitiably in this moment that people like her, the painfully introverted, would always be in danger- in danger many times of themselves, but many more times of the society that they were trying to escape for it had never loved them, had never deemed them worthy of the so called rewards of capitalism, with its very thinly veiled implication that the capitalist world did not care about art, and particularly not artists. She thought about Joan of Arc, and began to weep quietly. Today, if there were a Joan of Arc, they would have deemed her insane and numbed all her visions down to mere exaggerated hallucinations as they would pump her body full of Librium. They would burn her in their own way, the modern way.

But Laura was no Joan of Arc, which was probably a good thing, but she had always wanted to be just as brave- she had always felt that insanity could not stop her from being brave, and that it could perhaps even help. But she did not feel brave right now. She felt too weak to live, too weak to continue loving, as she tried to love Anna properly, but often failed. She did love her, though, but she would never realize how much until they were long parted, and she would come to forgive her anything. There would always be another chance waiting in her heart for Anna, one that begged to be validated but which would continue to beat and whimper softly in abeyance. She wished she were like Joan of Arc, that she could have foreseen this miserable future, and perhaps find something holy in it.

But she could not find holiness in anything anymore, not even in writing. All she saw in her own words was her own damnation. She began to write another poem, feeling the damnation was something she craved, thinking that the only way to be as brave as Joan of Arc was to also burn:

"As I walk through the valley of the shadow of Death I begin to limp, unable to walk out of it.

Suddenly I am paralyzed, and the shadow is moving quickly towards me.

How can something imaginary seem so real? And what is wrong with me that it does?

The shadow overtakes me and I am forever in its thralldom. I cannot get out of the valley,
So I say to myself: 'I think I'll stay here.'
As it is, I have no other place to go.'"

'Terrible writing,' she thought to herself, and ripped the poem up. As she had written it, though, the hallucinations had stopped, but in her madness and distress she had not noticed this. She wouldn't realize for a very long time that this writing, what she called her damnation, would also be the martyrdom that would set her free, would be the thing that could eventually make her brave-that damnation actually implies salvation. But she did not have the energy to write anymore, so her imagination ran free once more, baleful and untamed.

She was not sure how long she had gone without sleep It felt like an entire week, but then again, time did not seem rational anymore. It seemed random, erratic, that it did not follow a certain pattern, but did whatever the hell it wanted to, sometimes turning a week into a month, other times a day into a year. She was not entirely wrong in this view, but was feeling, as her defenses against the quantum mechanics and metaphysics that consciousness (but not the unconscious, which was ruling her right now) found logical ways to deal with were crumbling, making it so she could painfully feel everything. She could feel the lack of anything logical in the workings of the universe, particularly its ghost like manifestation, time. She could feel everything the ego, as it was disintegrating in her skull, protects us from. The human mind simply cannot live that way. That is insanity, having to face the truth unarmed.

And it was very sad, that the insane, whom would always be facing terror when they faced normalcy, were vilified so. Few people know but the mad themselves, but there is actually a melancholy tenderness in them, and in their troubled souls lies the most gentle goodness, something the world has always been seeking, but has not been humble enough to register that it can be found quite easily, (as it so desperately wants to be found) in the mind of a lunatic. But this goodness is not considered normal. It has become the mark of madness. Christ himself was probably mentally ill, but no one takes that into consideration, nor the fact that it was probably what drove him to be kind.

Unfortunately, Laura did not consider this at the time, either. She had fallen for the rhetoric the sane are constantly bloviating against the insane- she believed them when they told her she could never be kind, and could never be brave, because she was too ill. What she did not know was that the sane are rarely brave, rarely kind, and that they do not leave a mark on history, but come from obscurity and then go safely back into it, without ever having said a word. There was something in her that refused to live this way, so she had no other choice but to be mad.

Anna wanted to go to the grocery store. She thought it would do Laura some good to go out in public again, as she had not left their bedroom in many days, and she also thought it would help bring her back to the real world, doing something as routine and innocuous as grocery shopping. Laura wanted to beg Anna not to make her go. She knew she couldn't do it, that it would probably scare her to death, because as it was, she was afraid to go outside where she thought she might be justly murdered.

She thought, in her deranged, private way, that she had somehow angered her father, who worked for the Air Force long enough that the Air Force had committed an act of biological warfare against the town of Astrum, the town where she and Anna lived, by dropping an AIDS bomb on it. She did not take time to register that there's no such thing as an AIDS bomb, or the fact that her father was no longer in the Air Force, but these things, this reality which she was becoming acutely aware of its fragility, did not exist anymore. She thought every citizen in the town of Astrum, including herself and Anna, all had AIDS now, and that it was entirely her fault. She didn't know how she was going to face this public she believed she had destroyed irrevocably with her thoughtlessness.

But she went to the grocery store with Anna, because she was afraid to disappoint her even further.

There she was met with the curious, but hateful looks she had expected. There were hand sanitizer dispensers everywhere that people were fighting to use as Laura hung her head in shame. No one said anything to her, but she could see them all pointing, and heard them call her an anti -Christ under their breaths as they walked by. She looked at the flag hanging outside.

That year, a year Laura would try to do anything not to remember, the flags were always at half -mast. One tragedy would happen and the flags would be put at half- mast for a week or so, then as soon as the flag was about to be raised to its full height again, another tragedy would take place and they would have to be lowered immediately. It went on like this all year, until the flags, for 365 days straight, were at half- mast.

Laura looked at the flag now, hanging sadly half way down its flag pole, looking like a symbol of something broken as it blew in the wind without majesty, but with an air of defeat. She thought the flag was currently at half -mast now because of the AIDS epidemic she had supposedly caused. She covered her face with her hands and wept silently once more.

"What's wrong?" Anna asked.

"The flag," Laura whimpered desperately.

Anna shrugged. "It's always like that," she said. This only made Laura feel worse.

She was entirely incapable of doing something this ordinary right now. Every face seemed to be sneering at her, wanting to kill. All the food looked like poison. She had not been able to eat for the past couple days, in spite of Anna begging her to. She just couldn't do it. It was an impossible act for her. This was another reason Anna was taking her to the grocery store, because she thought it would make her hungry again. She did not have even the slightest idea that what she was doing was actually very cruel, that she was trying to force Laura back into a world she was now terrified of, because she believed it truly hated her. Maybe it did. Anna had also dragged her along because she needed help, but Laura was completely useless. Anna would get frustrated at her, and she would cringe at the sound of disappointment in her voice. No one understood what poor, pitiable Laura was going through right now, but how could they? None of them were schizophrenics.

When they had at last finished grocery shopping, they went out to the car. Laura was relieved. She could chain smoke again, though she had just lost her job and couldn't really afford cigarettes. Anna gave her the carton of milk to carry. She immediately dropped it and it burst onto the ground.

Laura looked at it with horror. To her it symbolized a dead infant, or a skull that had just been crushed. She looked at Anna with real fear in her eyes, but Anna didn't notice. "Can you go back in and get another one for me?" she asked.

Laura wanted to say, "No…please…I can't…please don't make me go back in there," but she was afraid to be that honest, so she merely gulped back an incipient sob and barely managed to get the word "oh..Oh… okay" out. Her heart felt like it was going to burst like the carton of milk did, wasted on the pavement, dripping and flowing all over the parking lot. As she walked away she tried not to cry from her terror, even though Anna was no longer looking.

As soon as she got back into the grocery store she was lost, and had forgotten what it was Anna had asked her to get. She then tried to call Anna but found she had forgotten her number, as well. Her own girlfriend.

After half an hour she found what appeared to her to be a carton of milk, as she hoped desperately that was what Anna had asked for.

"You need to call your dad! You need to go to the hospital!" Anna almost screamed. Laura had only gotten worse over the past few days. She still had not slept, barely ate, and had now stopped speaking. Anna handed her the phone. She dialed a series of numbers she hoped were her father's, but no one answered the phone. Instead she got to a voicemail that screeched: "IF THIS IS MY DAUGHTER, THE UNGRATEFUL USURPER, THE SCOURAGE OF SATAN, PLEASE DIAL NINE!"

Laura shook her head sadly. "I can't," she barely managed to get out. "He's mad at me."

Anna took the phone from her and redialed the numbers. She hung her head sadly. "That wasn't your dad," she said. "Try again."

But Laura just ended up dialing the same set of numbers, and reaching the same voicemail.

"You need to call your dad!" Anna said again, this time actually screaming. "What's his number?"

Laura hung her head miserably. "I…I don't remember," she said in an abstemious, haunting whisper.

Anna then hung her head as well, feeling both dejected and scared. "Okay," she tried to say with patience. "Hold on, I'll be right back. Please don't hurt yourself while I'm gone," but Anna was less worried about that than she had been. The last time she had left Laura alone it was when she was working- a whole nine hour period, and when she had gotten back Laura was sitting in the exact same place, staring at the same spot on the wall. The lights hadn't even been turned on. She hadn't moved. It had been nine hours, but to Laura it felt like five minutes.

And now Anna was gone for five minutes and it felt like nine hours. Laura was done speaking. When her father picked her up he bombarded her with questions she could not understand, and she had merely held up her hand in surrender and shook her head with horror and melancholy when he would try to get her to answer. At the hospital they would say she was catatonic. She wanted to scream, but even that sound would not escape her tired lips.

At the hospital there were pamphlets everywhere advertising their hospice care. On the front of all these pamphlets was a picture of Christ's crucifixion, and they read, "Go peacefully with God." At this Laura assumed they were going to execute her. She was very glad. When they stuck a syringe in her arm she assumed it was a lethal injection, and she laid down on the hospital bed pillow and smiled serenely on the faces of her family that were etched with worry and fear, but Laura felt at peace. "Go peacefully with

God." But she did not believe in God. She would go peacefully without Him.

She continued to stare at her family and thought to herself, "I wanted to die with Anna, but my family is nice, too." Then she thought of how she would never see Anna again, who she now assumed hated her because she hadn't shown up at the side of her holy deathbed. She had wanted Anna to be her psychopomp, her guiding light that would eventually turn into the most placid, easy going darkness. Laura had always thought a true lover was really a psychopomp. But Anna wasn't here, so Laura decided firmly she would die without grace. She would be damned to hell without the viaticum of a last look from her lover. She began to weep silently, as she thought to herself if Anna loved her, if she had ever loved her, it must have been very difficult for her. Laura knew very well the pain of loving something that is cursed.

Suddenly she felt her brain was bleeding, and that the blood was slowly dripping from her temple down her face. 'Good,' she thought to herself. 'It's working,' but she wiped the imagined blood off her face compulsively and erratically, until the skin on her face became chapped and raw. Her mother forced her hand away from her face and held it restrictively. Laura began to squirm. Again she wanted to scream, but still could not. The doctor came in.

He would not speak to her, he spoke to her family. Laura looked at his long, beaked mask with the glass eye holes and thought he must have been the psychopomp.

"I'm very sorry," he said to her parents. "But we have to take her to Gymnopedie. No one else can help her."

"Even God cannot help her," she thought she had heard him say as he walked away.

…And Gymnopedie was not exactly a holy word, either.

Chapter III

Il medico della peste stared at her through his glass eyeballs, analyzing her with an infuriating detachment, and one could not sense that there was even a real human being behind the mask, just another doctor living in fear that he would be infected with the same disease he was attempting, without love, to cure. Lilith thought that must have been impossible. How can one heal if one themselves is not slightly diseased?

"You are angry with me," il medico della peste said evenly.

"What's your real name?" Lilith suddenly asked.

"I can't tell you. Why are you angry?"

Lilith leaned back in her chair and lit a cigarette. "I don't hate you," she said gracefully. "I don't hate anyone, I just hate certain peoples *weltanschauung.*"

"And you hate my *weltanschauung?*"

"Yes."

"Why?"

"Because it implies that the world is valid through your eyes only, through the eyes of the normal; through the eyes of those who have never been sick, and who are granted the comfort and the privilege to wear a mask, while I cannot hide the madness on my face."

"I can't take off the mask," he said. "It's dangerous."

Lilith huffed. "You say the world is only valid through your glass eyes, but you wear those glass eyes out of fear."

"You're not making any progress, Lilith."

"You told me to speak my mind, and I'm doing it." She put out her cigarette. "Where do you get a mask like that anyway?" she asked.

"You have to be a doctor."

"I could be a doctor."

"Yet you chose to be a patient."

"No one *chooses* to be a patient, particularly not a mental patient."

Il medico della peste stared at her evenly, though Lilith could not see his eyes behind their glass containers. She wanted to rip the mask off of him and cough into his mouth.

"Dr. Cotton is coming tomorrow," il medico della peste declared wearily. "He will probably remove a part of your colon."

"I suppose I won't miss it."

"And Sideshow is tomorrow, as well."

At this Lilith's face fell. She hated Sideshow. She hated "the outsiders," as she called them, the way they would come in and taunt the patients at Gymnopedie, reminding them cruelly that they were the ill, while they, these spectators, were the well. Lilith supposed if being well meant you always had to be in the audience it wasn't worth it. She hated the audience, and not for their *weltanschauung,* but for their lack of one. She hated them personally.

"I want everyone to be on their best behavior," il medico della peste continued.

"Why don't you ever ask *them* to behave, as well? They treat us like we are animals in a menagerie!"

"Well, that *is* what you are."

"We're not animals," Lilith said stiffly, but without conviction. She was too tired for conviction.

"Well, all human beings are technically animals, and the mentally ill, well, they have a tendency to embody more...*atavistic* traits."

"We're more human than you," Lilith spat, "with your goddamn beaked mask. You're the one who looks like a monster."

"Do you want to go back in the Uttica crib again, Lilith?"

Lilith's eyes flared up, this time no longer with anger, but with an animal terror.

"No...please."

"Then show some self -control. Sideshow is tomorrow. Wear your best clothes and be on your best behavior. Make a good name for this hospital, and perhaps the visitors will not taunt you."

"Last time they threw rotten vegetables at me."

Il medico della peste shrugged. "We are all animals," he repeated. "Your therapy session is over, you may now go back to the ward...You're not making any progress, Lilith."

Lilith went out into the ward and sat next to Fredrick Law Olmsted. His case was particularly sad. He was actually the architect who had designed Gymnopedie State Mental Hospital.

"Kirkbride was a bastard!" he shouted. Lilith politely ignored him. She wanted to talk to him about architecture. When she was a kid she always dreamed she would grow to become an architect, but everyone told her she could not draw well enough, that she was no good at math, and the worst thing of all, the thing they all said that had made her give up much too early, was the cruel pronouncement, "you are not an artist, Lilith."

"Hey, Frederick."

"Kirkbride was a bastard!"

"How did you design this building?"

"Kirkbride was a bastard!"

Laura lay in her hospital bed at Gymnopedie, at last weeping without restraint, loudly, so everyone on the ward could hear her. Gymnopedie State Mental Hospital was not the gorgeous building Fredrick Law Olmsted had initially designed. It looked nothing like it did during the days Lilith had stayed there, sometime in the mid nineteenth century, when Fredrick Law Olmsted was still alive. Now the hospital looked like an administrative building. The beauty of the initial architecture was replaced with sterilized looking, long reaching hospital wings. It was strange how the hospital was now set up. It now had a transept. It was now designed like a cathedral without any of the beauty, but the religious madness was still there.

A chaplain would come speak to the patients, and bibles were handed out regularly along with more pamphlets saying "Go peacefully with God." All this made most of the patients think about was suicide, how they had never once actually *seen* God in anything, and how they had waited their whole lives trying to, eventually coming to the conclusion that one has to be dead to be in a state of grace.

Laura was a little different from them, though. Most of them were incredibly simple minded, mentally feeble, and therefore their imaginations could not reach as far as God, in spite of how they strove for it. Laura saw God in some things, though. At certain times when she had made love to Anna, in other people she would grow fond of almost magnetically, even sometimes in her writing, and very occasionally, in herself. Right now she found God in her weeping, in a long repressed instinct.

A man walked by and looked in at her lachrymose state. He looked like a man she already knew. He looked like her friend William Olmsted. She thought it was him. Immediately she stopped sobbing and her face became stone like.

She had a strange, ambiguous relationship with William. Most of her hated him, but even more of her naively fancied the idea that she loved him. She, even though she was living with another woman, sleeping in the same bed with her, taking all her meals with her, would still not let go of the parochial, Christian idea that she must be heterosexual, and this thing that she had with Anna, she would often try to convince herself was not love, even though in her darkest moments it was Anna she always cried out to. It was unfortunate, though. Often times she would cry out to William, too, and she would soon willfully ignore the obvious, glaring fact that when she cried out to William he never answered, but remained in stoic silence, trying to hide the smirk on his face as he would say something derisory like, "is this a cry for help, Laura?"

This man she saw looking in on her at Gymnopedie was not William Olmsted, though. It was just another one of the nurses at the hospital, another man without a name. He looked at Laura's hardened expression and quickly apologized. "Sorry to interrupt," he said, not realizing carelessly that this might sound like a disaffected irony, like something William would say with his sexy smirk and his "the devil may care, but I certainly don't," attitude. Laura was firmly convinced William was in the hospital with her. It was not that far a stretch of the imagination. William was mentally ill, as well, but had certain ways to escape it. He never had to face it head on the way Laura did. Or maybe he did, and that's when he'd grab the needle and disconnect from his synapses, becoming comfortably empty, having taped the sickness' mouth shut for at least an hour, until it was time for another injection.

It was strange that Laura liked him, as he was often cold to her. Perhaps that was what she liked. But even more so, his cynical desperation, his terrible, ubiquitous loneliness. He seemed to her less like a person and more like the doomed anti- hero in a Kafka novel- like Josef K, charged of crimes he hadn't committed, yet had at the same time, the sin of yearning, the crime of being a man. These are arbitrary faults, what we all have in us, things that we cannot help as God created them in us, and yet He hates us for them. And, poor Laura. She had committed the sin of pessimism, of introversion, two things society refuses to forgive or understand. And all she had ever wanted was to be in love, but she never felt she was optimistic enough for it, and had never learned how to think wishfully. She could only think realistically, philosophically, and love is nowhere to be found in realism or philosophy. Only the love of knowledge, the love of wisdom. And knowledge and wisdom, eventually, will demand all of you. They will not let you love anything mortal, or anything mortal love you. And yet the immortal will not care for you, either. This leaves you with nothing but the cynical desperation, the ubiquitous loneliness, the inability to feel optimistic in love when you only love things that are too haughty to feel.

Laura thought of all this, and wondered if it would ever be possible that she could put them into words. She sighed heavily as she thought she could not, as she did not think she had the eloquence in her to do them justice. Someone knocked on her door.

"Laura," the nurse called, "would you like to join us for group tonight?"

"Group what?"

"Group therapy."

"What will you be discussing?"

"The evil of drugs and alcohol and how Jesus can save us from them."

Laura found it very hard not to roll her eyes as she lay back in bed and curtly said, "no thank you."

The nurse huffed. "Honey," she said indignantly, "how are you supposed to get better if you don't go to group?"

"I'll get better alone, or I won't get better at all."

"You can't get better alone."

Laura, in spite of her dire need for independence, realized somewhere that this was true, but still she had trouble accepting it. And when she would finally get better, she really would do it without much help from others, besides a couple of incredibly benevolent friends she had not met yet. She would do it mostly alone, and she would end up only half healed, but this was good enough. Half of her would have to remain ill if she was ever going to write.

Laura didn't say anything to the nurse, but turned around in her bed, her back facing her.

"Well," the nurse said to her back. "Tomorrow we want you to participate in the positive thoughts group. This will be mandatory.

You have no choice."

"I know I have no choice," Laura groaned. "That's what made me crazy in the first place."

"Are you an artist?" the nurse suddenly asked.

Laura groaned again. She wanted to say yes more than anything. If she were an artist there would at last be some reason for the superfluous, but constant pumping of blood in her chest. But, as low as she felt right now, she couldn't find a reason in their being a reason to live. "No," she said stoically, with an air of finality, but also with a barely covered soupcon of longing and regret that she would continue saying no to this question, as she would be unaware of her own creativity for years to come. "I'm not an artist."

"Well, I'm going to sign you up for art group," the nurse said, now cheerfully. "I think you might enjoy that."

'I don't enjoy things anymore,' Laura thought to herself, but spoke nothing out loud. She refused to reveal herself to anyone at this point. Even if she had known she was an artist, at this time she would have kept it to herself.

Chapter IV

Lilith calmly brushed her hair as the men and women were staring in at her with a bitter, hateful curiosity in their eyes. They were disappointed. They expected her to be mad and do mad things- that was what they had paid for, to be entertained. They threw a rotten vegetable at her.

"Do something crazy!" one of them yelled.

Lilith sighed. "Perhaps I'm not crazy," she said levelly, with as much patience as she could muster, for she had never had much of it, and particularly not for other people, who had never once shown it to her.

The man laughed a rotten, cruel laugh. "She thinks she's not crazy!" he cried, and the rest of the audience started laughing, as well. "Well then what got you locked up in Gymnopedie State Mental Hospital?"

"I tried to kill myself."

"Well, I wish it would have worked, you're incredibly boring."

Meanwhile, in the ward, a woman was screaming and ripping her clothes off as the male spectators of Sideshow were hooting wildly and throwing dollar bills at her. The orderlies quickly ran towards her and put her in restraints. This made the men even more lascivious.

"I'd like to chain her up, too," one said with a leer. Lilith suddenly felt nauseous. How is it that people can convince themselves they're good when they say things like that? Merely because they have jobs and can function in the parameters of civilization, without being civilized? Merely because they were not locked up in Gymnopedie, but got to pay to watch those who were? Is that the difference between the abnormal and the normal? The one who is naked on the stage and those who are laughing at them in the audience? She began to throw up on the floor.

"Someone call an exorcist!" a woman called menacingly, holding a cross up to Lilith's face.

"Apage!" one of the more educated barbarians yelled. "You witch!"

The woman continued taunting her, which made the bile that was crawling out of her throat even more acerbic, even more potent. "If I hold this cross too close to her I wonder if she'll burn!"

"I am already burning," Lilith said quietly. More laughter.

And the nurses and orderlies and Il medico della pestes stood stock still, themselves perhaps amused as well. "Lilith, would you like an anti- emetic," Il medico della peste asked her with mock compassion.

"No, thank you," she said. She wanted to vomit. It eased the nausea she felt every time she looked in the faces of the sane. It was so strange to her, that the insane were given "moral treatment," but never the immoral.

"Douse her with cold water," Il medico della peste called.

"No, please," Lilith groaned, but the nurses were already there with the buckets of frozen water and they poured it up her nose and into her mouth. It washed out the vomit, but she also thought she might drown. She coughed violently and fell to her knees. She vomited again. The crowd cheered.

Lilith looked over to the nameless lunatic in the corner. He had been in restraints for so long that this flesh had actually grown over them. She had never even heard him say a word. She wondered what could have possibly been so violent about him. She reached out a hand to him. He would have taken it in his, as he was so dying for tenderness, but of course the restraints would not allow him to reach that far.

"Aw, look, they're lovers," the woman with the cross mockingly cooed.

"Don't touch him, Lilith!" an orderly yelled. "He's extremely dangerous," but Lilith would not let go. This man whose flesh was too big for his chains, was all she had right now.

"Lilith!" the woman cried, now shoving the cross in Lilith's face. "So you are a demon, ain't ya? Burn, you little heathen!"

"I am already burning," she said softly again, as the orderlies ripped her from the man in the restraints and carried her away after wrapping her in several cold blankets. She shivered violently. She looked along the walls of the ward which several inmates were chained against, crying and shitting themselves. She wanted to reach out to them, but she felt she was just as damned as they were, so what help could she bring? She did not realize that the damned can only be saved by the damned, as Jesus Christ himself was damned, and had to spend three days in hell.

…Of course Lilith had to stay seven years in hell, though.

It was visiting hours at Gymnopedie. Laura was only allowed two visitors at a time, usually her parents. She felt incredibly sad that it was never Anna who came, and she would not find out for another few days that her absence was due to the fact that her parents would not *let* Anna come visit her. Laura was starting to catch on to this, though.

"How are you, sweetheart?" her mother would ask with such schmaltz, sickeningly sweet, like tainted honey. Laura barely repressed the urge to roll her eyes.

"I'm fine," she said succinctly. "I was just hoping to see Anna."

"I'm sorry, darling."

Laura had tried to call Anna, but had still forgotten her number. Instead, through sobs, she had called an elderly woman, who was kind enough to try to help her, until of course Laura mentioned that it was her girlfriend she was trying to get hold of. Anna could have called her at the land line at Gymnopedie, but anyone trying to reach a patient had to have the password, which Laura's parents also refused to give to her, in spite of the fact that she had begged them.

"Your father and I were hoping you'd come move in with one of us when you get out of here…"

Her parents, fortunately, were divorced. When they had lived together it had been like living in a nightmare, and Laura's insanity had taken roots in that home where the plates were always smashed against the wall, the clocks were destroyed with hammers, and the knives were sometimes pointed at her father's throat. But they would always say it was the marijuana that had made her mad.

"No," Laura said firmly. "I want to live with Anna."

"But she hasn't even seen you or called you!"

Laura's eyes flashed. "How did you know that?" she asked.

Her mother pulled the usual trick she pulled, benefitting off Laura's "illness," as she always called it, by attempting to make her feel like she was not rational enough to make a valid argument. Many people would do this to her, though. "Don't you remember?" her mother said with the same false sweetness, and now also a hint of histrionic worry. "You told me."

"No I didn't," Laura said, keeping her ground.

Her dad interrupted. "It's true," he said faintly. "We don't want you to see her. She's a drug addict, Laura…"

"And I'm crazy. We understand each other. We try to help each other." Laura was too weary to start a real fight with them, though, so she would not mention the truth, that it was obviously the mere fact that she was a female that they did not want Laura to live with her the way she did. The nurse came in.

"What's going on?"

Laura saw her chance. "They won't let me see my girlfriend!" she cried, exasperated.

The nurse looked to her father. "We don't really approve of her roommate," he said.

"Girlfriend," Laura corrected.

Her father ignored her willfully. "Her roommate is a…"

"Girlfriend."

But her father continued. "The roommate…"

And Laura could not take it anymore. "GIRLFRIENDDDD!" she screamed, pounding the table that was next to her in bed in her room at Gymnopedie. Her father became still, not saying a word. The nurse didn't want to deal with it. She left the room.

"We don't want you to live with her again," her father said firmly.

"And this is what's making me crazy," she said softly, her voice not matching her rage. "The assumption that my life does not belong to me, but to both of you."

That night Anna had called Laura's mother at three in the morning weeping.

"Please let me see Laura," she had cried desperately. "Please!"

Her mother, who was, in spite of some of her violent, irascible tendencies, a kind person underneath it all, could hardly tolerate the sound of weeping without attempting to alleviate it. That, and she had heard the sincerity in Anna's voice. She truly missed Laura, and so her mother, hearing these declarations and deluges of longing realized that Anna really did love Laura. She called her back.

"Don't tell Laura's father, but I will take you to see her tomorrow."

It was a surprise when they came in. Laura had been expecting her mother, but not Anna. Her eyes lit up, and the pair embraced immediately.

"No public displays of affection," her mother softly chastised, and when Laura gave her an angry look she added, "it's the hospital rules." It wasn't. Her mother was just made uncomfortable. She did not hate the gays, but she had not really been exposed to them yet- it was not something she had grown up around, and it was particularly jarring to her to see it from her own daughter.

Laura and Anna ignored her, though and held hands across the bed. Her father looked away and immediately got up and left, giving his ex-wife an angry, almost betrayed look.

"I don't think he likes me," Anna whispered.

"He has his own problems," Laura whispered back, and Anna smiled.

"No PDA," her mother said again, but they continued to ignore her.

"I brought you some books," Anna said, as she grabbed her small purse, (what she often ironically referred to as a "satchel") and pulled from it four books. It was a couple Kurt Vonnegut books, a Tolstoy, and a Dostoyevsky, all of Laura's favorites. Her eyes became wet with delight as she almost snatched them from her.

"I bought her some books," Laura's mom protested weakly.

"Well, the more the merrier," her daughter responded, and her and her lover continued talking and giggling together like two small school children, ones that often had sand kicked in their faces, but would readily stand up for one another in spite of the risk. They had a safe haven with this unspoken law. Already Laura felt less crazy as she spoke to her roommate/girlfriend.

"Your laugh sounds different," her mother interrupted, speaking to Laura.

Anna shrugged and smiled. "It sounds the same to me." Laura simply laughed.

The visit seemed too short to Laura, but after Anna had left a wave of peace and reassurance swept over her. She felt at ease knowing she still had the only semblance of sanity she could rightfully call her own, the only aegis she had when facing the world that was so different from her, the only thing that was keeping her together in this horrorshow of a *bildungsroman,* in these incredibly painful formative years that were made even more painful by the fact that she was different even from the standard oddness of the day, the incredible isolation that comes with having a truly original mind, that seems unbearable and almost impossible to manage when you are young. At least she still had the one person who would always sympathize with her, even after they parted, her first, most true lover.

…It would never matter that her parents couldn't understand it.

Chapter V

Lilith lay on her bed with her hands taped together, lying on her chest. It looked as if she were praying, and as she stared at the ceiling she appeared like Joan of Arc in the Carl T.H. Dreyer film "The Passion of Joan of Arc," looking towards God for grace in the throes of her torment. That was a strange movie, Lilith thought to herself, but she had liked it. None of the other patients had… Apparently the film had been lost for a very long time, and had been hiding in Gymnopedie State Mental Hospital. It had given Lilith hope, because Joan of Arc was so clearly mad, but her madness was what made her holy. Or perhaps she wasn't mad. Lilith remembered learning that all her visions had come true.

It was strange. Lilith believed Joan of Arc had seen God, but she still didn't believe in God, nor, even, did she believe that Joan of Arc had been mad. She wrung her taped together hands. She had taped them herself, in order that she would not masturbate.

She was a compulsive masturbator, like many of the patients at Gymnopedie were, but most of them were men. Lilith remembered her second day at Gymnopedie. She had found a man masturbating in the ward where everyone could see him, but she kindly ignored it. She would not tell an orderly. The mad are never able to have even the briefest moment of happiness for free. They have to sacrifice more than they will ever own for it, and when they do not have anything, they have to steal it. In spite of her understanding of this illness, the men in return were quite cruel to her for suffering the same affliction. A man may rob for the chance at joy, but a woman is forbidden that right. They said she was "unholy: a woman that even God would not touch." God was a compulsive masturbator, too, Lilith had decided. That was how the Earth had been born, out of one supramundane entity's divine loneliness. And we are not very good company, but neither is God, Lilith thought. She was glad He would never touch her.

Being unable to touch herself at the moment was painful. She could not stop thinking of Adam, of his graceful naivety and unwavering obedience. She did not like unwavering obedience, but she thought there was a certain strength in naivety, a strength she had never been capable of as now she twisted her trammeled hands and groaned as the sweat fell down her cheeks in large, flowing rivulets. She almost thought she should pray, but she had long forgotten how to. Actually, she had never known how to, not even when she was young, and perhaps it was because she never was young, as the mad are forbidden even from the right of youth's brief purity. She remembered herself as a child: Brooding, quiet, sullen, withdrawn, always buried in a book, always noticing everything but never saying a word about it. She was exactly the same then as she was now, bereft of spirituality, and captured in the manacles of her own device. She still thought about Adam, and this made the urge for release all the more dire, and she struggled against it uselessly. She writhed like an animal as she tried to get her hands out of their trap.

"There was a knock on the door.

"Go away," she groaned.

"It's me." It was Adam.

"Please untie me," she begged.

"No. You know this is good for you, otherwise you would have never done it to yourself."

The sweat began to cover her body, evoking form her flesh a subtle, but foul odor, and she thought at last she was burning in Hell, that God had finally made good on His threat to punish her. Punish her for what, though? For masturbating? For being a woman? *For being a woman who maturbates*? She continued to twist through the thin sheets, staring blankly at the cross on the wall. Adam blushed. He would not admit it to himself, but he was aroused. Aroused by her suffering. It was what he liked about her, but still, even in moments like these when she was trapped and helpless, he always thought she was dangerous, and not because she was insane, but merely because she was not like other women.

"If you want I can read to you," he said.

"Go to hell!" she spat.

"I'm going home," he responded stiffly. "I just wanted to say goodbye to you on the way out."

"Is it really a sin to masturbate?" she asked with a wild, dark, crazed look in her eye.

"Yes," Adam answered without thinking. "It is the crime of philauty."

"I do not love myself."

"But you lust for your own flesh."

"My own flesh is damned!" she screamed, rearing up in the bed and her hands, still in their paradoxically praying position, seemed glued now to her heart. She looked like a religious icon, until you looked at her face. There she looked like a madwoman, desperate and without God. "I hate my flesh!"

"Then why do you do it?"

"I cannot help it," she said pitifully.

"Does it make you feel less alone?"

"No. It makes me feel even more alone. I don't even get a particular joy in it anymore."

"Then why do you do it?" Adam asked again.

"I don't know," she groaned. "I have given up on the idea that there is a rational explanation for any kind of human behavior, even my own. No one understands me. I do not understand myself. I am my own animal and my own behavior is still foreign to me, still new."

"You're twenty six and you still can't rationalize yourself?"

"No, because I've never been in the habit of lying to myself. That's why they call me mad."

"Whatever you say, Lilith," Adam responded coolly, unable, due to his normalcy, to believe anything too honest. Lilith's eyes rolled into the back of her head, and she lay back down in bed. The urge to touch herself had at last left, after she had spoken to Adam and remembered what a bastard he actually was.

Laura spent two weeks in Gymnopedie, which, in the modern world, was the average time spent in a mental hospital. They diagnose you without being thorough and give you a mélange of drugs that will initially make your suicidal tendencies grow worse, to a point of crisis, until you finally "plateau," as they call it, and you will no longer be capable of feeling high or low. This disaffected niveau sounded like death to Laura. She couldn't see, without highs or lows, how it would be possible for her to write. So for years she would not take the medication they had prescribed, afraid more than anything, of it taking away her lows. The highs were nice and quaint, but the lows…those were truly exquisite. Poetry was so easy when they came to rule your life, and how does one even feel the urge to write without them?

Besides, the best part of being a writer is when you get really good at suffering, when you begin to suffer with a certain artfulness, a certain nobility. You eventually become a professional in pain, and then pain will not bother you anymore, because you are good at it; at last you are good at something, and it is the only thing you're good at, so you cannot abandon it.

Laura did not realize that the medicine would, in the end, not really change her that much. It would never stop her from being so painfully different. And she had yet to grasp an understanding of how different she actually was, though Anna would often try to tell her, but she refused to believe her. Can you blame her? No one wants to hear that about themselves, particularly someone who is truly different, for they know the difference lies in the mind, and with this difference haunting your head, your head will become unraveled- your mind will take on the surrealist abstractions and hallucinations of hell. Your mind will mimic it perfectly, like a mirror help upside down reaching below the confines of the Earth, into the heart of it all, into the terror that keeps the planet rotating. You will suffer such a longing for your disappointed idealism that you will have nothing else in your life but your creations, and you will often hate them. You will be just like God in this aspect.

Take pity on the original. Do not envy them, even though they have something that you don't. It is not always fun. There is much greater pain felt by the writer than the one who reads.

And the way Laura's mind worked, she was afraid of how different she was, but she was even more afraid to lose it. In many ways, her alienation was what had created her.

Before she left Gymnopedie for the first time, she had to talk with the ward's psychiatrist, Dr. Ubermensch, so he could determine her sanity. Dr. Ubermensch was a kindly old man, asthenic and educated. He took a liking to Laura because she was a fledgling intellectual, just as he had been when he was her age, though he had never been insane. This was where his genius fell short.

He became Laura's psychiatrist for the remaining of her years, where he would prescribe the medication she was at first unwilling to take from his office, and they would talk about books and how her life was going. Laura grew to like Dr. Ubermensch, as well, because he would always ask about her writing, continuing to encourage her not to give it up. "It can perhaps help you better than any of us" he had once said with a faint smile, and Laura was glad at last someone understood that this was not a mere hobby of hers- it was the sole thing that kept her alive.

She sat in the chair across from Dr. Ubermensch at Gymnopedie. He took off his glasses and looked at her calmly. "I saw you reading Dostoyevsky the other day," he commented in his mild mannered way.

"Yes," Laura responded softly. "He's one of my favorite writers."

"Some of his work is pretty grim, but always thought provoking. Is that the way you write, too?"

"Yes."

"Nothing wrong with that. You know, Dostoyevsky was also

considered mentally ill." Laura smiled at this. She had always felt in her heart so deeply that it could not be arrogance, that she could one day be the shadow of Dostoyevsky, that she could perhaps pick up where he had left off. She had suffered from epilepsy when she was young, as well. She was lucky, though. She had outgrown it during adolescence, and her epilepsy had never been as bad as Dostoyevsky's. She merely had absent seizures, which were the mildest kind, but it was still jarring at times: Most of her childhood she could not remember. The only thing she really remembered was not fitting in- her incredible struggle with coordination, her inability to focus, the way they had all called her an "idiot." She also remembered certain thoughts she had, thoughts about death. She was seven years old the first time she wondered what it would be like to no longer exist.

Dr. Ubermensch continued. "What is necessary for curing insanity is that we find a way to rid you of all your unnecessary burdens, and really, most of them are unnecessary, except your intellectualism."

"What do you mean?"

"You seem to have the world on your shoulders. This is difficult, and I sympathize with you, but the world is a necessary burden."

Laura nodded, understanding exactly what he meant.

"You will always be someone who weeps at the things others laugh at," Dr. Ubermensch said with sadness in his voice, feeling genuine sympathy towards Laura and her necessary burden, "but there is strength in this. It's easy to become callous, it's an instinct, and to fight that instinct is another necessary burden, one that only the few can bear. And you are so young, already trying to do that. It's no wonder you ended up here."

"But I shouldn't give it up?"

The doctor smiled. "No. *Weltschmerz* is no great crime, and in fact, it is the root of all tenderness. I just think you need to talk about these things more; write more, explain them to Anna…"

Laura nodded. "It is so hard, though, to divulge a necessary burden. I almost feel as if I'm doing something wrong…"

"The world is everyone's burden, not just yours. Others try to ignore this fact, though, and that's where you come in. Make it so obvious that they cannot avoid it anymore."

Laura smiled. "Okay," she said. The doctor smiled at her once more, a weak, but gentle smile.

"You can go back home tomorrow," he said. "Just remember to take your medicine, continue writing, and talk to people more. Many people love you, Laura. That is nothing to be ashamed of."

…And so the next day she left Gymnopedie State Mental Hospital, thinking she would never come back to it again.

This was naïve of her.

Chapter VI

Lilith walked across the hospital grounds, casually observing the brilliant architecture and wondering how a man like Frederick Law Olmsted, a man once at the height of genius, had so easily succumbed to madness- how he was once near a king, but now suffered like a peasant. She supposed that was what to be a genius was, to be like a God, and the Gods are always mad. She walked next to him in silence. Frederick didn't say much, besides that Kirkbride was a bastard.

"Look at that building," Lilith said with gentle encouragement. "You made that. You made something so much bigger than yourself."

Frederick scoffed. "It is nothing but a chamber of horrors!" he denounced in bitterness. "I just managed to make it paradoxically beautiful on the outside. Gymnopedie is not a holy word!"

"What does Gymnopedie mean?" she asked. "I'd always wondered."

Frederick shrugged. "I used to know," he said grimly, "but I have forgotten."

"I don't know," Lilith whispered, her head hanging low. "It sounds like it was once a holy word."

"Of course it was! Madness itself was once a holy word!"

Lilith considered this and remembered the Joan of Arc film they had all watched. She recalled the scene when she had burned. "What have they done to us?" she asked sadly.

Frederick didn't say anything. He had used up all his words for the day.

They walked across the grounds in a hoard, all of the mad, all of the once holy who, by public opinion, were now demons. Lilith quietly and circumspectly took in her surroundings, as she had always done. There was a graveyard. It was right between the butcher shop and the chapel. She could see the rotten meat hanging on hooks, could smell the fresh blood, as the bells from the chapel rang and the dead stayed still, like a clock's pendulum that has broken and now hangs in restful paralysis. She shuddered. She did not want to be buried there, in between a chapel and a butcher's shop, on the grounds of Gymnopedie, that was only beautiful on the architectural façade, that was a work of art where artists stayed to die.

They passed these things, and Lilith was relieved. They walked into the carpentry workshop. A nun was standing there, painting a wooden crucifix. She was painting it red.

"Hello," she said to the patients absently. "Today we will be making coffins, so those who are buried here can be buried well."

Lilith cleared her throat. "Will these coffins be our own?" she asked.

The nun was not fazed. "Yes," she said without hesitation, "so you can be buried well."

"I want to be cremated!" a nameless lunatic piped up.

Lilith barely suppressed a laugh. "Well, I don't want to die at all," the nun quickly retorted. "But no one gets what they want."

"You don't want to die?" Lilith asked with a raised eyebrow. "But don't you think you're going to heaven?"

"Nothing is certain," the nun responded vaguely. The church bells continued to ring, a loud and discordant ring, melodious only in a haunting way. The nun passed everyone their tools and their long planks of wood. Lilith thought she must already be dead, and this was surely hell, and the devil was a nun and a man in a plague doctor's mask. The devil was a psychopomp.

The nun, Lilith realized, was not who she thought she was. So many people are not who they think they are. Perhaps we are doomed to be consistently wrong about ourselves. Then Lilith pondered herself. All she had ever thought of herself was that she was mad, different in a way that would always make it difficult to adjust to the deep rooted evils of social law, and apparently, in this way, she was right about herself. But how could she be insane if she was self -aware? Was that the mark of the sane, being totally blind to your humanity, your instincts, even when they manifest? She shuddered once again as the bells continued to ring their hollow dirge. She wished she wasn't self- aware. She wished she could be like everyone else who could be evil in a mundane wa, then suppose they were the ultimate good. They never had any trouble sleeping at night. They never had to tape their hands together.

Lilith built her coffin quietly. She found she actually quite enjoyed it. Hers was different from everyone else's. She built it like a crucifix, and drove in the nails were a person's hands and feet could be hammered in. She then mixed red paint with water and splashed it all over the coffin. It looked as she intended it to look. It looked like great, flowing rivulets of blood dripping down. The nun raised her eyebrow as Lilith calmly inscribed the words, *Iesu Nazarenus, Rex Iudaeourum.*

"That is a strange coffin," the nun said with slight disapproval.

Lilith merely smiled absently. "I have a bit of a messiah complex," she admitted.

"Do you really want to be in such pain like that on your deathbed?" the nun asked with probity. "Do you even know how Jesus Christ suffered? Do you really wish to emulate that?"

A manic, almost evil look came into Lilith's eyes. "I like pain," she said.

The nun walked away, feeling as if the girl could not be saved. This, unfortunately, was the popular opinion of the insane at the time, and I think, it might even still be. It is so much easier to give up on a person then to try to help them fight for themselves, and people always choose what's easy, no matter how cruel it is. Most people do not have the strength of mind necessary for strong convictions. Most people are not profound enough to really have faith.

"That's enough," the nun called. "You may all go back to your wards."

Lilith was sad. She had really enjoyed making that coffin. "Do we get to keep our coffins?" she asked.

"You will not see them again until the day you die," the nun replied grimly. Lilith shrugged her off. She didn't mind. She was always looking for another reason to be happy about her own death.

She walked next to Frederick again as they strolled through the grounds. "I have to show you something," he suddenly said.

Lilith was shocked. "You're awful talkative today, Fred," she observed.

He ignored her, but beckoned her to follow him. He led her through the cemetery. All the plots were identical, a line of white crucifixes, not a single name on any of them. It was not death that had robbed them of their identity, it was madness, and even more so, the stigma against it. Lilith grew sad as the bells that echoed through the graveyard tolled their horrible song of a God without remorse, of a God who is never troubled by His creations, who does not give a damn about them. To be so lucky.

DING! DING! DING! DING AN SICH!

Lilith could feel it reverberating in her skull. She felt just as heavy but hollow as one of the bells. She could feel the same song in her, the same lamentable cry, the same horrible melody, in it a longing for death, in it a plea for remorse from a world that has abandoned remorse for the ease of cynicism. Lilith grabbed her temples. Her head was buzzing. Her thoughts were mutilated. She then looked at the carcasses at the butcher's shop. All that blood.

"Here," Frederick suddenly said, pointing to a large mound of dirt.

"What is it?" Lilith asked.

"A mass grave."

"What?"

"This is where the inmates used to get buried, in a big pile of each other."

"Better than dying alone, I guess."

Frederick snorted. "They tell you when you're a child that you can be anything you want. They don't mean it, but it is true."

"I don't know. When I was a child I didn't want to be an inmate at Gymnopedie."

Frederick didn't say anything, he just stared blankly at the mass grave, a small tear at the corner of his eye, but it would not fall. "I never in my wildest dreams thought I would be an architect," he whispered. "Nor that I would build with my own hands my own prison's walls."

"That's just called being an adult," Lilith responded with acrimony. She also stared at the mass grave. "They tell you when you're a child that you can be anything you want, but when you become an adult they do anything to make you feel helpless. I can't understand it. I can't understand other people."

Frederick sighed. "I can't either, and I am supposedly a genius. Intelligence never gets rid of the confusion, and it can drive a wedge between you and other people. "

Lilith nodded her consent. "I have knowledge, but no wisdom."

"You're still young, but you are already lonely. It is good to keep at a distance from other people, though. With them the confusion becomes panic, and then that panic becomes hysteria."

Lilith pondered this for a moment, then shot Frederick a quick look. "I want to be buried alone," she said. "Not on top of everyone else. I want to be buried in the coffin I built, my own prison I built with my own hands."

"You want to be buried with your art. So do I."

Lilith scoffed. "You want to be buried with Gymnopedie State Mental Hospital?"

Frederick didn't say anything. He continued to ponder the mass grave and sighed. "Why do they hate us?" he asked ingenuously. "Does being insane mean you are not allowed any dignity?"

"Apparently."

Suddenly Frederick leaned in and gave her a hug. Lilith was shocked, so shocked that at first she did not put her arms around him in return. She had never seen Frederick touch another human being before. She felt special, different, one of the few people who can keep a great mind company. She returned the hug, and they held each other silently for a few moments in front of the mass grave. For a moment Lilith thought she had seen it moving. Frederick withdrew, attempting to smile at her, but he was too sad, too mad. Lilith could not smile, either.

They walked back to Gymnopedie matching one another's strides perfectly and not saying another word. After that Frederick would not speak again for several days, and then he was released from Gymnopedie, leaving Lilith to live there alone.

Chapter VII

Laura did manage to stay out of Gymnopedie for a year, though. This was also the year she decided to take writing seriously. She wrote and self- published her first novel that year, "Ten Ways to Disappear," which she followed with a brief novella in the same year titled, "A Man of God." Both were works of complete literary garbage, but it was the start of what would be a great, almost obsessive and pathological ritual, that would become her reason to live.

It took her a very long time to get good at it. She started a third novel, "The Midnight Manifesto," but this one she was unable to finish. She considered this a great failure and she deeply despised herself for it. She had hoped it would be her masterpiece.

Her and Anna broke up, once Anna discovered her callow infatuation with William. Anna and William got sober, though, and William moved away, so eventually Laura stopped thinking of him. She met someone else, another man. His name was George, and he, in the end, would destroy her life for many years.

When they first met he would effusively shower her with love's pleasantries- with declarations of an intense, incredible devotion he had supposedly never felt before. He told her he wanted to spend the rest of his life with her, and she was thrilled. She had never loved anyone this deeply before, though she was terrified to show it. She would not let George anywhere near the inside of her head, let alone the inside of her heart, and she would curse herself as an evil woman for how cold she was, but she would come to find that these defenses were justified, because George never meant a damn word he said, and particularly not the words he spoke to women. He desperately wanted them to be true, but they were not. Truthfully, he was in love with another woman just as Laura had fancied the idiotic idea she was in love with William when she had been living with Anna. In a way, she got what she had earned for her mistakes in her first love, who actually had meant the words dripping with sweetness, who actually would have spent the rest of her life with Laura if Laura would have given her the chance.

George, on the other hand, drove Laura completely out of her mind. He made it obvious he was in love with other people, he did not attempt to hide it, and as much as he would accuse Laura of being too reserved, he would be just as callous to her in return, quickly dropping the initial schmaltz that had merely been an actor's brief stage appearance. But still he was never honest.

And Laura loved him helplessly, to the point where she could no longer get out of bed when she woke in the morning and immediately thought of all his beautiful words he was saying to other women. And yet still the thought never struck her that he was just like any other man that lied his way through love with an almost sociopathic grace for a chance of a brief release that meant nothing to him, that he could just as easily live without. She still thought of him as the most special man on the planet, the most tender, the most intelligent. She did not realize for some time that he was merely the average chauvinist, only one with a good vocabulary, and a nature of artificial poetry that women often wanted badly enough to be real that they would force themselves to believe it was. It was sad, though. Those moments when she and George had first met, the scant weeks of their incipient love, had been the most beautiful moments of Laura's life, the most intoxicating, possessing a quality she had thought might have been the last remaining bit of true magic in the world, but while they had been the most intense happiness of her life, they were also the most brief, and they were quickly followed by a long episode of insanity and an almost permanent hopelessness. She did not write for an entire year.

Then she would spend many years searching for a man who actually was the things George pretended to be, for the things he pretended to be were truly beautiful. It had become unbearably sad to her that this beauty was a farce, leading her to believe that most beauty was a farce. She was not entirely wrong in this, but there is still a little bit of it left in the world, the genuine beauty that does not need to put a mask on, and she would never stop searching for it, though this search was unconscious. She had given up on it consciously. She had repressed beauty more than she had ever repressed horror.

She had also lost the will to live, and along with it the primeval fear of dying. This is a grave state of mind, but so is the fear of death. Either way, whether you yearn for death or if you try to flee from it, both extremes lead to a life of misery. The best thing one can do is try not to think about it at all, but that is more often than not impossible, particularly for someone, like Laura, of philosophical tendencies. For them death is all around, even in beauty, and especially in a kiss. Laura used to kiss George with burning desperation, hoping it would eventually finish off its work of slowly killing her. He drained her with his kiss. She knew she loved him when he had stolen from her all her ambition, but was not kind enough to leave in its place the comfort of complacency, only a dissatisfaction so great she felt only death could cure it, the inhuman emptiness, and the ubiquitous thought that her only possible future was no future at all, just a daunting, ineffable nothingness, a mute *effes*, which was disturbingly better than the present. She was a person who had been granted the ability to love copiously, but never to love in happiness.

And, of course George would not provide this for her, either, as he himself was also incapable of it, and he wanted his lover to be just as hopeless as he was, just as without faith in love. This broke Laura almost indelibly, for she was a secret idealist, and love had been the only thing she had ever hoped for or demanded from life, but life had made it sour due to her impertinence of asking of it anything, when it is so often unwilling to give. She had to rid herself of life so she could rid herself of love.

She tried to kill herself again, after a long sleepless night and a fight with George. She had called him, thinking he had already left her. George of course had no idea what she was talking about. "I love you, I love you, I love you," he had begged, but in her fit of insanity she suddenly realized how little he believed in anything he said, that words were a casual thing to him, whereas to her, they should be heavy with significance if they are to be spoken, and especially when they are written. He rushed over to her house to speak with her, but the words did not make sense. She was unable to retain most of them, but she remembered that he told her he liked the way she thought he was such a tender person, because in reality he wasn't. He had chosen this moment to finally be honest with her, the moment where he assumed she could not comprehend it, but the words stuck with her for a very long time, this confession he had made of his cruelty, how he had, in a roundabout way, admitted that he took great joy in fooling her. But she immediately buried this under her psychoses, kissed him and told him she loved him, but this time she felt like she did not mean it either. That was what had made it easy to say.

The next day work was difficult. She thought her co -workers were planning on murdering her when she got home. She did not care. When she got home she not only left the door unlocked, but open, begging these imaginary hitmen to do their job.

She got home and she drank heavily and masturbated repeatedly, through tears, while at the same time indulging the hallucinations in an almost gluttonously self-destructive way. Across the hall she thought she heard George raping all her friends.

They pretended they liked it for his ego, and he shouted at the top of his lungs the whole time, "This is what Laura does to me! I told her I was raped as a child and then she raped me!"

Laura cringed in fear. She did not remember having done this, but she assumed it must have been true. She drained her entire glass of wine in one gulp, and began to masturbate against her will once more.

"Look at her!" she heard George yell once more. "Now she's even raping herself!"

She cried, but she continued. Then another one of her friends' voice popped up. "I've never really liked Laura," the voice said. "But I didn't know she was capable of this."

"She is Satan!" George declaimed in return. "The way she treats her friends is vile! And I've never been so depressed in my life. I'm nothing to her but a sex slave!"

At this Laura orgasmed without pleasure, whimpering as she did it. "I'm so sorry, George," she whispered, wishing there was some way she could repent. "Oh, but there is," the imaginary voice her mind had assigned as George said to her, reading her thoughts. "Kill yourself. Do it now. Please go back to hell."

She went to bed to lay down, meanwhile feeling like she really was the scourge of the planet for not killing herself as George suggested. She heard a loud bang and saw a flash of light outside her bedroom window. She bit down hard on her knuckles. She thought George had just shot himself.

"My God," she whispered. "My God. What have I done?"

Then she heard George's voice again. Her mind had resurrected him almost immediately after it had killed him. He was the disturbed Christ of her imagination. She went back into the living room to continue drinking her wine, hoping it would make her sleep. Then she heard George and all her friends gathered in front of her window. They were singing a funeral dirge.

"Pick up the pills and slit your wrist. Pick up the pills and slit your wrist. Please go back to hell. Please go back to hell. Please go back to hell."

They repeated this mantra over and over again, George singing it the loudest, at the top of his lungs, his voice unwavering. She sank into herself. This was the first time she had ever heard any amount of conviction in his voice.

"This is bullshit!" one of her friends cried. "The one thing we've ever asked her to do and she won't do it!"

"She still hasn't killed herself yet? What a fucking monster."

And then George came in once more, at an incredible volume.

"PLEASE GO BACK…TO HELLLL!"

Laura started to cry. She thought they were right. She thought she was a monster for not having yet carried out the suicide that would satiate them. It was all they had ever asked of her. It was the only way they could be happy again, was to live without her. Still she did not have the courage to do it. Still there was a little bit of defiance left in her.

"PLEASE GO BACK TO HELLL." All her other friends left, but George stayed in front of her window, singing his death song to her long through the night. She kept drinking hoping the wine would kill her. She closed her eyes as George kept singing "PLEASE GO BACK TO HELLL!" The sound was, in a sick way, comforting to her. She imagined now that he was the psychopomp, and if she just continued listening to him with her eyes closed she would just slip into death naturally.

"PICK UP THE PILLS AND SLIT YOUR WRIST!" George absolutely bellowed, and then suddenly he stopped. There was silence for a moment, and Laura thought she really might die at the moment of relief. That was all she had wanted from the beginning, just silence.

Then George started speaking again. "There is no hope for you, Laura," he said. "You have no future, you have no past. If you really love me you'll do it. You'll pick up the pills and slit your wrists, pick up the pills and slit your wrist…"

These were the magic words. She couldn't bear the idea that after all these awful things she imagined she had done to George that he would not ever know she loved him. This was something she was afraid of even when she was sane, for with the deterioration of her mental health always came with it the inability to express herself. The majority of the times she was with George she wouldn't say a single word to him, and soon it would be like that with everyone else, as well. She was unable to speak again, this time not for a couple weeks of psychosis, but for an entire year of it.

She ate all the pills in her medicine cabinet: the Remeron, the Risperdal, even all her birth control pills. Then she picked up her shaving razor and dragged it across the skin of both her wrists. She did it horizontally, though, and the blade was blunt, so she did not bleed that much, and the lacerations were superficial. She was too upset to notice, though.

She lay down in bed and waited for death. 'This time it will work for sure,' she thought to herself. 'And George will know I love him.' She let the blood from her wrists pool onto her pillow, feeling there was something artistic about that. Vomit crawled up her throat, but she swallowed it.

Then finally the bliss of the drug induced sleep. At last the silence. *Enfins muet!*

The next morning she did not awake until one of her coworkers, a woman named Darcy, stormed into her house. Darcy had seen the door wide open and then the blood on Laura's pillow and she immediately panicked, suddenly afraid that Laura's paranoia at being murdered may have been accurate. But then she saw the two slatted, horizontal scars from the razor on both wrists. She sighed, but not with relief. She realized Laura had done this to herself.

She shook her awake. "Laura," she said, trying to be as calm as possible. "Laura, you're a couple hours late for work. Everyone is really worried about you."

Laura woke feeling more groggy than she had ever felt in her life. She looked at Darcy with a true, profound confusion, and tried to lie back down. "Come on," Darcy begged. "You have to go to work. What happened to you last night?"

"It didn't work," Laura groaned.

"Did you try to kill yourself?"

Laura didn't say anything, but at last Darcy forced her out of bed. Laura went to change out of her pajamas, completely forgetting Darcy was even still there, and she stripped naked in front of her. Darcy politely looked away. "You got nice tits," she said, trying to lighten the mood, but Laura ignored her. She was disoriented, in a haze of medication, unable to comprehend reality. Darcy had to help her get dressed.

"I don't think I can do this," Laura whispered.

"It's okay," Darcy responded. "I'm sure you'll get sent home, I just want to bring you to work so everyone knows you're alright."

"I can't leave the house," Laura whimpered, begging.

"I'm sorry, Laura, but I don't really want to leave you alone right now."

"I just wanna sleep…"

So Darcy took her to their workplace, the dough manufacturing room at Roland's Pizza. Roland's Pizza was owned by Anna's family, and they had, in many ways, adopted Laura. They genuinely cared about her, and when Anna's uncle Jacob saw the scars on Laura's wrist that she was too confused and too thick in a state of both drug induced and psychotic delirium to hide, a tear welled up in his eye.

"Laura, do you need to go to the hospital again?" he asked very quietly, in a conciliatory manner.

Laura's voice, in return, was completely hollow, devoid of any emotion. "I'm fine," she said glibly.

"Well, to be honest, Laura, you don't look fine," and he shot another glance to her wrists. "Can I please call your dad for you?"

"That's ok, I'll call him when I get home."

"What happened to you last night?"

Laura didn't say anything.

"Laura did you? …Again?"

But she had already exhausted her ability to speak. She merely shook her head no, and Jacob bit back his worry when he could see in her eyes that old numb, blank look of terror that always meant she was lost in a place where they could not reach her. Jacob went to speak to Darcy.

"Do you have her mom's number?"

"Yes."

"Take her home and then call her mom, and make sure she gets there quickly. We don't want her to try it again."

"Do you really think she tried to kill herself?" Darcy asked.

Jacob sighed. "I don't know, and I don't really want to know, either."

Laura's mother picked her up quickly and drove her to the hospital. She was in the ICU for two days, where she was incredibly lethargic, unable to move, and unable to sleep. She just lay back in her hospital bed and stared at the television, which only confused her more. She tried to read instead, but the words were blurry and incomprehensible. She started to cry with frustration, feeling afraid that she would never be able to read again, which meant she would never be able to write again, either. And still the hallucinations were happening. She thought she heard the other patients at the ICU screaming that they wanted her to leave, so she tried to disconnect her IV. Her mother stood up and panicked.

"What are you doing?" she asked.

The doctor ran in. "I have to leave," Laura said firmly. "No one wants me here."

"You can't leave," the doctor had said. "Do you need me to explain to you why you can't leave?'

This was what the doctor had said, but what Laura heard was: "no one wants you anywhere, so you might as well stay here."

"I think she's getting a little agitated," her mother said.

The doctor nodded. "Well, she doesn't seem as lethargic as yesterday. There's a little bit of progress."

Laura crawled back into the bed helplessly, as she continued hearing the screams from the other patients for her to get out. She turned on the news.

"Oh no, don't watch that," her mother said, and immediately changed the channel. "That's a little bit too heavy."

Laura wanted to scream at this. How condescending it was, as if Laura wasn't already well versed in the evils of the world, as if they didn't live safely inside her skull. Her mother was like this even when she wasn't sick. She thought if Laura stopped thinking she would be better again, that it was the intellectualism that was making her "ill," as she called it. But Laura didn't love anything else. And it was true, many of the things she learned did make her sad, but she felt like she had to learn them in order to not be on the wrong side of history again, as her Aryan WASP family had always been on the wrong side of history, the side of those who are never its victim. And how, she wondered, could her parents say they wanted to protect her from this planet's darkness, (something she did not want to be protected from,) when they had taken her to Dachau when she was a baby. They had lived in Germany then, when her father was in the Air Force. She didn't remember anything from that time, not even Dachau, but she had always felt like something had happened to her there, that in the earliest, most fragile years of her subconscious, when she had been exposed to the most shameful evil of Earth's history, that she in reality *hadn't* forgotten it, that she would never let herself forget it, for she knew the memories, particularly the collective memories, that we as humans almost instinctually repress for their shame, were the most important to remember. This is the way that history is allowed to repeat itself, when we forget it, for it can never truly be obviated. It is always living whether we care to recognize the fact or not, and if it does not live inside our minds, it lives in the present. This was why it was important to Laura to be an intellectual, to be someone who never forgot anything. This would greatly contribute to her depression, but she had decided with certainty in her youth, perhaps even in infancy, that she would rather be plaintive than one who laughs at those who history needlessly sacrifices, or even worse, one who does not think about them at all.

She wrestled the remote away from her mother and turned the television back to the news. They were talking about nuclear weapons. This at least was something she could concentrate on. The doctor walked in again.

"I'm terribly sorry," she said. "But she's going to have to go back to Gymnopedie."

Chapter VIII

Lilith wasn't feeling well after Frederick left. Gymnopedie became unbearable to her now that she didn't have a friend, and the few times Frederick had actually spoken had been fleeting moments that were quite dear to her. She loved his wisdom. She loved the way he could sometimes seem so sane, even in the throes of madness. She wondered if she was like this, too. She knew she possessed a certain amount of profundity, therefore she couldn't be entirely hopeless. Perhaps her mind, even in its sickness, could still do great things, like Frederick had. Perhaps she could build something the world would never forget, and then it wouldn't matter anymore that it had long forgotten her, and left her abandoned to the anonymity of madness.

But with Frederick gone she didn't feel like attempting anything. She would not leave her room for several days. She would not bathe until it was time for hydrotherapy and she was forced to, when they would douse her entire body with cold water and leave her naked and freezing. This was somehow supposed to help her mind.

At last she got out of her room, though, and into the narrow world that was the hallway of the ward, which wasn't any less grim. A new patient was being admitted. Lilith gasped. It was another celebrity. It was Vaslav Nijinsky.

Nijinsky was one of her favorite artists, and she pushed through the crowd of the insane who were pissing themselves freely and staring with either numbness or catatonia at the unbearably white walls to get a closer look at him. He looked very tired. The doctors gathered around him and began to lambast him with questions, but Nijinsky would not answer any of them. He just shook his head doggedly, with such an incredible meekness that it could be mistaken for tenderness, and it actually was. Nijinsky was just as gentle as his ballet movements were graceful. He was deathly silent, but it was a monastic silence, a silence that existed because the owner of the mouth did not wish to hurt anything, a silence that wanted to be blessed, saint like. It was the silence of Heaven, the silence of God.

Lilith stared at him with wonder in her eyes. Suddenly she could not help herself. She reached out to him. She got an inch away from his face but then stopped, seeing he had flinched when she had gotten too close to him. She hated herself for this. "I'm sorry," she said, and Nijinsky smiled at her weakly. The doctors escorted him to his room, and Lilith followed them.

She looked in at him as he sat on his bed. He looked exhausted, but he would not go to sleep. He looked solitary enough to be singular, to be entirely alone, being someone of a brain so unique it was not Earthly, but supernatural… and therefore it inspired fear and mistrust. He was someone who isolation looked natural on, for his super- humanity could not be understood, perhaps not even by himself, and he did not think like anyone else but perhaps the paraclete. His mind, even when he was sane, had never been his own. It had always belonged to the world, even though the world could not make sense of it, and he did not think with the brain but with the soul within him that was composed of centuries of ancient language that occidental values had long washed over with their flood. He was simultaneously the past and future, but he was never the present. He was the ghost of epochs, the specter of time, which to him stood still even when it was ongoing. That was why he could not speak. There were no words to express the freedom and the terror of living in a world without time. And it suddenly struck Lilith how strange it was that the people who express human nature the most clearly are the ones who are so strikingly different from it, that perhaps Nijinsky understood time and communication better than anyone after having lived without them.

And then there was Lilith, who was just like a number of madmen whose messiah complex had failed to make them a better person.

She reached out a hand to him, slowly this time. He did not flinch. "I'm Lilith," she said.

Nijinsky smiled and shook her hand, then gestured for her to sit on the bed next to him. She did so with great delight. But still he would not say anything, he just liked the feeling of having someone next to him.

"This is a terrible place," Lilith said. "I'm sad to see you in here. You deserve so much more than this."

Nijinsky would not say anything, but he wanted to show her his appreciation of these words with motion, and he grabbed her hand and held it. Lilith smiled from ear to ear. It had been a long time since anyone had touched her. The last time was when she had hugged Frederick by the mass grave, and that was several months ago now. "I don't think you're insane at all," Lilith whispered to Nijinsky. "I've seen you dance. That is not madness. That's the small amount of beauty left in this world."

Nijinsky shook his head, disagreeing with her, but he still did not take his hand away from hers. He felt comfort in another human being for the first time in what had been years. Recently he had not felt human at all. Recently he had felt more like the bastard son of a disgraced God, a half super-human and half pitiful, unacceptable wretch. As he held Lilith's hand, though, something of his old self was restored to him, the part that had taken up dancing in the first place, in order to reach out to other's without words, which he had always found inadequate in properly describing the loneliness, the horror, and particularly the beauty. Suddenly, with a quick motion, he got up from the bed. He began to dance.

Lilith clapped her hands wildly in ecstasy as she watched his body contort in what, she felt, was an act of contrition, and even more so, a begging for mercy not from God, but from man. He moved as if he were water, as if there was no place where he could not flow, and no part of the human mind that he did not know, and no part of it which he could not express perfectly with his silence. His motions were ghost like- they were the haunting of beauty, as if beauty were dead but could be temporarily resurrected with human grace, with mercy. There was mercy in Nijinsky's movements. It was a reprieve from annihilation, it was proof that there could be gentleness in mankind, as he performed each motion with thorough precision, but most importantly, with tenderness, as if he were the world's lover, a genuine lover that didn't want to break a single heart, but would mend them skillfully. Suddenly something came over Lilith, a swell of emotion she thought she had successfully killed a long time ago, and whose renascence was just as painful as it was joyful. She got up and she started dancing.

Nijinsky emitted a soft, barely audible chuckle, and Lilith laughed along with him, glad he had at last made a sound, a noise of protest. She could not dance. There was no grace in her steps, but she at last got a taste of freedom in her prison, something she thought could only be obtained in dreams. They danced for half an hour until one of the orderlies came and demanded they stopped. Lilith slumped down on Nijinsky's bed, completely out of breath. The orderly glared at them, but the pair went on smiling. Nijinsky sat next to Lilith. He handed her something.

It was a dead rose he had been carrying in his pocket. It was dead, but still beautiful.

As with Anna, Laura's parents would not let George come see her at Gymnopedie, either. This time it had been at Laura's request, though. She did not want to see him, mostly because she did not want him to see her- docile from drugs and with two obvious scars on her wrists. She didn't want him to know she had tried to kill herself, and what was more, she still remembered clearly all the things she thought he had said to her, the "please go back to hell," that still rang in her ears as it was her mind's echo. Her mind had become hollow. There were no thoughts left in her head, only vague fantasies and the will to die.

She barely spoke in this second two week long stay at Gymnopedie, and when they released her it was because they thought she was stable, not because she was better.

The nurse came by every hour to ask her the same series of questions: "Any thoughts of suicide, racing thoughts, feelings of helplessness, etc?" but Laura knew the correct lies to say in order to get her out of there. And then more questions:

"Have you been going to group?"

"I don't like group."

"Well, you can't get better if you don't go to group. Besides, you might learn something."

Laura wanted to say they did not teach any of the things she wanted to know, as she found with all institutions, but she felt too exhausted to speak, and in fact, the whole stay at Gymnopedie she had perhaps said only twelve words. She just stared into the distance. Her mind, these days, was either empty or tohubohu, void or *chaos* and void, there was no temperance left in it, no milder season, only an abyss that at times could no longer bear its emptiness, its near nonexistence, so it would then fill itself with fire. Her hallucinations, her madness, were the natural process of creating something from nothing, as the universe itself was created, and thus she would, out of the nullity of her mind, create a new universe that was too wretched to describe, though she lived in it. This was why she could not speak. And her mind could not bear itself if it did not create something, even when it felt the only possible thing it could create was its own hell.

And there was no more light in her eyes. Her eyes, those eyes she hated with their WASPish blue, were now completely black, and never betrayed any emotion in them. They were dim and stared without focus into the distance, unconsciously observing nothing. She was in hell, but she would not let herself feel it. She would adjust herself to it as she had always done.

At last she worked up the nerve to call George, though. She called him on the hospital's courtesy phone, and was surprised when he answered. He normally never answered number's he didn't recognize, but he had been waiting to hear from her. "Hello," he said with light trepidation.

"It's Laura," she responded laconically.

"Oh!" he said, pleasantly surprised. "It's good to hear from you."

Laura didn't say anything for a moment, as her heart beat rapidly and she found herself actually enjoying the uncomfortable silence they usually shared together, their mutual half fledged prize, that in the end would not be enough. At this moment she enjoyed it, though, realizing she had missed it dearly, in spite of its awkwardness. "How have you been?" she finally asked, nervously.

"Oh, I'm okay," he said. "It's been an up and down week, but I'm healthy, I suppose. How are you?"

"I'm fine," she quickly lied.

"I'm so glad you got hold of me," he admitted. "Your mom intimated to me that you never wanted to talk to me again."

"No," Laura said in a piling, pathetic voice. "I just thought you might hate me."

"No!" George said in the same voice. "I was worried, not mad."

"Ok, good."

And again the thick, but eerily pleasant silence. "I miss you, kitten," George said.

"I miss you, too," but her voice was hollow, refusing to betray the yearning its owner actually felt quite acutely. It was true, she had entertained the idea of never seeing him again, because in her heart she knew his love was dangerous to her, but she was not strong enough to actually go through with this. In the end, she would always want him back.

"I get out tomorrow," she said with hope.

"Well, I'm busy tomorrow, but I'm sure I'll see you soon."

Laura hung her head. She did not like the prospect of having to go another few days without seeing him. He had been all she thought of the past two weeks. "Okay," she said evenly, trying not to sound as disappointed as she was, but she was not entirely surprised. George had only ever spent one day a week with her.

"Well, I'm at work, I gotta go. I love you."

"Bye," and she hung up quickly. She was still too frightened to tell him she loved him, at least when she was sane.

Chapter IX

"Why do you always have to be on top?" Adam asked angrily.

"Because that's the only way it's pleasurable for me."

"Well, I don't like it," and Adam rolled her over so he was now lying on top of her, attempting to dominate her, something that was indomitable. Lilith struggled against him.

"I don't want to do this anymore," she said.

"Shut up." Adam penetrated her and she put up one final struggle. He quickly took his fist to the side of her head and knocked her out. Lilith was glad. At least she didn't have to be awake for it. It was strange, as much as she was driven towards masturbation, she didn't really like sex that much, though she could almost never say no to it, either. And the times, such as now, when she did say no, were the worst, because her refusal was usually disregarded.

Adam, on the other hand, was self- satisfied, feeling at last like he was a man. Lilith always made him feel like less of a man, because he knew (though he would not admit it) that she was much more intelligent than him. This made him hate her. To him it upset the balance of things, that it was not natural, and particularly the times when they had sex and she demanded to be on top of him, that could not be normal, either. 'Well, no more!' Adam thought. 'She may be intelligent, but she's not a man.'

He finished quickly, then dragged her body back to her room. An orderly walked by.

"Lilith giving you trouble?" he asked.

"Yes. I had to give her a sedative."

"I didn't know janitors could administer sedatives."

Adam blushed crimson. "They gave me some just in case."

"I'm surprised you knew how to use them."

Rage flared inside Adam's gut, making his face all the more rubicund and glowing. He was so tired of being called stupid. So what if he didn't read a lot of books, like Lilith did? He was still a man, wasn't he? He was still deserving of respect. "They're not that hard to understand," he said gruffly. The orderly raised an eyebrow at him. It was a stroke of luck for Adam that he didn't actually give a damn about the patients.

"Well, carry on," was all he said, though he still felt suspicious. He saw parts of the girl's clothing that had been ripped. He ignored it, and tried not to think about it. Adam dragged Lilith back to her bed. He thought about raping her again, but decided he was spent for the night. He kissed her forehead as he left. It was less a gesture of love than a gesture of irony. He turned around and saw a shadow looming.

"Who's there?" he asked with panic. He thought it might be the orderly, and he was soon to lose his job. Then he saw a leg step out from the shadows, trembling. Then a hand, also trembling. He almost screamed when he saw the hand had a knife in it. The face of the man with the knife half appeared, the other half still covered by darkness. Adam reared up, putting a fist into the air, and as he did this the man in the shadows raised the knife higher. Suddenly Adam recognized the man. It was another patient. Vaslav Nijinsky, he believed his name was. Some kind of famous man, though Adam knew nothing about him.

"Are you going to kill me," he asked pitiably.

Nijinsky said nothing, as he always did, but threw the knife across the room straight for Adam's chest. Adam dodged it. He picked up the knife and went running towards the man in the shadows, but he had already disappeared with the night, as the sun was rising blood red and without mercy in its sky, in the nothingness it lived in. Lilith woke up.

"What the hell are you doing?" she asked Adam.

"There was a man here…he…"

"Did you rape me?"

Adam placed the knife on the pillow right next to Lilith's head. "Yes," he said with cold finality. He knew she would not stab him. She did pick up the knife, though, inspecting it thoughtfully, thinking she would kill Adam, but she knew the truth. He was a man and she was a woman. She was an inmate at a lunatic asylum, and he had a respectable job-she was not sane, and he supposedly was. He was protected by God and she wasn't. She threw the knife vehemently to the ground, relishing in the echo of the cold, hard steel bouncing off of the linoleum. It was the sound of blood that deserved to be shed, but would not be, for it was the blood of the white man, which is untouchable in its mercilessness.

"Get the hell out!" she screamed.

"Don't tell anyone. Please."

Lilith deliberately bashed her head against the wall, over and over again, and the plaster started to crack, leaving a crooked, jagged line coming down from the ceiling to the head of the bed, like a disruption of orderly perfection, a disturbance in time, a piece of Lilith's artwork, which was only an aesthetic manifestation of her madness. The orderlies came running to sedate her.

"Who can I tell?!" she screamed through sobs. "Who will believe me? Even you will be able to convince yourself I'm lying, for you are a man, a white man, and can therefore sin freely without sin leaving its stain on you!" The orderlies shoved a needle in her side as if it were Longinus' spear. Her eyes rolled back into her head and she fell back onto the pillow, comatose.

…Nijinsky was still in the corner, shrouding himself with the remaining shadows. No one else would bother to look into what had happened that night, but he had seen everything. He had seen Adam carelessly dragging Lilith's seemingly lifeless body across the cold linoleum floor. He had seen the lump on the side of her head, and the bits of clothing that were torn, exposing her breasts. He knew what had happened to her, what had been done to her, how the soupcon like shred of remaining free will she had was stolen from her, forcefully.

He knew damn well what had happened to his only friend that night, and he planned to avenge her.

That night Laura had a dream. It was about her parents. They were still young, about Laura's age, perhaps a couple years older, and they were taken into a room with a dashing young scientist wearing a long lab coat and looking into a mirror. Her mother was pregnant. Even as Laura slept she got a sense of her own body behind the subtle but growing bulge in her mother's stomach, as if she were looking into a mirror, too. She could see herself as a fetus, curled up like a carcass and blissfully sucking her thumb, hoping she would never have to leave the safety of this womb, because she already knew what lay outside of it, things like Dachau and Gymnopedie.

The scientist brought the mirror to her parents. Now she could see herself as she was, with the scars on her wrists and the nullity in the eyes. "This will be your daughter," the scientist said drolly. "She will be bisexual and insane. She will drop out of college to pursue an inauspicious career in the arts. She will be a patient in a mental hospital."

"Oh dear," her mother said, and her father shuddered.

"Can we upgrade?" he asked.

"Oh yes, but it won't be cheap."

"That's fine," her mother said. "I don't want my baby to be… ill."

"Or a homo," her father interjected.

"That's fine," the scientist said, and he smashed the mirror where Laura's face was and it disappeared. Laura was relieved. Then the scientist grabbed another mirror and displayed it. In it was a face somewhat like hers, but without the dead eyes, and smiling with a cap and gown on, holding up her college diploma. "This will be your new daughter. She is completely healthy and straight as they come. She will graduate with honors from MIT…"

"That's more like it!" her father said. Her mother also seemed relieved.

"But what will happen with the other one?" she asked. "The one who is…sick."

"She's gone now. You've done her a favor. She does not want to be born."

And then the scene faded and she woke up. She was not angry

with her parents. She perhaps would have done the same thing if she had ever had the privilege of being normal, of being someone who can pass judgment on the sick because they are not sick themselves. She rubbed the rheum out of her eyes, pressing her fists tightly against her eyelids. At the back of her eyeballs, where her skull met her brain, she could see the imprint of two swastikas . She opened her eyes with horror.

Then she closed them. Still she saw swastikas behind her eyes, dancing in front of her brain. She felt sick. She looked towards the picture, the picture her parents had given her solely because they wanted to forget about it. It was a picture of her and her father in front of Dachau. She was in a stroller screaming only the way an infant or a madman can, screaming like a lost and deranged soul, abandoned by the rest of the world that likes to turn away from grief coldly, unable to look it in the eye. Her father was behind her, a pale, grim look on his face, as if he had also seen something he wished he never had.

And then behind them was the towering wall of barbed wire and the furnace.

She had shown this picture to her psychiatrist because she appreciated how surreal it was, and she wanted to explain to him that this was how her mind worked, in the abstractions of horror. Ubermensch had not understood, and kept her for further observation.

Laura shuddered as she looked at the picture. She did not want to think about it, but she felt this was the only way she could get the swastikas out of her mind, if she could reach back into some buried and forgotten hollow and remember the silent, but ear splitting screams she had heard that day, the howling dust of thousands of the dead, the *habal de garmin*, "the breath of the bones," and the resurrection of pain she must have witnessed like a contorting shadow on the walls, looming over the tomb of the nameless. She tried to remember this so she could feel human again, as recently she could not even feel compassion towards herself, as recently she had become an animal's corpse.

She closed her eyes. Still the swastikas were there. She screamed, but quietly, looking around for something she could gauge her eyes out with. She tried using the edges of her bedside table. Nothing. Just a faint bruise on both of her eyelids. The nurse walked in.

"You're leaving tomorrow," he said curtly. "But until then you should join us for group."

Laura groaned, but nodded her consent. Luckily the nurse had not noticed the bruises on her eyelids.

She got out of bed with trepidation, feeling unhappily deathless, never willing to come to terms with her artificial *athanasia.* She did not want to live forever. She did not even want to live another day, but she looked past her misery to her future and she saw an emptiness that would not end, an infinity with nothing in it, just words that got sucked back into the mouth like void they came from. And perhaps not even that. Laura thought she was never going to write again. She had decided that the mere idea of it was hopeless, and that she had no talent- that she had been fooling herself whenever she had decided she was a creative person. She now thought she was the opposite. She thought she was the vacuum that ended all creativity, which turned passion into a void. She felt like this because everyone she'd dated, Anna and George, were both creative, and both of them, in the course of being with her, had also lost sight of their art. Laura felt like a monster for this. She felt like some kind of emotional tyrant, like a succubus of ambition.

She did not take into account that Anna and George were also depressive characters, who, like Laura, could easily lose ambition, as ambition lives in some hearts, but merely haunts others. And then those it does not touch at all, those are the lucky ones. Lucky, but lifeless.

Laura walked the circular hallway, or "ward" of Gymnopedie, each direction it took being a dead end. Her heart, she thought, worked in the same cycle, and this was her *athanasia*. This was why she would not die, because she had a Sisyphean, ouroboros shaped routine that barely held her world from falling into abysmal depths she would have preferred over the way she lived now, just like a clock, middling, anxious, and cyclical. She would die every night just to wake up alive again in the morning to restart a quotidian set of hours that were identical to the ones that preceded, and identical to the ones that followed, like an endless mistake, repeated punctually over every twenty four hour period, when it would make so much more sense to die and cease this rote of oblivion and mindlessly forgetting in order to get by.

She paced the circular ward numbly, almost running into the walls that very closely confined her like a rat in a labyrinth, but a simple labyrinth, one that doesn't lead anywhere yet still goes on forever even with its enclosed finitude. She sighed at the thought of this. This was her whole life, pacing around a small, circular hallway, imprisoned to the same faces, imprisoned to the act of waking up daily with the same diseased brain. Life felt so limited to her, like a journey that is short, leading nowhere, but still exhausting in spite of the brief distance from the first hour to the last. Such a small space to travel, while you are merely a speck of dust in the cosmic year, a subatomic particle with a half-life.

Not even that. A quarter life, and still that is too much. And here we are, all walking around only half alive with the rest of us dying.

The Anpin twins were staring at her. Their names were Zeir and Erich, one of them having a small, petite, and gentle face, while the other had a long, fathomless, and haunted one. Other than that they looked exactly the same. They stared at her, reading her thoughts. They knew she hated the ward, and she would rather be in her bedroom, reading about them. They both gave her an identical, eerie smile, and walked past her holding hands, inseparable. Laura tried to think nothing of it, but that long face with its valleys and shadows, and the invisible notion of echoes running along its lines of premature age. It was an image she could often not get out of her head. It seemed like four faces in one; one for each direction, staring across light years, across the dimensions of universes, which lie far beyond the realm of time, and across the distance of the universe itself, which is limited. And at last, staring into the void of infinity, the void we came from, and which granted us death as asylum. Laura shuddered. 'To have a face like that,' she thought to herself, 'a face like the face of God. A face that is mired in ugliness, and cannot separate itself from the world.'

…She tried to ignore the strange thought in her mind with its ever increasing rapidity that it was not a face, but a mirror. She hated mirrors, as the pitiless depths that scared her the most were the ones she could look at within herself.

We are created from the random particles of the universe, and the universe was created from nothing. This nothingness is in us, as well. That is why we are all so empty.

Chapter X

The next day Laura got out. The first thing she wanted to do when her mother picked her up was go to the library. She knew in her heart that she was not ready for the real world yet, so she wanted to go to the place she had loved since she was a child, because it seemed so much like the *opposite* of the real world. It was always quiet there, and learning didn't come at such a terrible price as it did everywhere else. At the library it was free, natural and yet supernatural at the same time, but with a quiet grace in its strangeness, unlike anything inside Laura's head, where the numerous oddities screamed as if in torment after having been kept behind her eye sockets for too long without ever coming out of her mouth. The library was an exotic place, exotic without the terror.

Laura would often go to the library and wish her brain was the same as it was: packed full of information, of stories and manifestoes, of ancient woes and intricacies, but still organized and peaceful. Her mind only possessed the former- a half knowledge of a half universe, but it was organized like the universe, as well, like an aleatory hell with only empty blackness enveloping it, which was often times the only thing in her head that made sense, but which scared her just the same-the thought that in her quest to know everything she was merely learning more about the depths of nothing. She shuddered and tried to breathe in the comfort of organized *episteme* she could not obtain herself, but it was different now. She did not feel the same magic she always had. It, like enlightenment and its brevity in the mind, had already faded, swung like a pendulum back into the chaos, the lack of order, the lack of sense. The timelessness of the library, she thought, was now marked by time just like everything else, and would one day be ancient and incomprehensible, just like the books and the language they were written in. Now, even in her place of solace, the entropy was still all around.

She tried not to think about it and immediately gravitated towards the foreign film section, as she always did. She picked out another Jean Luc Godard movie. There was always another Jean Luc Godard movie at this library. It had several works of all the great foreign directors: Bresson, Fellini, Bergman, Michelangelo Antonioni, Jean Cocteau, Luis Bunuel…Carl T. H. Dreyer. She had picked Godard today, though, and the film "Vivre sa Vie." As she picked it up and inspected it in her small hands suddenly the magic was back, then faded just as quickly, but at least she had felt it for a moment, and briefly the memory of art came back to her, and the thought that really, though she would not assign herself any purpose at the moment while her mind was forcing its solipsism on her entire being, that she was really quite devoted to art, and for a moment she even thought it was the sole reason she lived, but this thought quickly faded as well as she also remembered living never has a reason.

She went back home with her mother, who would not let her be alone at the moment, even though it was Laura's implicit wish to be so, but her mother had never understood this. She took Laura's near pathological need for solitude as a part of her illness, and believed it made her worse. She thought it was unhealthy that Laura lived alone, and she would soon do everything within her power to encroach upon her monastic lifestyle, which, in the end, would make Laura feel trapped, helpless, and more than anything else, insane. And she wanted to scream at the top of her lungs to her parents, to Dr. Ubermensch, to her co -workers, and even, to George: "I am not insane, I'm just not like you."

So she watched Vivre sa Vie with her mother, who criticized it the whole time, while giving Laura side long, disturbed looks, as if Laura had done something unspeakable by merely watching it.

"This is horrible," her mother said. "I hate this."

"Well, you're free to leave," Laura grumbled.

"What was that?"

A long, agonized sigh. "Nothing."

"I don't understand what's going on in this movie."

"I can explain it to you."

"You mean you think this makes *sense?*"

Laura sighed and tried to tune her mother out when it got to the part in the film where Nana goes to see "The Passion of Joan of Arc." Laura raised an eyebrow. The title of that film stirred something in her, as if she recognized it, and had some knowledge of it which had been forgotten, but not enough to where it did not incite vague phantoms within her.

She watched Nana as Nana watched "The Passion of Joan of Arc," both sets of eyes being completely glued to what they were seeing, the woman who was playing Joan of arc on the screen being filmed within the screen where Laura was watching; The way her hair was so short, and her eyes almost filled with tears, but not quite, and the way she seemed so mad, but at the same time, so pure, as she constantly looked up to the sky to God. And for a moment Laura even wondered if madness really *was* pure, a thought she could perhaps never discuss with a sane person. It would not be something they could ever wrap their heads around, considering what they had been taught. On the screen Nana was crying. So was Joan of Arc, and Laura felt a tear roll down her face, as well.

She looked up the film on her phone, found out that it was directed by a man named Carl T.H. Dreyer. She also found out that it was lost for many years, until it was found again, in a mental hospital. The article would not say which mental hospital, but Laura already knew. It was somewhere in a memory that existed before she did, but had still found its way into her mind, and had still emerged past the fog of decades to be remembered again. It was what Plato called *anamnesis*. Laura knew the mental hospital the film had been found in was Gymnopedie.

She laughed to herself, quietly enough that her mother could not hear her.

"So this has happened to me before."

Lilith and Nijinsky sat quietly, watching The Passion of Joan of Arc. Nijinsky had never seen it before, or at had at least so indicated by the shake of his head. Now he was completely absorbed by it, in rapture. He saw the way Joan of Arc always looked skyward, and immediately imitated it, but not in mockery, in wonder.

Then they got to the scene where she was burned. Nijinsky watched her mouth gape in screaming, but the whole time still looking towards God. Then it was over, just like that, as if it had never happened. Nijinsky stood up, a sad look in his eyes, but a smile on his face. He started dancing, with eyes looking at the sky, begging for mercy, but also in a silent, undemanding appreciation of God.

He contorted the way a person who is burning alive contorts, and Lilith gasped as she actually saw flames begin to gather at his feet. Nijinsky, without looking her in the eye, as he was still making his upward supplication, while at the same time, holding both hands, palms upwards toward the ground where the flames were, motioned for her to be silent. The flames danced and he danced within them, always looking at God, not seeming to mind that he was burning.

Lilith vaguely remembered something she had read somewhere, something she could not place, but which at the same time devoured her with shocking clarity. She remembered a passage in a book, that said something like, "Heaven and hell are mirrors of each other," or "The ground is the same as the sky," or something like that, for it was still muddled by the derangement of memory that madness brings, but Lilith remembered it the way one remembers a ghost, in a corrupted kind of way. She thought for a second it might be a passage from the bible. "As it is above it is below." That's what it was.

Then she thought about Jesus, and the Harrowing of Hell. She had seen it in a Hieronymus Bosch painting once. The painting had made it seem abstract and senseless, and Lilith supposed it was. She thought about Christ's Descent into Hell, and she wondered if perhaps this is the only way you can get to Heaven, is to burn first, making yourself something sacrificial. She turned to Nijinsky for the answers, but could not make sense of him anymore through the smoke. She could see he was still looking up, still dancing, but it appeared he was stretching endlessly in both directions, towards the sky and towards the ground.

As she watched him she felt herself suddenly lifted off the ground. She saw Nijinsky as she flew upward. His skin was not charred at all. He still looked like a masculine version of a porcelain doll, the perfect martyr, a hermaphrodite. Then she was on the ground again. The flames, which she realized now she had imagined, were gone, but Nijinsky was still looking helplessly but without fear towards the sky. She moved to touch him, but something inexplicable and magnetic stopped her. She trembled with fear as a wicked smile came across his face, and he then looked at the ground, placed both his hands on it, and heaved the Earth. It seemed to move for a second.

Then Lilith remembered there was no sky and there was no ground, nor a heaven or a hell. Just a white ceiling with the paint peeling off, and a cold linoleum floor. They were still in Gymnopedie, a narrow, suffocating world. They could not reach to the expansions of the world without forms, the world of metaphysics, "the soul," with its flames that ravage you, but also guide you through the darkness of the unknowable, as if you are your own torch, a martyr for the ego, waiting for the moment when you can taste your enlightenment like blood in your mouth, at last consumed by it, turning to ashes.

But Gymnopedie was no Garden of Eden. There was no knowledge of good and evil here, only the slow draining of memory into utter oblivion. It was not a gnomic fairytale, it was not paradise, but Lilith felt uncomfortable with the idea of paradise, of possessing anything she might feel she couldn't afford to lose. And paradise is always lost. It sinks under the ocean and can never be found again, it is obliterated by an earthquake, a tidal wave, a war, unwanted by both nature and man, in spite of how man yearns for it, in his soul he knows he does not really want a world where his primitive instincts for flesh will be hindered.

Lilith and Nijinsky sat next to each other, neither saying a word, as they most often didn't. It was an *amour sans paroles*, the best kind. Suddenly Lilith's tongue became possessed with the need for speech. She rolled around one word in her mouth, trying to keep it locked in there, but eventually it escaped. "Chashmal," she said.

Nijinsky smiled. "Chashmal," she hissed again, though she had no idea what she was saying, or if it was even a real word. It was.

Chashmal, the "speaking silence." Such is the nature of madness. Such is the nature of love.

Laura was at work, outside on her smoke break, when the phone rang. It was Anna. She picked it up nervously, unaware of what to say.

"Hello?"

"Laura?" the voice cried desperately.

"Yes."

"It's me." Anna always said that on the phone to her. "It's me," because Laura would always know who she was, and there would always be a certain intimacy between them. As soon as Anna had said it Laura felt relieved. She felt as if they had never actually separated, not really, anyway. In heart, but never in spirit.

"Hey," Laura repeated again, feeling far less uncomfortable with the mechanical act of speaking when she was speaking to Anna. If only it could be this way with George, but he made her so nervous, and they had never been close like her and Anna had been. They had never lived together for years, in spite of the general disapproval that it evoked, and they had never truly been themselves around each other, for George was always trapped on the big screen, portraying a feeling he had never actually felt, while Laura was trying to hide that she truly had.

"I heard you had to go to the hospital again," Anna said seriously.

"Yea," Laura replied succinctly, dismayed.

"Are you okay?"

"I am now."

"I was really worried about you. I didn't think you would ever have to go back there."

"I didn't either."

"You need to take your medicine, Laura."

Laura sighed into the phone. "Okay," she said numbly.

"I tried to call your mom, but she hates me."

"It's okay."

"I was really worried about you," Anna repeated.

"I'm fine," Laura blankly lied.

"Well, I gotta go. Call me if you need anything."

"Okay."

…And they simply could not help it. By now it was instinct, this comfort, this familiarity and freedom of self they couldn't find in anyone else. And they would not let it die completely. It was the only thing worth holding on to.

They said "I love you" as they got off the phone.

Laura spent most of her time now reading, and often the words would not make sense. It was like reading a script from a language one used to know but has half- forgotten from abeyance, and now when she read it was as if she were listening to a drunk man, every word slurred, so she could only understand his speech to point where she had a vague idea what he was saying, after piecing it together slowly in her head. This was how she felt in conversation, as well. George would come over once a week, and she would not say a word most of the time, while he would bloviate about his internal struggles, about his lackluster past that was a faux torment to him, that he refused to forget because the pity it inspired in him for himself was all that validated him, even more so than his intelligence, or his apt artistic abilities, both of which he had mostly abandoned due to a mixture of laziness and the surrender to aging. He was a lot older than Laura. Between them there was a thirteen year gap, as Laura had barely entered her twenties and he was rapidly approaching his forties. But still, this was not where the communication gap came from.

Mainly, it was an inability on George's behalf to understand Laura. He was an extremely perspicacious man, but his tastes were different than Laura's. The works of art he liked to force upon her were usually kitsch, intelligent but twee, whereas Laura liked works of art that could move her and terrify her with their diagnosis of man as a half made beast. These things George generally didn't like. Not because he was not intelligent enough to understand them. He was, but he felt like they were pretentious and overbearing with their hopelessness, and, in turn, he felt the same way about Laura.

She rarely talked to him about what she was reading, and when she did he was polite enough to feign interest, but he did not understand. He did not understand that these works of nihilism and despair were all that consoled her, because they would remind her repeatedly who she was, and who she would someday have to become. They set her path clear before her, and they were the sole object of her life that comforted her though they spared her from no detail of the world's senselessness, but they did remind her that some people will never be able to shake off the sadness, who do not feel terror numbly, but acutely, in constant instances of panic, and that these people have learned there is a prize to this indefinite depression, because it is were profundity lies, and through this profundity, art.

Perhaps if she explained this to George he *would* understand. He certainly had his problems with major depression, as well, though he wore them like a badge of honor, while Laura wore hers like a mendicant's tattered rags, a stigma she firmly attached to herself so other people would leave her alone. It was strange. George was perfectly capable of understanding Laura, but he *chose* not to, partially because he wanted her to remain enigmatic, and partially because he, in spite of his declarations of similar mental illness, didn't really want to be as mad as she was.

Laura was reading The Tales of Hoffman one of the times he came to visit. She read the story about the lover who was an automaton, and she realized with great pain that this was the way she acted when George was around, unnaturally compliant and hardly animated. And this was why the man in the story had fallen in love with the automaton, because she was pretty and didn't say much. And this was why George was in love with Laura, as well.

Some men will always prefer an automaton over a real lover, over the wildness and untamable nature of flesh and blood, because it's easier, and they do not really have to be in love.

Laura told George the story about the automaton lover, and he thought it was interesting. What she had desperately wanted to ask him, though, was if this was the way he had felt about her, but she already knew he did. He would often compare her to dead women. And besides that, she was afraid of a conversation that personal.

That night they had sex, like they did every Friday night, as Laura felt herself becoming obliterated by the insistent drag of his *widerhonlungsdrang* into old age. She would accompany him into the nullity and boredom of growing old, but he would never kindle or abet her passions of youth. Still, she liked fucking him, because it was the only way they were ever intimate with each other. George would always whisper "I love you' into her ear when they had sex, and Laura never knew why, it was supposed to be sweet and tender, but to her it felt dark and empty. As they had sex that night Laura felt mechanical and awkward. She thought she heard something inside herself that was making the sound of a cog moving in slow repetition. He kissed her and she wanted the machine to break.

Then he left the next morning, as he always did, not to return again until the next Friday, and perhaps not even then, as he would some days just not show up. Laura hated those nights. Those nights she would get even more wasted than normal and end up scrubbing the baseboards of her apartment for hours until it was morning with a tattered, unusable kitchen sponge.

George always woke up early. They went to bed early, too, as they usually ran out of things to say or movies to watch to avoid conversation around ten or eleven p.m. And while George would get up, Laura would often stay in bed, even though she was awake, because she could not get out of it. There were times where she even didn't make it to work because she could not get out of bed. George, who should have known how this felt, would often call her lazy for it.

He sat on her loveseat for a moment, drinking Dr. Pepper and listening to *The Howard Stern Show*. She heard his soft chuckle at certain parts of the radio interview and she wanted desperately to be near him, to talk to him, to put his hat on his head and kiss him goodbye as he went to work, to do all the things normal couples did besides just sex, but she knew it would never be like that. She was too crazy.

He left and she stayed in bed.

In her incessant sleep she had a dream. Zeir and Erich Anpin were standing over her bed. She looked at them curiously. She had always thought Erich's long face was a little scary, but now she looked at it and thought it was beautiful, even though it only portrayed nothing, it was nothingness at the moment she craved. Then she looked at Zeir's face. It was just a corruption of Erich's, a compact version of infinity, an abridged, bowdlerized, and bastardized work of art. Still, out of both of them, Zeir was the only one that would speak. "What are you doing here?" she asked.

"Oh, nothing," Zeir said cheerfully. "We essentially have no purpose."

Laura groaned and rolled over until they were gone. They didn't disappear but turned into two beams of light coming in through the window, one hitting her in the eyes, the other in the mind. She screamed. It burned. Suddenly she knew she was no longer a woman but had just become a man. She felt like her name was Judge Schreber.

Her mother and brother walked in. Laura looked at them through gritted teeth. 'Who the hell gave her an extra key?' she asked herself. She got up to use the bathroom. She stood up over the toilet and unzipped her pants. She screamed. There was no penis there.

"Where's my dick?!" she screamed, groping mid-air for the missing phallus.

"Excuse me?" her mother asked.

"Where's my dick?!" she screamed again. "I'm trying to piss, but my dick is gone!"

Quickly her mother called her father and she was rushed to the hospital. "Where are you taking me?" she asked with fear in her voice.

"To the doctor," he mother said sweetly, talking to her as if she were a child. "They're going to give you medicine."

Suddenly Laura saw the hospital looming in the distance and she began to scream. "NO!" she cried desperately. "THEY'RE NOT GOING TO GIVE ME MEDICINE!!"

In Laura's mind she thought they were going to publicly execute her. A nurse was waiting for them in the front of the emergency room with a wheelchair made of plastic, and Laura screamed more as he wrestled her out of the car into the wheelchair. She was shaking all over her body. Her mother went to hold her hand, but Laura quickly withdrew it. Her mother looked in her eyes. The look of paralyzed, absolute terror- it was too much to even weep over.

They took Laura into an isolated room. They tried to inject her with something, a lethal injection, Laura thought, and she squirmed and screamed more. The nurse looked to her mother. "Hold her down," she said. Her mother complied while Laura wept as the injection went into her side.

"What did I do wrong?" she asked, her lip trembling from the tears. The nurse didn't say anything. Laura looked to a small surveillance camera that was in this isolated part of the hospital, then quickly looked away, as she imagined it was not only watching her, but televising her, so the whole nation, and perhaps the world, could watch her die. Still she did not know what she'd done to inspire such hatred, but she considered herself lucky that they had given her the lethal injection instead of hanging her.

Then the nurse and her parents left. *Enfins seul!* She huddled up her legs to her chest and stared numbly at the wall. The voices persisted. She thought every person who lived in the city of Astrum, where she lived, was in the waiting room, cutting themselves. She heard a voice she did not know.

"We're gonna fill this hospital with blood," he said as he dragged the razor over the same wound that was already bleeding profusely even as the nurse was trying to dress the wound. "And what's more, we all have HIV." Then a horrible, nasally laugh, and the continued sound of blunt steel dragging across flesh, a symphony of razors. Laura trembled. 'This is what I've done wrong,' she thought to herself. 'This is the revolt I've caused…No wonder they executed me.'

She heard the sound of innocent mothers with innocent children trying to get out of the hospital, but the other men and women who were openly bleeding would not let them leave, and the level of blood that was dripping onto the white linoleum floors had turned into a flood that was ankle high. You could not walk through the hospital without trudging through it, hoping you didn't have any open wounds the blood could mix into. The hospital was quickly condemned. A nurse said over the loudspeaker, "You will never be able to leave. We're all going to die here, slowly."

Laura threw the thin blanket over her head and wished the chemicals from the lethal injection would work faster. The things science does for us these days. And then she saw herself on a television screen, huddled like a fetus, and then a shot to the denizens of Astrum, who were cut in ribbons, laughing as they were bleeding. The blood level had gone from ankle high to waist high. "We're gonna drown!" a woman screamed.

"Yes," another voice that Laura did not recognize said. "We're all going to drown in blood." Then the same horrible raucous, nasally laugh, the laugh of death as it mocks us every day. A child began screaming, and Laura covered her hands over her ears.

The hospital staff left Laura alone in that isolated room for hours, as she was on the edge of the bed, expectant with fear, waiting any moment for the deluge of blood, which she thought had filled the hospital by now, to come crashing into her bourgeois little room, and the blood would fill her mouth, nose, and eyes until she could not breathe or see, surrounded by the other corpses in the river of tainted *sang*. She trembled, looking to the door for when the blood would burst in. Another nurse walked in.

"We're going to need a urine sample from you."

Laura responded in a language even she did not know, some ancient *ursprache*, Adamic, probably.

"What was that?" the nurse asked. Laura shrugged and pissed into the cup.

Shortly after that the ambulance at last took her to Gymnopedie. In the ambulance they asked her the same barrage of questions they always did: "Do you have a heart problem?" "Do you have epilepsy?" "Has anyone in your family suffered a similar experience?" Laura barely answered these questions, but simply nodded or shook her head to indicate yes and no.

When they got to Gymnopedie she immediately lay down in bed, because she had not slept the night before. Zeir and Erich Anpin looked into her room, Zeir smiling his usual freakish, empty, and forced smile, while Erich's face remained stoic as always. They left a bouquet of flowers on her chest. She grasped the flowers with both hands folded over her chest and lay as still as she possibly could. Her art didn't imitate life, it imitated death. She was still frightened. She thought the hospital was full of man sized spiders they were locking her in with so they could eat her alive.

She realized she smelled bad, very bad. But she was too tired to take a shower. She tried to sleep, so when the spiders ate her at least she would not be awake for it. She closed her eyes and waited.

Chapter XI

Lilith walked through the ward despondently. She had an appointment with an *Il Medico della Peste*, and she was not particularly glad about it. She didn't feel like any of them had a cure, just hideous masks Maybe there was no cure, and if anyone had it they would have to be sick themselves. Someone like Geread de Nerval, or Judge Schreber, they perhaps had the cure. But not *Il Medico della Peste.* How can you heal something you are frightened of? Lilith wondered about this and thought perhaps this was why she had done no good to other human beings, as well, because she was and always had been, afraid of them. Even more than they were afraid of her. She was like a spider. People would scream when they saw her, and she would have screamed as well if she had a voice, but she didn't, so she just scurried away rapidly in silence, back to the artistry of her home, back to the thread like noose she liked to dangle off of . Lilith decided she liked spiders. She supposed she looked just as horrifying as they did, that all human beings did.

She walked past Sylvia Plath and Anne Sexton on the way.

The two were arguing over whose suicide would be more glorious. Lilith rolled her eyes. She saw Nijinsky, playing with a cat, and he smiled at her his typically warm and enthusiastic smile. She saw a spider drowning in the bucket of water used to collect the drainage from the leak in the ceiling. She gasped and he smiled at her again, knowingly. He quickly saved the spider and let it out of the window.

At last she got to *Il Medico della Peste.* "Hello," the voice coming hollowly out of the beaked mask said to her. Lilith sighed with relief. This was *Il Medico della Peste* that she liked, the only one of them she liked.

"Hello, *Medico.*" She couldn't see it, but he smiled. He opened up a satchel. In it was a hoard of rats.

"Are you going to induce fever?" she asked. He nodded.

"Well, I hope they don't have the plague," she said ironically. *Il Medico della Peste* tried to laugh, but he couldn't. He let the rats out of the satchel, dumping them onto Lilith's body. They began to bite her. "They are diseased," he admitted.

At first it hurt, but then she became used to it, each bite feeling like nothing more than a slight twinge, a dull ache like her conscience or longing for love that she had learned to ignore.

"I'm sorry I have to do this," *Il Medico della Peste* said solemnly.

Lilith shrugged. The blood was running down her legs and arms, but she looked incongruously peaceful, like a religious martyr. *Il Medico della Peste* collected the rats and put them back in his satchel. They bit him a couple of times, too. "You'll get a fever in a couple days," he said solemnly. "Then I'll be back."

"How is this supposed to cure me?"

"It's complicated."

"So you don't really know, either."

"No," he said honestly. "I am just like you. I take orders from doctors."

"You're not like me," she said with anger. "There is a large gap between doctors and patients." She pointed to his mask.

Il Medico della Peste sighed. "I'm not really allowed to, but if you want, I can get you a mask."

"Why would I want a mask?"

"To hide."

Il Medioc della Peste suddenly grabbed another satchel. "What's in that, diseased fleas?" Lilith asked. *Il Medico della Peste* pulled out a typewriter.

"I brought you this today," he said plaintively. He felt bad that he had the rats bite her, but for some reason he had felt like he had to do it. Looking back, though, he did not know what the reason was. "Also for when you need to hide."

Lilith looked at the typewriter with wonder. "You want me… to write?"

"I think it will help you get out of here. I do want to see you get out of here."

"Honestly," Lilith said through sad eyes. "I don't think I have anywhere else to go."

"Of course you do. The entire world is not in this hospital, only the darkest part of it…"

"And which is that, the patients or the doctors?"

"Both, I suppose."

"Then I suppose this darkness is everywhere, in everyone."

"Good," and he smiled behind his mask once more. "Write that down."

"Take off your mask," Lilith suddenly ordered.

"W…what?"

"Take off your mask. You see, this is what I'm hiding from, people who have abandoned being people so they can become personas. And I hate that it is the personas, not the people, who are always accepted for who they *aren't.* Take off your mask before it swallows you. I don't want you to forget who you are."

Il Medico della Peste thought about it for a moment, then did as she ordered. He had a gentle, timid face. He was young and attractive, a little gaunt in the cheekbones, but with nice, softly etched brown eyes, short cropped dark hair, and charmingly thin lips. "My name is Mel," he said a bit cautiously, but stuck out his hand for Lilith to shake it. She marveled at this. None of *Il Medico della Pestes* had ever touched her unless they were operating on her, removing bits of her colon and the like. She shook the man's hand.

This time she actually got to see his smile. "It's nice," he said. "Not being in the mask. Now, I'll show you how to use the typewriter."

Lilith sat in silence next to Nijinsky, as they always did, and it was an unusual, but blessed comfort. A woman walked in through the front door.

"Another is entering the nursery," Anne Sexton said cynically, but Lilith and Nijinsky ignored her. Lilith looked to the patient. She could not tell if they were a woman or a man, but they smiled at her, a sweet, thin, albeit a bit ironic, smile, and she smiled back. The nurses registered the new inmate and walked them through the ward. Lilith didn't know what came over her, but she got up to follow them. Nijinsky did not try to stop her, while Anne gave her a funny look in her cool, *haute- monde*, superior intellect type of a stare, but she did not try to stop her either.

"What's your name?" Lilith asked the new patient, once she had caught up to them.

"Benjy," they responded laconically.

"No," the nurse admonished him the way a mother admonishes a small child, "your name is Alice."

"No, it's not," Benjy said succinctly, but with sweetness in his voice. "My name is Benjy. I'm a man."

"You're a woman."

Lilith looked at Benjy more closely. Now she could see the feminine characteristics of the face, as well as the obvious fact his breasts were taped down.

"I'm a man," he said again, still calmly, with the sweetest patience, and Lilith felt herself spellbound. She had never wanted to admit it, particularly not to any of the staff at Gymnopedie, but there was something polymorphous about her sexual appetite. It could take many forms, responding with titillation to the gaze of a woman the same way she did as a man, and particularly someone who was a little bit of both. Benjy of course noticed the flustered, hungry look in her eyes. He winked at her. Lilith felt naked under his studied, curious, but politely vague stare, covered by nothing but rat bites.

"I'm a man," he said again to the nurse, but remained looking intently at Lilith. "And I want to fuck women."

That night Lilith didn't bother to tape her hands together. She masturbated, for the first time in her life, without shame. Her parents and the staff at Gymnopedie would have liked her to feel shame, but at last, in this glorious moment, she refused to. She felt it would be cruel if she had. She would not be ashamed of Benjy, because even if he really were an anomaly like the rest liked to think, she now discovered that anomalies were beautiful. To be both man and woman must be to get closer to being the Anthropos, she thought. It must be the most pluterperfect state of humanity, being free of the sadomasochistic dualism of the sexes, to be a perfect balance of both. Lilith had at last found something to worship.

And they will always try to make you feel ashamed of what you worship if it is not the same thing they do, but all they worship, Lilith realized, was neither Godlike nor human. They worshipped the material: money, the automobile, Ford, Rockefeller, American consumerism. Lilith, (like everyone else, truthfully), could not find within her the ability to worship what she could not see, but she would not worship what was clearly empty, either. She would worship the human who had the clearest resemblance to what, when she was a child, had envisioned as God, which, she remembered, had been a hermaphrodite.

She masturbated for the first time with lucidity, with pleasure, and not her usual silent, luridly fantastical abreaction of a past trauma that still titillated her thirst for masochism. She masturbated with love. It was healthy.

Adam watched in the shadows behind her slightly open door the entire time. He was aroused, but at the same time he deeply hated her. Regrettably, this aroused him even more, and he wanted to hold her down with both fists and release his long pent up thirst for sadism onto her naked, unwilling body. She had humiliated him by always being the dominant one in sexual situations. All he knew is he would never let her get on top of him again. He would never let a woman make him feel so weak, and he hated both of them, both himself and her, for making it happen in the first place.

He couldn't tell what it was, but something about Lilith still made him feel weak. Even at this very moment, when she was beaming with glory, pleasure, and long sought after self- love at last achieved in an instant of devotion, he felt like she had acquired something he would never have, because it had never been within him. His hate began to rise. He couldn't understand how someone who knew they were a prisoner could be so free.

Laura awoke and at last took a shower. There was graffiti in the shower stall, it said "Just what I needed: another cold shower whit a black boy." Laura scoffed. That idea actually sounded nice to her, intimate, as she was unable to feel an intimate connection to anything at the moment; at her best, a book, but never a fellow human being. The obfuscated cloud of derealization that followed her everywhere made landscapes change and shift until it seemed like they were no longer there except for in her imagination, which, in spite of imagining them, couldn't find any meaning in them. She felt alienated from her own creations, and everything around her took on a certain *jamais vu* quality that made her surroundings impossible to comprehend or relate to. She could not even understand herself these days, whom she felt was too empty and deranged for explanation. She could not reify herself, or the world around her that seemed *au hazard* in its blind groping of chance.

She inspected her body numbly. She still hated it. It was still fat, unseemly, and without beauty. It was a mirror of her mind, which devoured without creating. Even when she had sex with George, it was still just another form of mindless bodily consumption, mixed with expectant, wishful thinking she knew to be naïve. She looked at her grotesque, barely animated human frame and saw it was covered in small holes, bites, she thought. The nurse came in.

"I think I have bed bugs," Laura said as she was coming out of the shower. The nurse inspected her arm that was covered in small, round demarcations.

"Those are cigarette burns," the nurse said mildly. Suddenly Laura remembered vaguely, as if it were a scene from a movie she had watched a long time ago, in black and white, in a different language, and therefore did not feel as if it were something that had actually happened to her, but she recalled without much strength of memory now a blurred vignette where she had burned herself over and over again with a lit cigarette.

"I'll get some salve and bandages to dress your wounds," the nurse said curtly. Laura nodded. After the nurse left she lay back down in bed, as recently she spent most of her time in bed, sometimes sleeplessly, at other times sleeping for twenty hours in a day. She looked at the awkward figure of her naked body and for a moment thought about masturbating, but decided she didn't have the strength at the moment to put herself through such a psychological melodrama. She had always been a compulsive masturbator, but recently it had been taking up all her time in the rare hours where she was actually awake, but would still remain in bed.

Sex with George left her aroused but unsatisfied, always wanting more, always wanting something he could not, or more likely refused, to offer her. It was easy to tell by the way he fucked her that he didn't love her, in spite of the fact he would often whisper it in her ear during this empty but perfumed vision that to him was more like an act of solipsism, and to Laura a desperate plea of devotion that went unheard. So always after he left she would masturbate immediately, recalling what he had done to her the night before with eidetic clarity, but it was always without pleasure, without lust. It was more like an emotionally masochistic act of penitence.

And she would often recall the first time they had sex, when his whispered cries of an incredible love had sounded so real, and how beautiful it was, how cloying and tender. Now when they had sex it felt forced, cold, hideously empty, and unnatural. It had transformed from its initial moment of beauty into a grotesque landscape of surrealism. It had turned into another facet of Laura's madness.

And she wondered why it is that things that are so spellbinding at first eventually wear away into something dull and mechanical. Perhaps it is just monstrous time that robs beauty with the repetition of age, but Laura felt as if the initial thrill of beauty was perhaps nothing more than the briefest hallucination before we are quickly dashed back against the rocks of reason on that intoxicating wave, and we find we are in an ocean just like any other- profound but merciless, without rational purpose. Beauty makes us mad, and so, perhaps, madness is what makes us see beauty. It is a quick derangement of the senses, a fleeting episode of schizophrenia before the ennui of sanity quickly sets back in and makes everything around you comfortably dull once more.

The nurse walked back in and dressed Laura's wounds. Laura wondered what had made her do it, and what was making her so crazy. Her unconscious, she supposed. She sometimes arrogantly fancied herself as a genius, and therefore her unconscious was even more boggled with ancient mysteries and terrors than other, more normal people. The higher the intelligence, the more mangled and ruined the mind is. Still, her unconscious was made of the same things all people's subconscious are made of, sex and death, but, being able to think in a higher realm, it was mass death, and sex not for creation, but for destruction, as she often felt that the creation of human beings was really a destructive act; the blind groping for the illusion of love, the thrusting, the imminent looming of death always connected with any pleasure .

But what made her the most sad, the most angry, was that the id, the constant impulse in us to kill and fuck, was who we all really are, just a sordid group of rapists and murderers, while the rest of us, all the more noble qualities of our minds, are just a pretense used to hide our real intentions we ourselves are not even aware of. We are just monsters repressed by affectations. She became depressed, and as soon as the nurse left, lay back in bed. She wondered what the genius' id must look like. She supposed it looked like the nuclear bomb.

She imagined the big banging noise that was the same noise that began everything, a noise of pure destruction, creating a universe. We mirror that process, Laura thought: out of the chaos of sex, into a womb. She wanted to kill the staff at the hospital, she wanted to kill most people, who she felt only found life bearable because they had never thought about it. Another nurse walked in and she groaned.

"Laura, you're wanted in art group."

"I don't wanna go."

"Well, you can't just stay in bed all day. Besides, you like art."

Laura didn't have the strength to argue with him, so she compliantly joined the art group. They were painting crucifixes today, to bring them peace. She wanted to scoff. Why is it that we can only find peace in another person's doom? The cross is a reminder of an ancient torture enacted by tyrants that possibly killed millions. How could she find peace in that? Why didn't they make her paint an electric chair or a noose? Wouldn't that be just as religious? She only wished that people knew that God is actually a great burden, the only thing we have in common with Him being that we perhaps do not exist, either.

However, though she refused to admit it, she did enjoy these art therapy sessions very much. She made a somewhat irreligious cross. She painted it white at first, then mixed water with red paint, splattering it all over the crucifix so it looked like drops of blood. She painted three dots where the nails would have been, and wrote *Iesu Nazarenus, Rex Iudaeorum* on its top. She wrote other Latin phrases, *Qou Vadis, Domine,* etc., and the name HILLEL in big letters in the center. Everyone, even the insane, looked at her curiously.

"What language is that?" someone asked.

"It's Latin."

"It's very…interesting, Laura," The occupational therapist said with trepidation, a look of concern and unrest being obvious in her eyes. Laura's art often made her feel uneasy. It made the other patients feel uneasy, too.

"Well, it's obvious you're creative," someone piped up, trying to be positive.

Laura shook her head doggedly. "I'm not creative."

"Why do you think that? Because that's what your boyfriend tells you?"

Laura didn't say anything. She still had such devotion towards George that he had practically been sanctified in her eyes. She thought he was the perfect, ultimate human being. It must have been her who was the rotten one.

Occupational therapy was over and the therapist took all their crosses and put them in the cabinet. Later she would get rid of Laura's.

She sat in the activity room, which was really just a small room to watch TV in. She searched through the movies timidly, but she knew she would find it. And there it was, The Passion of Joan of Arc.

She watched it mostly alone, with a few brief interruptions from the other patients who, upon seeing that the film was in black and white and silent, immediately became bored with it, thinking it wasn't enough of a spectacle because it was not built implicitly to entertain. They would have preferred to watch Joan of Arc burn in person, where the fire would be colorful and the screaming loud. Laura was disappointed. She could not even find a refuge in the insane, who, besides anxiety, poverty, and a miserable past, were still like everyone else. The only other inmate at the hospital she felt inexplicably connected to was Erich Anpin, who was, by nature, a mute.

She felt martyred just like Joan of Arc, being the special brand of insane that is particularly sensitive to metaphysics and the inherent existential conditions of living. She was odd even among the odd, strange even among strangers. She began to think that she really did not think like other people, and therefore she should always keep her mouth shut, for her thoughts, due to their possible rarity, would only be met with hostility, and secretly, fear. She slumped down in her chair, buried under the weight of her depression, watching silently as Joan burned, also silently, looking to God for a vision that was clouded by ashes and tears. No one else thought like her, either, and that was why she was burned, for possessing a spirituality the prosaic *endoxa* of man could never hope to understand, and which they privately envied. Laura's mother walked in.

"What are you watching?" she asked cheerily. Laura didn't feel like talking, so she simply passed her mother the DVD case with a silence so thick and a docility so profound it was obvious the other human beings in their obstinate refusal to understand her, had at last broken her completely, leaving her helplessly alone, aided in life by nothing but a compliance that was really a beseeching for her loneliness to remain undisturbed; her loneliness, which had now become another nervous compulsion.

"Oh dear, don't watch that, it will depress you."

Laura didn't say anything. Perhaps she liked being depressed, she thought. It made her feel more like a human, while at the same time it distanced her from other humans, who, honestly, she couldn't comprehend, either, but was able to make an effort to through the detached lucidity of her sorrow. That is the curse of intelligence, to be able to understand how everything works except other people.

"I like it," Laura said very quietly. Erich Anpin walked in and sat next to her. Laura watched him. He looked at Joan of Arc as if she were one of the few people who had ever actually known him. She understood this feeling. They watched the movie in silence while her mother eyed them curiously, feeling the way almost everyone felt about them, that they were something profoundly disturbing. Perhaps she was right, but they had their purpose. The lonely will always find comfort in what disturbs others.

Zeir Anpin came in as well. "I've seen this movie," he said

mildly, to all effect appearing as if it were not something that had ever affected him. Zeir was deranged, but he seemed to have a way of denying his past. It was an incredibly normal quality for someone who was so strange, but she supposed people accepted him because they had no choice. Erich, on the other hand, they didn't even think about.

"Who are your friends?" Laura's mother asked.

"They're not my friends," she replied stiffly. Neither Zeir or Erich seemed upset about it.

"It's very sad," her mother said in an eerie, absent way.

Laura raised an eyebrow at her. "What is?"

"What happened to Joan of Arc."

"That was what happened to any woman who thought for herself in those days. The word 'witch' really meant 'feminist.'" As she said this she shot an intimidating glare at Zeir, as she felt he was something so empty and contrived he had all too easily become the scourge of the planet, though he was perhaps the planet itself. Zeir was still unaffected, always comfortably blasé as he pulled a lighter out of the pockets of his pants and pulled on its trigger, giving her a threatening look through the flames.

Her mother almost screamed. "You're not supposed to have lighters in here!"

Quickly a nurse came in and wrestled the lighter away from him. Laura didn't care. At this point she didn't mind the idea of being burned alive. She would not even scream, and she certainly would not look towards God. She had nothing in common with Joan of Arc, whose madness was the madness of God. Laura smiled to herself as she thought her madness was probably made by the devil instead. "If it were still acceptable for them to burn us today they still would," she said stiffly, deliberately disconnecting herself from what she was afraid might be the truth as she spoke it with an air of doomed prophecy.

Erich tapped her on the shoulder. He had written something down. Erich was a writer, but he had the inveterate tendency to destroy everything he'd written, but still his characters remained bewildered and half alive like human beings. He handed her what he'd written, in all caps:

GOD IS NOT LOVE. LOVE IS GOD.

Laura smirked. "I'm not sure I believe in either," she said. Erich then gave her a very sad look and burned the paper.

"Where are you both getting lighters?!" the nurse screamed with nervous agitation. Laura looked at him and shook her head wearily.

"They are both completely senseless," she said.

Between the two of them she had nowhere to run.

Chapter XII

It was another sideshow today. The sane came in droves to crash in upon her intrapersonal world of undisturbed madness, tainting the purity of her psychological difference. They would refuse to understand her, as always. They would mock her instead, because that is much easier.

But Lilith was begrudgingly relieved that today they were not there implicitly to laugh at and torture the patients. They had all come to see the great Dr. Egas Moniz preform his miracle lobotomy.

Personally, Lilith found the procedure to be medieval, and if he ever prescribed it to her she knew she would kill herself instead. That was the breaking point for her. She no longer cared if her mind was alienated and scorned, she had grown used to that since childhood, but the thought of it being taken away from her completely, that was too much to bear. It was strange, though. She hated her mind, realizing that a mind, particularly an abnormal one, is a great burden to anyone. It was what tortured her body, and debased her soul, if she still had one, but she most likely didn't, so therefore her mind, in spite of being ruinous and cruel, was all she had. And besides, without it she could not write.

The spectators and patients crowded around the operating theater. Lilith quickly became depressed when she saw the patients, the people she believed should know better, to have the same sickening look of bloodlust in their eyes as did the sane. They wanted to be entertained, as well, and nothing entertains people more than their own cruelty.

The patient strapped to the chair was squirming and screaming. Lilith recognized him. It was Andre Korsakov, a Russian émigré whom America had turned insane. He looked Lilith directly in the eye. "LILITH!" he yelled, a high pitched, agonized yell. "DON'T LET THEM DO THIS TO ME!" Lilith turned her face away from him, tears falling out of her eyes when she realized she was like everyone else, too cowardly to be kind…too cowardly to be anything but a spectator, and though she did not feel the sick satisfaction of sadism that was a catharsis for the others, she was still not brave enough to put an end to it. She was not even brave enough to save her own life, how could she possibly save anyone else's? She inspected the crowd with their wry, toothy grins. She decided the only difference between barbarism and civilization is that in civilization you can murder without getting blood on your hands. Dr. Egas Moniz entered with his long beaked mask and what looked like two ice picks in his hands.

Lilith at last worked up the strength to look at Andre. The look of terror in his eyes, it was too much to even weep over. At last he would be simplified. Throughout growing up we are complicated by the things surrounding us that we cannot control but wear us down every day into too many unnecessary circuits and synapses. To be inevitably robbed of the simple, naïve nature one had as a child. That is truly life's worse degradation. But to be forced against one's will to be simple to the point of mindlessness. That's even worse.

Everyone in the audience, including come of the patients, cheered when Egas Moniz put two ice picks through Andre's eyes sockets. Lilith looked away as he screamed once more. Nijinsky put a hand on her shoulder, but she remained silent and in agony. She had long been exposed to the evil humans were capable of. She had read somewhere once that if they were not capable of this evil, they wouldn't be capable of good. Lilith then felt like good was a pyrrhic victory, if millions of people had to die to save the few who are already privileged. She had also read somewhere that evil exists because of free will, so we can choose to be good. But most of the time we choose evil, because it is much easier. Does that even count as free will, or is it just wishing to be rid of it? She didn't want to think about it anymore, as she watched Andre's free will being forced from him *because* of evil. And yet she did not think that Egas Moniz, by principle, was an evil man, at least not consciously. It was his subconscious that was making him do this to people, in the name of helping them, but really it was an excess of intelligence that made him want to harm them, without him even being aware of it. Lilith shuddered. No matter how much you *want* to be good, you can still be evil without realizing it. We are all capable of it.

"It is not fair that we're all locked up in here, most of us for trying to kill ourselves," Lilith whispered to Nijinsky. Benjy, who was sitting behind them, raised an eyebrow and also listened to her, his curiosity towards the strange woman who was seemingly martyred by insanity, almost as if it were slowly sanctifying her. "All people have the right to kill themselves." And then at last she looked at Andre's face. There was something on it worse than terror now. It was pure emptiness, as if the supposed evil that had just escaped his body had taken all of his soul with it. He was sane now, as sane as it gets, which is to have no brain or no will, to be dead where you are walking. The look of numbness and nullity on his face, it made Lilith feel like she was looking into a mirror. It was the same look she had on her face most of the time, of complete docility only an automaton could understand. "Tis better to kill yourself than someone else," she added, spitting as she said it and glaring at Egas Moniz. Andre had been her friend. Sure, he was raving mad, but it had made him human. Now he was a bastardization of that.

"And no one can live without killing something," Benjy added from behind them. At last Lilith looked at him. "Those who attempt suicide know this."

Lilith sighed and put her head in Benjy's lap. He stroked her hair lovingly, but immediately the nurse came and forced them apart. Lilith hung her head as Andre was rolled off the stage, a completely blank look in his eyes where there had once been fury, devotion, and on special occasions, the rare moments where it hadn't been beaten or medicated out of him, passion. As soon as the nurse left Benjy put his arm around her chest. Lilith tried to smile, but could not. She was too well acquainted with the almost religious nature of despair. She looked to Nijinsky. He was dancing in his seat, an incredibly mournful, slow dance without his usual grace. Andre was also Russian, from a place this American institution refused to understand, would prefer to fear. As Nijinsky danced his kinetic lament he wondered how much time he had left before something similar would happen to him.

At last they all left the theater. Sideshow was over. It had been even more horrible than usual this time, because someone, Christ like, had been martyred, and not for salvation, but for entertainment.

Laura sat in the TV room at Gymnopedie, waiting cautiously. George had finally gotten fed up with not being able to visit her, so today he was coming with her mother. Laura was excited to see him, but she still felt the same sense of despair upon thinking that if he came he would perhaps find out how insane she truly was, that he would learn indefinitely that she was actually quite different from him. George generally only liked people who were similar to him, and he was already feeling the communication gap between their separate loves of both low and high art, though he thought he had successfully dulled Laura down a little bit by constantly impressing his less serious, less dismal nature on her.

They walked in, Laura's mother and George. Laura held her breath for a second when she saw George. He waved at her. She tried to smile when she waved back.

"Hello, sweet pea," her mother called. Her forced smile quickly abandoned her face. George looked around, observing the hospital, because he had secretly wondered what it was like there, and had even secretly wondered what it was like to be Laura, though he was afraid to ask her. Also he had a keen eye for detail, and noticed everything so acutely it would send him spinning into a blind panic when it would all grow too large and encroach upon his safety of simplicity. Truthfully, George was mentally ill, too, but still he could not relate to Laura, who was insane in a very different way. And for the year that they were together Laura would have to bear the weight of both their neuroses in silence, without ever divulging to George the secrets of her madness, while he elucidated his in lengthy, desperate detail. It did not help her get better, and secretly, George didn't want her to. If she got better than he would have to as well, but he didn't want to, and he didn't want to be alone again, so it was more convenient for him if they were both insane and Laura didn't talk about it too much so he would not have to force out the little bit of sympathy he had left for others, the rest of it being implicitly devoted to himself.

George approached her. "This place is really weird," he whispered.

Laura shrugged. "I'm used to it."

George grabbed her by her shoulders and shook her. "No. Don't get used to this, please."

Laura smiled. Perhaps he really did care after all, but it was impossible to tell. They embraced and Laura felt the smoothness of his pale, thin flesh, and she couldn't help but wonder, if beauty is only skin deep, perhaps love is too. She wanted to hold onto it, though, to hold onto him, but he always withdrew quickly. Truthfully, outside of the bedroom, they never touched each other much. They couldn't even get skin deep, not for very long. But George was stamped in Laura's mind like a recurring dream or ancient imago, almost a Moloch. She could not get him out, and when they did touch, always in the dark, always abashedly, she felt like it was not enough, that something crucial was missing. But it was all that was keeping her alive.

George didn't stay for long, and they didn't talk much. Particularly not Laura, who was always stunned speechless around him, and by what, even she in her deep, tenacious love for him would never know. But perhaps it was this love that made her go quiet, into the depths of a soul that without him was barren. It was the love that made her feel so alone.

A knock on the door. Lilith quickly answered. It was Mel. He ran into the room surreptitiously, quickly shutting the door behind him, then taking off his mask.

"I brought you an *Il medico della peste* mask," he said hurriedly, amazed by his own rebelliousness which had previously been forgotten for the sake of a mask. He handed her the mask, and she took it by the long beak the way a person might take a knife by its blade.

"Thank you," she said. She knew he had taken a great risk for her.

"Do you want to put it on?" he asked.

"No. You're not wearing one, so I shouldn't, either. It wouldn't be fair."

"Is that why you hate the doctors here?"

"Individual insanity is not a plague," she said, feeling tired from having to explain this so often, "it is a human right. Now, insanity *en masse*, *le fou de foule* is. But that is the kind of insanity we never lock up, though it's the most dangerous. That is the insanity we accept only because it's not solitary."

"Well, people don't want to feel alone."

"And they like to feel together at someone else's expense. They feel included by excluding. And I am always the one that gets excluded, just because I don't mind being alone from time to time."

"But even you don't want to be alone all the time."

"No, but other people want me to be, and I acquiesce to their desires."

"That's not true, Lilith…"

"Then why do the doctors wear the masks, if they don't think we're a contagion?"

"I'm not wearing a mask."

 Lilith didn't say anything. "Why did you want that mask if you don't wear it?" Mel asked her.

"I don't want to wear it around other people. I want to be completely naked around other people, which is why they hate me. They do not feel comfortable with the honesty. But when I am with myself, I cannot face me. I must lie. I need a mask when I'm alone. I need to be invisible to me. I suppose that means I'm not really comfortable with my own honesty, either. "

Mel changed the subject, as he was beginning to feel uncomfortable. "Have you been using the typewriter?"

"Every day. I find it's the only time when I know what I'm doing. The rest of the day is spent in blind panic."

Mel nodded. "So it comforts you?"

"Yes. The only thing that comforts me is art, and even that is painful."

Mel didn't say anything, but tinkered with his removed mask, as if he wanted to put it back on. Lilith of course noticed this, and turned away from him. "Sorry," he said stoically. She merely shrugged.

"Can I put it back on?" he asked.

"I thought you liked not wearing it…"

"I did at first, but now I feel…strange."

"You're afraid of me again."

"I'm not afraid of you."

"Then why do you want to put it back on?"

Mel didn't say anything for a moment, but continued absently fingering his mask. "I am afraid of something," he said at last. "But I don't know what. It's not you, though."

"It may not be me, but I remind you of it, whatever it is, don't I?"

"Yes," he barely whispered, then put his mask back on. "You can put yours on, too," he added.

"No," Lilith spat angrily. "I am not afraid of whatever it is. How can you be afraid of something nameless?"

"Because it is nameless. Because I do not know it, and can't put it into words. Perhaps even if I did know it I still couldn't put it into words. That's what really scares me."

Lilith looked towards her typewriter distantly. She nodded as she began to stroke it almost the way a lover would stroke her, if she had one, but she didn't. At least she had a typewriter in its stead. "I can understand that," she said. "If I can't put things into words I have no reason to live." Then she sank into thought, and realized there were plenty of things she could not put into words, because words could not describe them; beauty and terror. She would do the best she could to elucidate them to herself, though.

"I have to go," Mel said seriously through the beak of the mask, making his voice sound like a *creux neant musicien*, but this was usually what Lilith heard when words were spoken, the *creux neant*, the universe itself. She had no idea how it didn't make others insane like it had made her. She tried to look into Mel's eyes, but it was impossible through the thick, round goggles of the mask. She felt sad. No one would ever attempt to see things through her eyes for fear they would then forever be associated with madness. And maybe they were right. Maybe if they saw the world through her eyes they would have tried to kill themselves, too. She tried to explain that to them, that they would have behaved no differently if they possessed her same weltanschauung, but they generally found a way to live without one. She suddenly knew what it was the Mel was afraid of. He was afraid there was some reason in insanity.

"Leave then," Lilith said coldly.

"I'm sorry," Mel said. "I know I've let you down today."

"It's okay. Everyone does in the end. I am particularly easy to neglect."

"Why do you think that is?"

"Because I can make it by myself, so others don't feel guilty leaving me alone."

"But you don't want to be alone, do you?"

"I don't know anymore. I suppose it is easier, and you get used to it after a while."

"No," Mel said defiantly. "Don't get used to that." She wondered if she had any other choice, though, when God Himself wanted her to be alone. Mel left, squeezing her hand as he walked out. Lilith decided she still liked him, even though he *had* let her down. She could tell he was trying, but there were some things about her he could never get close to, due to his unnamed fear, which was all the more real when it was ambiguously undefined.

Lilith went to the bathroom. She looked into the black cement wall where the mirrors were supposed to be. She wondered for a moment what she looked like. She had long forgotten, but she supposed it was easier to know herself if she didn't have a face. How can anyone possibly not become insane when they try to know themselves? Perhaps being mad meant you were someone without a face, a *cruex neant visage*. She looked deeply into the smooth, tenebrous wall and dragged her fingernail across it, then up and down. She did this until her nail was filed down into a stub, and her finger started bleeding. She was drawing what she imagined her face looked like.

And she looked into this makeshift mirror, this mimesis she had to pay for with her own blood. It wasn't a face, really, that she had drawn, but a skull, and like all skulls, it appeared to be laughing. Death mocks life like a nihilistic jester, someone who knows the emptiness of the world and finds it funny. In this way, Lilith was not like death. She couldn't remember the last time she had laughed, but then again, she couldn't remember the last time she cried, either. She was somewhere in between life and death then- life, which is always weeping, and death that is always laughing at its tears. She could do neither, though. She was somewhere in the womb, in between the rapid swing of the pendulum that cuts through nothingness and divides the world into being born and dying. Lilith supposed it would be what she looked like once she put the mask on.

And she did as soon as she got back to her bedroom. She put on the mask, sat at the typewriter, and began writing. This, she knew, was the only way she could be brave. She laughed to herself. "Now I'm the doctor," she said through a snarl as she kept typing. "Now I'm the psychopomp."

"I am a sick man, a wicked man." This was the first sentence of Fyodor Dostoyevsky's *Notes from Underground.* Laura had read it in high school, which was now about four years ago, but she had never forgotten that opening line. Now it was her mantra. Everywhere in the limited world of Gymnopedie State Mental Hospital she walked around saying it under her breath. "I am a sick man, a wicked man." With each step, it would not stop playing in her head. It was all she heard in her mind's eye, and sometimes it was so loud it actually became audible. People would ask her simple things, in hope of getting a simple answer, such as "how are you Laura?" and out of her mouth, involuntarily would come "I am a sick man, a wicked man." People generally ignored it, though. She said it at home as she cut herself: "I am a sick man, a wicked man," while she dragged the double edged razor slowly across her skin, savoring the slow leak of blood that came out of its tracks.

She sat in her room at Gymnopedie, rocking back and forth, repeating it over and over in a voice lower than a whisper. She stopped when she at last heard something else. It was a low humming, almost like the sound of a Tibetan monk's chants, but it came from a voice that was clearly not human. Laura knew that it was the voice of the void. She tried to get closer to it, but the closer she got the more far off the sound became, growing faint, but never disappearing completely. Laura had read about this before. It was called *trismos,* a wind that supposedly only the dead could hear. The dead, and the insane, Laura thought, as being insane could in some cases mimic death. And particularly in Laura's case. George often would tell her she was dead, and she knew he was right, but what he forgot to add was that the dead seek love only from those who are also decayed. But he was right, and she knew it especially now, as she was able to hear the *trismos.* What a fate, she thought, to be dead and still have to go through the motions and routine of living, like a puppet, rigid but spasmodic, pulled on invisible strings by a master who is not known. Her body hadn't died, but her will had, long even before the first suicide attempt. And when your will dies you are dead in a different, much more horrible way than the comfort of never ending sleep offered to those who are scientifically dead. You are dead in a metaphysical sense: the most important part of you is gone, but in its place is left some deranged spirit, a complete, unholy bastardization of who you once were, a phantom of your old, dead passions and your old, dead will. This phantom becomes your body, always naked and trembling, rigid but spasmodic, unable to be pierced by anything but razors, and even then you still do not bleed enough. A thick skin, but one that is made out of shadows. Laura didn't mind. She thought the dead knew things the living were incapable of knowing, such as the sound of the *trismos*, that beautiful, haunting sound without either melody or discord, that is not quite music but clearly where music came from. The sound of nothingness, the *creux neant musicien.*

She finally got to a spot in the room where she could hear it perfectly, as she was turned away from it, and it felt almost as if the sound was coming from the rear of her skull, a *sotto voce*, one that could suck in the rest of her body, and which was merely borrowing her head in this moment for its own unknown designs, for it was a sound she had not invented, but which had been around for all time, as many things in her brain had; the secret knowledge of the dead. She listened to the low humming and felt it slowly drag her in, distending her and breaking her apart. Suddenly it bellowed:

I AM A SICK MAN, A WICKED MAN!

Laura screamed, and it sucked her in completely.

Chapter XIII

After that Laura was able to go home, though everyone knew she was not better. Most of them, even her own friends, even George, assumed that her silence was really a stubborn refusal to become well, that she, in a deranged way, enjoyed this final self-destruction that all of them ubiquitously agreed she would not come back from. They were wrong, though, completely wrong. Laura did not enjoy this sickness at all, but she felt she deserved it. "I am a sick man, a wicked man," was all she ever said these days, as she thought it was the ultimate truth about herself. She assumed she could do no better than this senselessness, and art had taught her for a long time now that in senselessness, in the blindness of confusion, there is truth. You cannot discover truth until you first go insane; the truth hurts. Enlightenment hurts even more.

And Laura would get better, eventually, though her psychosis would be incredibly tenacious, and make several encores. She, in truth, was done with it before it was done with her. It would release her eventually, but take with it George, her ultimate love, who would eventually come to terms with the fact that he could not understand her, and that he was done trying. But Laura would learn to fill the void he inevitably left within her when he walked away; though she would not find a love like that again, one that consumed her sanity and ambition, she would at least be able to write again. This she, by necessity, taught herself, would have to be enough.

Shortly after Laura was released out of the hospital her mother moved into her already small by most standards one bedroom apartment. Her mother was technically homeless, and a stay that was supposed to only be two weeks quickly became six months, where Laura had to return to Gymnopedie at least two times, maybe three. I don't know. I have forced myself to forget the bulk of this time period, by necessity.

Her mother living with her did not really help. Her mother would often reorganize the apartment when Laura was at work, as she had brought her incredible load of meretricious chattel along with her, which, in spite of it all being garish and useless, her mother held quite dear, almost to the point of some kind of religious madness, as if it were not just overpriced furniture, but iconography. She would take all Laura's art off the walls, as she found it disturbing and without the forced, artificial charm she craved for her living spaces as well as her conversations. She would rarely let Laura leave the house alone, would not even let her walk to work, and would go so far as to follow her when she tried to go out with her friends, claiming always that she was smoking marijuana, which, according to her and the hospital staff, was what was making her insane.

And the only joy Laura had in life right now was her foreign art films and her strange books. In this way she was no different than when she had supposedly been sane, if she ever had been.

She had developed a rabid fascination for surrealism and all its facets. She read Artaud, Tzara, Breton, Alfred Jerry, Hugo Ball, Eluard, and Jacques Prevert. She watched Luis Bunuel and Jean Cocteau films. This were the only things that made sense to her, and made her feel a little less crazy. The thought that people had made such beautiful things from absurdity gave her hope for herself that perhaps one day she could do the same thing, and indulge this madness in a healthy way, thereby, making sense of it, thereby, getting rid of it. But her mother did not understand. She thought the films were sick and confusing. She could see no possible meaning in any of them, though Laura tried to explain it to her, but her mother thought every word out of her mouth was the most deranged lunacy, and in the end, she would write off all the art Laura enjoyed as the main contributing factor of her illness, though it would, in time, become the only thing to save her from it. Laura knew it could do this, and she tried to explain this as well, but again her mother labelled it as more madness, even though it was perhaps the only part of Laura that was sane, but, admittedly, this sanity first had to be born in madness. She could not explain this either. Her mother was another of many people who would not admit any validity to her point of view because it was, in some ways, frightening. But that did not stop it from perhaps being true.

George would not watch these movies with her because he thought they were boring and ostentatious, and her mother would not watch them with her because they made her afraid, afraid that in spite of her vehement protests to the contrary, Laura was right, and they *did* make sense. Really, Laura wanted to watch them alone, anyway, as she felt appreciation was easier and more genuine in solitude, but these days she was never alone. This certainly made her more crazy.

Laura did get lonely, particularly when George was around, but she generally felt better when she was by herself, even at the times it was lonely. This was much less lonely than being around people who could not make sense of her, which in these days, was everyone. This was another way that insanity was no different from sanity. Whether she was "ill" or well, she could not prevent herself from being strange. She had been strange ever since she was a child, and it had always been met with hostility, first by her parents, then the other schoolchildren, and now even her friends.

George came over that night. Laura always got black out drunk when he came over. Sometimes she would be blacked out for several hours by the time they had sex, which they did every Friday night, as scheduled, and she would wake up with both of them naked and wonder what incredibly stupid things she must have said the night before, but unfortunately, this was the only way she could speak, and she supposed her words must have been incredibly insignificant if even she could not remember them, that she must have spoken like everyone else did, without impact. It was good that she had given up writing then, she supposed.

And the sex must have been more nothingness, as well, a lust the resembled a black hole, all devouring but empty. She was often glad she couldn't remember it. Not because she didn't enjoy having sex with George, she did, but it was just easier to do it in a haze of alcoholic amnesia, so then she did not have to think about it, and did not have the hollow "I love you" engrammed into her mind too deeply. She knew George would leave her eventually. He was not the kind of person that liked staying anywhere for too long. She thought if she could erase the memory of him before it had even become a memory, as it was happening, she would not have to long for him too much when he did decide to stop playing her for the drunken, psychotic, miserable fool he had turned her into and at last mercifully break all ties. She was very, very wrong. She gave it a noble effort, and came shockingly close to her goal, but still she could not manage to black out an entire year. Much of George would stay with her for the remainder of her life, which was strange, because they never talked much, and truthfully never knew one another.

But Laura was the helpless victim to a freakishly apt memory. This is the curse of intellectualism, that you are not allowed to forget anything. Laura came to discover, by degrees, that to be an intellectual is not simply to hold a lot of information in your head, it is to force yourself not to ignore the truth no matter how horrible it is: It is to realize that the information in your head is a true story written in rivers of the blood of countless massacres, and to not let yourself forget that. It is to abandon the instinct to repress the fleeting awareness of your own capability of evil. It is to abandon the instinct to repress history. So why would anyone want to be an intellectual? Because it's not something you get to choose, it is another instinct. And it is alienating and painful, but in the end you do not regret it.

But it can greatly contribute to mental illness, as the two seem to go together. I still cannot tell if it was reality that made me insane or its alternative, which is also reality, or both; reality *and* reality.

And Laura was treading some incredibly dangerous waters. When she and George had sex it was almost always unprotected, not to mention the fact that they would both be drunk, as well, though Laura considerably more so. (She would still not come to terms with the fact that, though she loved George, she actually *didn't* enjoy having sex with men, and would not even for years after he had left her.) Laura had gotten prescribed birth control, but she was generally in too much of a confused, eerie daze to remember to take the pill. She would also neglect taking the medication that she would eventually have to begrudgingly admit, did help keep her sane. This combustible combination led her to her fourth stay at Gymnopedie.

This time it had happened at home, not at work, and I suppose that was merciful. Again George had not showed up to their Friday night appointment, which was all she looked forward to each week, and really, all that was keeping her alive, though the sickness of this love was what was slowly killing her, the philtre being more poison that medicine, but I suppose that was what had made it so intoxicating. George didn't come, so Laura decided to go to bed at 7 p.m. Cue the psychosis.

Laura suddenly started crying in her bed, and her mother and brother again rushed into the room to see her wide eyed with terror and helplessness. She made them sit down on the bed with her. She kept weeping as her mother kept shouting in her face, "what you're seeing is not real. What you're seeing is not real," over and over again, which, in spite of its intentions, wasn't helping. Laura took it as another cold hearted reminder that she was "ill," and would therefore never have a normal love, and that there would never be any truth in her perceptions, that were tainted with insanity. Besides, Laura wasn't having visual hallucinations. She wasn't even really having hallucinations at all. It was more like a feeling, one that is so irrational it cannot be described, not even in the meaninglessness of art, but which was still legitimate in spite of its fearful absurdity, or, more likely, because of it. It was the feeling that the devil was so close to being God.

At last her family left. She was glad. She could weep alone.

But they came back, and with them brought a team of paramedics. The paramedics shined a light in her eye, and she stared into it dully, not looking away.

"What is your birthday?" they asked.

She wouldn't answer. She did not have the strength within her to talk anymore. She was too overcome by this invisible, ineffable but rising feeling she could not put into words, so she wouldn't speak, feeling as if she had ultimately failed the one ambition in her life that she fancied, (perhaps irrationally , perhaps not) was her divine quest, and had previously given an existence that is otherwise hunted by this senselessness that was now overwhelming her, a hidden prize of rational purpose to guide her through it. But now she did not have that guide. Now she did not have words. She knew the answers to all the questions, but she was much too terrified to speak.

"What is your middle name?"

No answer.

"Who is the president of the United States?"

No answer.

"She's catatonic."

No protest.

So they carried her down the steps to her apartment in a stretcher and loaded her in the ambulance. Again she folded her hands over her chest like a decorated corpse.

As they loaded her in the ambulance she thought she was being accused of terrorism, and after the ambulance, they were going to put her in a helicopter and dump her into the ocean. She thought Vladimir Putin had usurped Obama and was now the president of the United States, and it was her fault, because she had bought subversive Russian literature on the internet. Her mother was in the ambulance with her, holding her hand. She heard her mother talk to the paramedics, and suddenly she felt as if her mother was going to take her place in the execution, that they had traded lives. Laura wanted to scream in protest. Sure, she had problems with her mother, but she didn't want her killed because of something foolish Laura had done. But still no words would come out, so she simply brooded over how horrible of a person she was, as she had been for months, though it had yet to redeem her. "I am a sick man, a wicked man…"

But this was all, of course, in Laura's mind, which only made it all the more real for her. You can escape reality, but you can never escape your own mind. But they didn't kill Laura or her mother, and Vladimir Putin was not president, and thankfully it is still not a crime to order Lermontov novels online. They took her to the emergency room instead. Laura thought it was a man's prison. She wasn't that far off. She thought all the male patients, or inmates, in her mind (though what is the difference? One is prisoner to the state, the other to their body,) wanted to sta her. Her dad came in, too, along with her brother. She wanted to beg them not to walk around the prison, thinking they would be killed too if they did. Still no words, and still the feeling that her passive wordlessness was a great evil, or at least a submission to it.

Everywhere around her she heard nonsensical screams, abstractions of horror, a cryptogram that she could not make sense of, but knew well enough to know its secrets were frightening. She closed her eyes. A doctor came in, a female. Laura was relieved. She asked standard questions.

"Are you sexually active?"

Laura nodded.

"Could you be pregnant?"

Laura shook her head.

"Well, we're going to make sure." Then they wheeled her to another room.

Lilith sat down compliantly on the bed. Il medico dell peste walked toward her, holding the various syringes. She wondered if she should be depressed, but she didn't feel anything. She almost felt this treatment made sense.

Now the terror in Laura's mind had reached its peak. To give birth in a man's prison? She then, in her wild, fantastical fear, thought that abortion had been criminalized because of her foolishness. She wanted to cry. "What have I done?" she kept repeating in her head as the doctors put her on a bed with a machine rigged to it and what looked like a small, but terrifying television screen in its center. They grabbed a rather phallic looking device and put gel on it. Laura screamed silently.

The obstetrician then tried to put the rather phallic device inside her, but Laura scrambled to the top of the bed. She kept shaking her head no, but not saying it. Her mother tried to calm her, and then the doctor tried to put it inside her again. The same reaction, and at last Laura spoke. "No...please."

Her mother whispered to the doctor, "she's a bit uncomfortable with these things."

The doctor sighed but understood. "Okay. We can do an ultrasound on her stomach."

Then they put the same gel they had put on the horrible phallus onto her stomach, and over that a machine that seemed to Laura like one of the scanners they use at grocery stores. The small, terrifying television screen lit up. Laura looked at it begrudgingly. She had never much liked television, she thought there was something insidious about it. This television was gray and black, with an odd triangle going down the middle of it, and in the center, what looked like a small, horrible creature, a death sentence in Laura's eyes. She was indeed, pregnant.

They took her again to the small, isolated room, but this time it was more like a hallway with a couple other hospital beds attached, a bathroom, and a glaring video camera. Laura lay down on her bed, as she was instructed to do, and then they left her alone for another four hours as they always did. In the next room, that was actually empty, she thought she heard George and their mutual friend Sam fucking. There was a basis to this paranoia. George was madly in love with Sam, and had even admitted it to Laura once. It was just something he expected her to put up with. She heard them fuck, and as they were fucking, they mocked her.

"You see, you're just not artistic enough for me, Laura. And, besides, Sam and I are both skinny. You have to be skinny to be an artist, not a fat ass."

Laura tried to ignore them as best she could. She wasn't angry at them. Again, she felt this was something she deserved. She did love George, but she also kept herself anchored to him because she felt he almost had the right to his emotional infidelities (and his physical ones) because all she did these days was drink herself stupid and read books he honestly didn't care about. How could he possibly love her? She was too ill.

"We're moving to New York together," Sam started trilling joyfully. "We've started a band together, and there's a recording studio in Boston that's interested in us."

Laura didn't say anything.

"We're leaving you behind," George added.

Eventually Laura couldn't take it anymore. She got out of bed and started pacing around the cramped hallway. The room right next to hers, the room where she thought Sam and George were fucking, was empty. She still did not think it was in her imagination, though, and she wasn't entirely wrong. George really did fuck Sam, about as much as he fucked Laura.

All the rooms were empty, except one room where a dilapidated looking man with a shaved head was thrashing around and screaming. Laura thought he must have had cancer. Then two doctors came in and injected him with something until he stopped moving. Laura became afraid and ran back into her room; again she had seen something she shouldn't have, and it was perhaps not a hallucination.

She lay back down in bed and examined her body, how fat it was. How could she possibly be an artist, be George's ideal, when she looked like a lumberjack? Artists had style; they knew how to dress hip. She generally just dressed like a lesbian. How could George possibly love her? He must be lying every time he says it, she thought, and again, this was not entirely mad, though it was one of the things that were making her so. She continued to stare at her disgusting, non- artistic body covered in the drab, impersonal clothes. She was not anything interesting. And then suddenly the thought struck her that she was actually a hermaphrodite. She felt completely certain at the moment in the conviction that she had both sets of genitals. Then George and Sam next door started mocking her for that as well and she became even more sure. They wouldn't lie to her.

At last a nurse walked in. "We're going to need a urine sample from you," she said calmly, then handed her the empty plastic cup. Laura went into the bathroom but was still confused. She didn't know quite what it was the nurse wanted her to do with the empty plastic cup. After a moment she sank down onto the bathroom floor and took off her pants. She was on the bathroom floor for almost half an hour until the nurse walked in. Laura quickly zipped up her pants. "I need you to urinate in that cup," the nurse reiterated. At last Laura understood. They were essentially drug testing her. Laura wanted to tell the nurse flatly that they would find marijuana in her system, but she didn't feel like making that much of an effort. She waited another twenty minutes for the urge to urinate to come, and then, in her state of delirium, got most of the piss all over the floor and some on her hands, but a little bit of it was in the cup.

Finally the ambulance came. It was the same sentence: two to three more weeks at Gymnopedie. Before they loaded her in the ambulance, they gave her a mélange of drugs, so her delirium increased and she was half asleep, unaware of what was going on as she was strapped into her stretcher. All she could remember was looking at the EMT and saying, "George won't love me anymore, now that I have both parts." The paramedic ignored her and they drove away.

People are particularly hostile to you when you're insane.

Chapter XIV

Lilith kissed Benjy passionately, in a way she had never kissed a man before, and she supposed it was because, technically, Benjy wasn't a man. It was strange. Lilith had never been a lesbian before, and had no desire to be with someone of the same sex when she was young, or even in her adult life until now. But every man she had been with had never loved her, but wanted to amuse themselves at the expense of her sanity, and, in some instances, her dignity. What Adam had done to her the other night, which only Nijinsky had seen and which she knew only Nijinsky would believe her about; that had been the last straw. She didn't think Benjy loved her either, but at least he respected her, and in many aspects, he did care. Lilith wanted to tell him what Adam had done- she knew Benjy would believe her, but the words would not come out. She tried to force them, but all she could do was kiss Benjy and hope that would be enough to get her by, at least for a little while, and she could forget Adam. It was incredibly sad and masochistic, which, was unfortunately, the way her mind usually worked, but in spite of what he'd done to her, she still loved him, almost as much as she hated him. But she hated him intensely, because the effect that his actions had on her had made her prisoner to her own silence, to the memory it left inside her that was now eating her away but would not force itself out of her mouth, as well as the personal knowledge that even if she told someone and they believed her, nothing would be done about it. There is no justice for women, particularly not in those times, and honestly, not in the modern world, either, and Adam had done the worst thing a sadist can to do to their victim, which is, to make them unable to speak. And it isn't even only the sadist that does this to a victim, but the rest of the world, as well, that doesn't feel it has the time for the compassion or the anger required to make this go away. The world is a sadist, too- not a natural sadist, but a sadist out of laziness, and it's in the habit of re-victimizing as a staple of this laziness.

Lilith tried not to think about it, but Benjy noticed her kisses now had a sluggish lassitude, as if her mouth may have been present, but her mind was no longer attached to it- her mind was somewhere else entirely, in a world that was far less pleasant than the blessed asylum of another woman's body instead of a man's: she was in the world where men have complete control of their bodies and can do whatever they like with them, no matter at whose expense. She was living in the American reality. Benjy stopped kissing her. "You're thinking about him, aren't you?" he asked stiffly.'

"Yes, but not in the way you think." Now would have been a perfect time to tell him what had happened, what Adam had done to her, but still the words got caught in her throat like a bad cough, an illness that is stuck inside of you, and will not erupt from the mouth. She realized now that this moment in her life where she had mostly been unconscious had made her considerably more mentally ill, and the thing that people would willfully refuse to understand was that it wasn't her fault: even before she had been raped it wasn't her fault. She had never chosen to be insane. She had never chosen to be a woman. And she certainly hadn't chosen to be a rape victim.

Benjy didn't say anything. He just shrugged his casual, dispassionate, but graceful shrug and continued to kiss Lilith. The door suddenly opened. It was a female nurse. She saw *Il Medico della Peste* mask in the corner, and quickly dragged Lilith away from Benjy by the hair. Oh, how they've turned us against each other.

"Where did you get this?" the nurse asked vehemently, pointing to the mask.

"I stole it," Lilith quickly lied.

"Patients are not to cavort with other patients, or allowed access to medical equipment!"

Lilith shrugged. "Sorry."

The nurse grabbed her, again by the hair, and led her this way all across the hospital grounds. She brought with her the mask. At last she stopped schlepping Lilith all along the hospital's gardens, away from the cemetery with the unmarked graves between the butcher's shop and the cathedral, and behind them to the mass grave. But now the mass grave was marked. It said *campus sceleratus.* The nun who had the patients build their own coffins was standing directly next to it, Lilith's coffin in hand. She put the mask on Lilith's face. "Get in," she ordered grimly, pointing to the coffin.

Lilith wasn't sure why, but she did as she was told. As the coffin closed over her, the nails she had placed herself went through her hands and she screamed, arms outstretched inside her coffin with the mask now forever stuck on her face, as if she was some disturbed apostle about to proclaim a drunken *kerygma* of lunacy, ready to make an offering of herself, quite unlike most human beings who prefer to sacrifice one another in hordes and hecatombs. Instead she would sacrifice herself; but she was not like Jesus. She was not like Joan of Arc. She had no cause she was dying for, besides simply wanting to be dead. There wasn't any salvation in it, only the incessant yearning for silence that had finally gotten too loud. The nun and the nurse opened the mass grave and interred her.

Lilith couldn't see anything with the mask on, but she felt the blood running down her palms in her sick, mock crucifixion. Her imagination had finally decided to kill her, with the help of the hostility of others. Now that this mask was stuck on her face, she wished she had never asked for it. She realized that she would decay much faster than it, and eventually be a skull with a mask on, and then eventually be dust with a mask on. This was no different than having flesh, she supposed. Then it got dark, incredibly dark, a darkness that cannot be understood by the human mind, though it is the darkness where we as a species collectively spent our infancy. Lilith could feel herself devolving, could feel herself going more mad.

She was under the ground for two hours in this tenebrous death cage with the death mask on until she heard the sounds of digging. This took another hour, and by now Lilith had pissed herself, and lost a lot of blood from her unholy stigmata. At last the coffin was wrenched open. Lilith bit down on her lip as the nails were ripped out of her hands, causing them to bleed more and for the wounds to get bigger. It was Mel. He was not wearing a mask. He held out a hand to her, and Lilith cringed as the garish sores on her palms touched his calloused hands, streaking them with blood. The deed had been done, the thing that he was so afraid of. He had been tainted by her imagination.

"Talitha cumi," he whispered softly as he grabbed her around the waist and helped her climb out of the chasm in the ground where they had put her. She didn't know what the words meant, but they soothed her. She briefly looked back and saw all the unnamed skeletons. That was almost her, buried with hundreds of other insane people. Somehow this seemed more comfortable than being dead alone. It took them another half an hour to climb out of the pit. By the time they resurfaced it was night, a particularly dark night, but not as dark as the coffin.

When Laura woke up she was upset to find herself in Gymnopedie. Again, she had thought the entire thing had been a dream. A male nurse walked in.

"I hear you're expecting. Congratulations!" he said cheerily.

"Expecting what?"

The nurse stopped short. "You're pregnant."

"No, I'm not."

"Honey, they did an ultrasound and a urine test. You're pregnant."

"Well, I'm not keeping it."

"Oh," the nurse said, faltering once more. "Are you going to put it up for adoption?"

"No. I'm going to get an abortion."

Il medico della peste put several injections in Lilith's arms. She took them stoically, not feeling any pain...

The nurse looked at her horrified, as if she were not a real woman, but a monster disguised as one. He quickly looked at her chart with shaking hands. "Well," he said slowly. "It says here it's an ectopic pregnancy…"

"What does that mean?"

"It means the fetus is growing *outside* your fallopian tubes. It will most likely miscarry."

"These are hormone injections," Il medico della peste droned in a disaffected monotone. "You see, we don't really want the mentally ill reproducing…"

Laura emitted a huge sigh of relief. She didn't really want to get an abortion. No woman does. But she also didn't want to have a baby, so she felt, in this moment, that God had come through for her for the first time. He was going to abort it for her. "Let me get the doctor," the nurse said, still with trepidation. "She will know how to explain this to you better."

Twelve minutes passed until the doctor and the nurse came in. The doctor looked at Laura briefly, making sure not to make eye contact. "I'm sorry, but your pregnancy is not valid…"

"Good."

"But you must know there are severe risks during an ectopic pregnancy. We may have to surgically remove the fetus, and there is a chance that you could bleed to death…"

'Good,' Laura thought again, but had enough sense not to say it out loud. At this point death seemed far less absurd to her than life.

"We will be checking your hormone levels every day. If they continue to drop you will no longer be pregnant."

"There you go," Il medico della peste said as he removed the last needle. "You will never be able to have a child now. I'm sorry

if this upsets you, but you must understand that as a mad person you lose certain rights…"

"You don't have to explain it. I'm well aware. Besides, I never wanted to have children, anyway."

"Oh, good."

"I do have one question, though. Are all intellectuals eugenicists?

For the most part…

Laura nodded that she understood and they both left. She crawled back into bed helplessly. She could not have this baby. Hopefully it would miscarry. She wondered about George. Her parents had probably already told him the news. She imagined he would be furious with her, and he had indeed told her mother that Laura had told him she couldn't get pregnant, and that was why he had never used a condom. Laura never remembered saying this to him, though. She threw the blankets over her eyes. How could she have a baby with someone who didn't even know her, and who she didn't know either? She never thought George would have lied like that. And she wondered sometimes if he even knew himself, or if he was so caught up in the pretense of himself he advertised that he had confused it for who he truly was. It was not him, though, Laura would eventually find out. It was just the false projections of his ego.

See, the ego is not the self, far from it. The self is really in the unconscious, where everyone is selfish and rapacious. No one is more in touch with the unconscious than the insane. Therefore, it is only the insane who know themselves, and this is what makes them crazy. Are we really locked in our unconscious, hidden from ourselves stealthily *by* ourselves? In the words of Arthur Rimbaud, *Je est un autre.* "I" is another. Then who is I, if we are not it? And what are we if we're not I? I don't know, but we are certainly not. Yet we aren't "we" either. Then what are we? *It. Das Ding.* I is the noumenon. It is as nonexistent as the perceptions it evokes, and we are these perceptions, not the thing itself which is trapped under layers of veneer, these perceptions we have of ourselves, who we suppose we should be, and who we suppose we are, which we often deliberately fool ourselves into thinking are the same. But we're not supposed to be anything, and we *aren't* anything, either. But it defends the ego when we pretend we are; the ego, which we have built as a fortress against all- inclusive selflessness and the shadows in the unconscious that still remember it. "I" is another, but it remains unseen.

And Laura was one of those terrible unfortunates whose mind, though still deluded like all minds, was deluded in its own way. Uniqueness of mind is always paid for with madness, though it is also madness' only blessing. A serpentine mind that is always eating itself. Something bordering close to the infinite, but not quite; a mock eternity, but one that actually does traverse both heaven and hell.

But she knew that no matter what happened, if the baby did miscarry or if she had to get an abortion, this would be the end of things between her and George. She knew he would never touch her again after this, and she was right. They never had sex again, by George's wishes, but secretly she knew that was all he wanted from her. Laura closed her eyes and tried to fall asleep. Right now during sleep was when she was the most happy, even during her nightmares, because no matter how horrible the dream, she couldn't feel it, not the way she could when she was awake. And when she was awake it was a nightmare that lasted for twelve hours each day. She forced herself asleep.

She quickly had a dream, in color, as she always dreamed, to make it all the more realistic and terrifying. She was the Virgin Mary, the *theotokos*, and she was at an altar in a church, kneeling before the large, baleful statue of Jesus, (her son, she supposed,) crucified. She was begging out loud for him to give her an abortion, for him to never be born. Everyone thinks Jesus had to exist for reasons of our salvation, but Laura knew better. She knew his death was senseless, like all death is. To try to find meaning in death is only to naively justify your own self destruction. That is what people really see in Jesus. And no matter how much Laura begged him to save her, he never lifted a finger from his nailed in hands, did not speak a word, did not even move. Laura knew that he was truly dead, and had been for a long time. He could not help her. But if he was dead perhaps the baby would be dead, as well. She felt the need to preemptively save it from its martyrdom, as she wished she had been saved from hers. It's hard to tell if comparing one's own mental illness to martyrdom is delusional or not. In some aspects it is true, particularly if you decide to make art out of your delirium. A day would come when Laura wished nothing more than to be completely exposed for all she was, the immense good in her, as well as the insidious evil, as we all have both, but few of us are able to own up to either. And she knew she would be hated for it. Honesty is often met with hostility these days. In this way she *was* a martyr. There is a thin line between delusion and truth, and they are always exchanging faces. No wonder we're all so confused.

Laura woke up. She had not been asleep long, since she had already slept twelve hours and her body had grown tired of it. Another male nurse was standing in the doorway. "Lunch time, Laura," he called. This was the only time she left her room.

Chapter XV

The next day her parents and George came to visit her. She saw her mother and George walking towards her room while she was reading in the main ward, but she didn't try to stop them. She was too shy. She still had that terrible fluttering feeling in her stomach, the sweating of the hands, the weird palpitations in her throat whenever she saw George. As he walked past she noticed he had gotten a haircut, and was wearing a nice shirt. She thought he looked particularly handsome today.

A few moments later they returned, looking bewildered, but this time they saw her, with a book swallowing her face and her knees pressed against her chest, hoping not to be seen at all. She was reading *The Idiot*. They sat down next to her and both awkwardly said hello. George was particularly awkward about it. "I like your little haircut," Laura said mildly to him.

He smiled. "Thank you."

"Let's go back to your room where we have a little more privacy," her mother interjected, and Laura numbly agreed. She was angry with her mother. Her mother had told the doctors that

Laura was living with her, not that she was living with Laura. Also she was trying to get power of attorney over Laura, though thankfully Laura's father had talked her out of it. That would have been unbearable. She was only twenty two, and as it was already, her mother would hardly let her go out without her. And she didn't want to talk to George, either. She was not prepared to talk to him about his son or daughter or monster or whatever it was growing misplaced in her belly and probably dying. And she was right. It was the first thing they asked her about when they got into her room, and now she realized why George had come to begin with.

"Are your hormone levels dropping?" her mother asked.

"Yes. They check every day and every day it gets lower."

George barely suppressed a visible sigh of relief. For the rest of the conversation it was mostly her mother and George who did all the talking, while she just sat on the bed next to George trying not to look at him, but staring blankly at an innocuous section of the wall. George looked into her face a couple of times, though she would not register his gaze, and he finally noticed what he'd been ignoring this whole time: the fact that all the light had gone from her eyes. They didn't even look blue anymore, but a horrible, yet dull black, while the rest of her face seemed to mirror this corpse like countenance, all around it being an air of utter defeat, of a resignation to something worse than fate. She looked just like a disturbed porcelain doll, half anesthetized to something that was killing her, but not completely, though the part of it she could feel was kept expertly hidden, and could not be seen on her face. Laura saw out of the corner of her eye George's look of horror, perhaps even of guilt, so she hung her head to the point where she couldn't see him at all. He got the hint and stopped looking at her. She was still pretty, he thought, but there was certainly a worm inside her that was eating everything in her that was alive and decaying it. But that was fine. She was still pretty.

After Lilith was caught with Benjy the two of them were strictly forbidden to see each other. Lilith missed him, but really they had never talked much. Lilith couldn't even see any ostensible reason *why* he was locked up in Gymnopedie, besides the fact that he thought he was supposed to be a man. That didn't seem so strange to Lilith. She herself had wondered many times what life would be like as a man. Certainly easier, she had decided. If she were a man she would have probably been published by now, and wouldn't have to keep her typewriter a secret. Mel had still been coming by to see her, and had even gotten used to being around her without the mask. He no longer seemed worried that she would infect him, because she perhaps already had. And he discovered he actually found it quite pleasant.

And of course there was still Nijinsky, who was always by her side, though he would not say a word. Even in his silence, though, Lilith found he understood her better than anyone ever had. He was a magical sort of human. He spoke loudest when he danced. Lilith would often occupy several hours a day watching him dance. Sometimes she would make him pose for her and she would draw pictures of his agile and contorted body, but she would never draw his face, to protect his anonymity, and besides his face didn't matter. It was the stance of his body, which, with superhuman grace, always depicted something incredibly human. She had Nijinsky and Mel. That was enough for her for now. And honestly, she still slept with Adam, as well, though she was terrified of being buried alive again in a coffin of her own design. But the terror was exhilarating, as exhilarating as the helplessness.

If Nijinsky found out he would be furious, though, as he was constantly and silently plotting Adam's demise. He didn't want to kill him, because he felt an artist should never kill, that they must be sanctioned above that, but he did want to find some way to get him out of the hospital where Lilith could not see him. Nijinsky knew about the mysterious thralldom he had over her, the way he satisfied her masochism, and the way she often distorted this masochism into feelings of love. Lilith had come to appreciate pain for a certain beauty it had in its plaintive landscapes, and nothing else had ever been able to make her feel more intensely, more passionately, than exquisite agony. Joy could be intense sometimes, but it was always brief, so brief it must have been worthless. But pain lingered, twisting the personality into refined complexities, and with this, a lingering, subtle beauty starts to rise, one that can only be seen by the trained eye, and which only pain can create and subsequently destroy.

And she wasn't sure if she was even capable of feeling anything else, so of course pain became love, yearning became too profound to regret, and love of the requited brand, became boring. She now subscribed to the opinion that if it didn't hurt, it couldn't be love, because you cannot be feeling if you are not feeling pain. She felt like those who weren't depressed were able to be so only at the expense of ignoring the world they lived in. She felt like those who loved without grief must have been incredibly empty, too empty to love. It was a sickly opinion, but no one has been able to disprove it so far. Besides, Lilith was built to hurt. She did it as gracefully as Nijinsky danced, who also danced because of some inner agitation that forced him to keep moving and in such strange ways, making him incapable of normal expression. These are the people who love best, Lilith thought, though their love is never understood- those who have to love in monastic silence, working hard for nothing.

But deep inside she knew she had to get rid of Adam. She could not deny the fact that he had raped her. She hoped soon Nijinsky's plans would take hold, so she could go comfortably back to not feeling pain, though it meant not feeling at all, and thereby, not loving. Love, she had decided, demanded sacrifices of things she no longer had the luxury to sacrifice, and other things she had never even had to begin with. She was capable of it, but she was not equipped enough for it. And despite her devotion to suffering, she did hope someday she could acquire a love that was normal and not extraordinary enough that it could actually last. She'd give anything to be boring.

She remembered a conversation she'd had with Mel only a couple days ago. He asked her if she ever thought about death.

"Often," she told him resignedly.

"And what do you think about it?"

Lilith had paused for a moment, wondering how she could articulate something that bordered on all three lines of the human interpretation of nature: thought, feeling, and instinct. "I think," she said slowly, "that we are all a work in progress for our whole lives, until we die. That's when we are finished, like a novel, and sometimes the ending is empty, not fulfilling, but the work is still complete. We are complete when we die, but at the moment of death, we still might be unfinished."

"What do you mean?"

"I mean, I guess we're all unfinished at the moment of death. It's only death that finishes us…"

"Well, of course…"

"But I don't mean finishes us as ends us, I mean finishes us as completes us, fills the emptiness that life left there."

"Lilith," Mel had said, also slowly, trying to be polite as he possibly could. "To find meaning in death is only to naively justify your self -destruction."

"And to find meaning in life is only to fool yourself."

"You find meaning in writing. Isn't that the same as finding meaning in life?"

"But I know I'm fooling myself. Essentially art doesn't mean anything either."

"Then why do you do it?"

Lilith shrugged. "I don't know, honestly. I suppose it does give some meaning to life, even though it's supposedly life's imitation. How can we find meaning in life's imitation but not life itself?"

"Because we make it…"

"Then it's egoism."

"No. Life is made by nothing. Art is at least made by something, *someone*."

"Isn't that the same thing as being made by nothing?"

Mel began to get frustrated. "You belligerently chose to be cynical!"

"I don't want to be fooled, particularly not by myself."

"Well perhaps nothing is a person. Perhaps that's God, and if we are all people, and people are nothing, perhaps we are God, too…"

"That still doesn't answer my question. How is the imitation better than the real thing?"

"Because it's easier."

"Art isn't easy."

"But the artist generally finds it more tolerable than life. That's why they do it."

Lilith at last conceded to him. "I suppose it's easier to

create than to be created, to walk around incomplete until death. Characters are incomplete until death, too, but at least they are not you completely, just your imitation. Maybe we're God's imitation, too, and there is more meaning in us than Him just like there is more meaning in art than life, despite it being an imitation."

"God is nothing," Mel said eerily, "and we are an imitation of God, an imitation of nothing, but not actually nothing. It is the same with life and art."

"Artificial nothing."

"That's what something is."

Lilith got lost in the memory. She was beginning to really like Mel. He had a philosophical nature as well, but it didn't make him feel hopeless. She thought this must take an incredible strength of character, to be acquainted with the folly of the universe without letting it mar you. Lilith wished she could be more like that. And she was starting to realize he wasn't as afraid as she'd initially thought, either. He was willing to sit with her without the mask on, and in some ways, indulge her madness, for he knew it bordered on truth, he just wanted to get her to the point where it didn't manifest as delirium anymore, or as moral hebetude, or as cynicism. It took Lilith a long time to realize cynicism wasn't necessarily truth. But life was pretty grim in the walls of Gymnopedie, living without a colon and with people like Andrei whose brains had been picked out. She looked toward Andrei. He always sat in the same chair now on the ward, staring blankly and distantly at nothing, saliva dribbling slowly on his chest. Lilith looked away, but it was too late. She already remembered what he was like before the lobotomy. He was a timid intellectual, a mild mannered freak. Now he seemed like the shadow of a ghost, not alive in any way. Nijinsky saw the distress in her eyes and squeezed her shoulder lovingly, but he still didn't say anything. Lilith was glad. For some reason she felt like language would taint the simple purity of his nature. "Nothing is more difficult than to be simple." Aldous Huxley. She was amazed she remembered that. Then she looked at Andrei, the dribbling torpor he had now become. That wasn't simplicity, it was death. 'Nothing is easier than to be dead,' she thought, but then she looked in his eyes.

In his eyes, he was not dead. In his eyes he was numbly horrified. 'Perhaps not,' she recanted.

Laura got out of Gymnopedie hospital five days later. She was terrified that she was still pregnant. Of course the doctors had not told her much, as they never did, but at last she had gotten a proper diagnosis out of them. "You have undifferentiated schizophrenia," the doctor had told her. "That means you have every kind of schizophrenia." Lilith had taken the news placidly, though the whole time she had been hoping it wasn't true. And of course it was even worse than her pessimistic imagination had devised.

"But you can still lead a normal life," the doctor had added.

'A normal life!' Laura remembered scoffing in her head. What crazy person has ever been lucky enough to have one? What crazy person has ever been lucky enough to even *want* one?

After a few days of being back home with her mother she at last got a period. No woman has ever been so relieved. She got lucky, extremely lucky, to the point where she had unwittingly cheated death. Instead of having to get the fetus surgically removed and perhaps bleed to death, it simply reabsorbed back into her uterus, and came out with the period.

And oddly enough, she was starting to get better. George told her politely that he didn't want to see her again until she'd gotten her shit together, and this motivated her. Honestly, she expected she was never going to call him again, though, because she didn't think she would ever have the nerve, and what if she didn't get better? In her mind, they had broken up, and she was trying to keep as busy as she could to not think about him. It worked at first, but of course she eventually caved. Most of the time she was very strong, but not in regards to George. With him she was soft everywhere, helplessly vulnerable, able to rely on nothing but the hope that he would be kind to her.

She called him again after about three weeks of separation, but for the short remainder of their relationship they would not only never have sex again, but never even sleep in the same bed together, and barely touched each other at all. They had a few final endearing moments, but it was not enough to keep George interested, especially as now that she was getting better and starting to be herself again, George was becoming intimidated by her. She, in her renascence, would be more creatively productive than he was, and this he could not live with.

And in the meantime things would get more tense between her and her mother. Her mother had bought them a bottle of port one night. Laura drank the entire thing, and, fed up with watching "normal people TV" as she called it to placate her mother's judgments of her outré interests, had put in an Andy Warhol movie. It was "The Chelsea Girls." During the movie her mother stated over and over again that she hated it, and Laura would ignore her, as well as the constant irruption of "you're still drinking!"

"Well, perhaps it's better not to buy a person you know to be an alcoholic a bottle of strong wine," Laura replied saucily. After the movie was over her mother shrugged and laugh.

"Well, I suppose it's a good anti- drug film."

"It's an Andy Warhol movie. I highly doubt it's anti- drug."

"Well, it didn't seem to mean anything."

"Some art is like that, but what it means is that life doesn't mean anything, either."

Her mother looked at her like she had just said something absolutely incomprehensible and insane.

"Why would they all do that to themselves? The drugs and what not?"

"It was hard to be gay in the 60s," Laura mused. "It's still hard to be gay. It's hard to be anything that's different, including mentally ill, and often all we have to turn to is hard drugs."

"Why?"

Laura sighed. "Because when society rejects you, automatically you become society's nemesis. If that's what people say you are, that's what you become. Besides, there is no other alternative. It's either a normal life, which people who are not normal, people like *me*, can't possibly live, or a life of ignominy. And really neither is enjoyable to us, but what else are we supposed to do?"

"I don't understand what you're saying. Laura, you're drunk."

"Yes, but that doesn't mean I'm not making sense."

"You're not! How can you say any of this movie made sense?!"

Laura shrugged. "It did to me." Laura's mother had often called herself a misfit, but now Laura wished she actually had any idea of what that was like. It is so strange that human beings can only comprehend the suffering they themselves have experienced, while any suffering that is alien to them they not only fear, but condemn. '*Homo sum,* Laura thought. '*humani nihil a me alienum puto.*'

Laura had always strongly believed that being human means

you are responsible for other humans and their atrocities, even if you do not like being around other people. But strangely enough, it *is* the misanthropes who take the bulk of this responsibility, accepting unwaveringly their share of guilt, though they are never loved for it. This is sad, because perhaps misanthropes actually love other people immensely, but stay away from them due to feelings of weariness towards them and their love being brazenly misunderstood. We always misjudge people, giving the ones who are empty and false, but particularly artful at deception, constant adulation, and shunning the ones who seem callous, but are sincere. But it is difficult. People are never who they appear to be. They are either much better or much worse.

Laura finished off the bottle of port and looked at her mother one more time, who was staring at her as if she had just sighted a UFO. That look her mother gave her, it was a look she could never forget, for she had been the butt of it almost all her life, this look that people had in their eyes when she spoke that clearly showed they thought there was something deeply wrong with her, that she was odd and sick. She supposed they were right, and she supposed she would receive this look for the rest of her life, especially when she was being rational.

But before she worked up the nerve to see George again, she saw Anna first. She figured George was probably with his ex- girlfriend right now, so she might as well be with hers also. Besides, Lou Reed had just died, and George wouldn't be able to understand how that was a loss to her. Anna would, though.

They went to the bar together, both dressed in ubiquitously black mourning clothes, and played Velvet Underground songs on the juke box.

"Are you feeling any better?" Anna asked.

"A little bit."

"Are you lying?"

"Not really. I'm feeling a little bit better. There's just one thing…"

"What?"

"I've given up on writing."

Anna sighed and drank her beer. "Why? You love writing. It's your livelihood."

"But I've never been very good at it…"

"I thought you were pretty good. I think you've said a few things that have never been said before."

"I don't know," Laura sighed. "I think I was fooling myself when I thought I was a creative person."

Anna scoffed. "That blows my mind. How could you think you're not creative? Laura, most people don't write Latin phrases in lipstick on their bathroom mirrors."

Laura giggled effusively. She remembered that. She had written Latin phrases all over their bathroom mirrors in lipstick, and all her and Laura's friends had laughed with endearment at how eccentric she was. Those were better times, even if they were all on drugs. Back then she was able to speak and write as much as she wanted, and she realized timidly that right now, in this moment with Anna, she had spoken more than she had perhaps all year, certainly more than she had ever spoken to George, and she was more herself in this instance than she had been for many months. Certainly more herself than she was able to be around George. She missed Anna. She had felt closer to her than she had felt to any other person, and now to be with someone who liked her solely for how distant she was, it was unnerving. And it was sad. She had never realized that she actually did love Anna when they were together, but now she did, now that she missed her and yearned for that closeness once more which she had abandoned simply to be a heterosexual. It hadn't been worth it.

"I think you're going to give up giving up on writing," Anna said with a reassuring smile. Laura returned the smile, her first real one in a long time.

"I hope you're right."

And thankfully she was.

Another sideshow, again to watch Moniz's miracle lobotomy. The patients sat with the "regulars" as Lilith called them with embittered scorn, after having been denied their empty joys for too long, and all of them, patients and regulars alike, looked hollow eyed but expectant, hoping to see something that would momentarily thrill them without putting them in any danger. That's the problem with the regulars; they don't know how to face death. The patients did, though, as they always knew it would be one of their own that would be sacrificed for this momentary thrill, that they actually *were* in danger. They knew how to face death. They even enjoyed it.

Moniz rolled out the patient and held up the two strange surgical devices that looked like ice picks. Lilith looked at them more closely. They *were* ice picks. 'How barbaric,' she thought. The modern world is always barbaric. She looked to see who the patient was. Christian, another patient that she actually really liked, who was harmless like all of them, too tired to think anymore. Her heart sank, and she hung her head to mirror it, falling limply against some invisible noose. Nijinsky eyed her with big, warm, sad eyes, but kept that numb composure of his that he had sacrificed a great deal for. Moniz indicated that the procedure was to begin.

Lilith looked all around the theater for Benjy, but she couldn't see him anywhere. They had probably done something worse to him than her. They had probably put him in the strait jacket. Moniz started to place the ice picks under Christian's eyelids. Suddenly a blood curdling scream and the brief sight of Christian drawing a knife away slowly. Lilith lifted her head with a violently quick jerk, resurrected from her invisible execution. Her heart beat rapidly. She looked at Nijinsky with fire in her eyes. "Did he just stab Egas Moniz?" Nijinsky smiled and nodded.

There was a few seconds where everyone was still, unable to register quite what happened. Then it was slightly delayed action by the orderlies and other staff that resembled immediacy, but was actually panic. Lilith chuckled. "They've always been afraid of us," she said with satisfaction.

Christian was wrestled to the ground and put in a strait jacket. He didn't put up much protest. He had done what he wanted to do. The entire audience clapped. They had finally seen what they loved seeing the most, which thrilled them more than life ever could: murder. Andrei tried to clap but no longer had the reflexive capability, so Lilith reached over to where he was sitting, just a couple seats away from her and Nijinsky, and grabbed his hands and made them clap limply, the way a puppet does. Andrei tried to smile, but didn't have the reflexive capability for that, either, which was sad, because Lilith knew he still had the humanity. But she smiled at him warmly to indicate that she knew what he had tried to do.

Several doctors were kneeling over Moniz's unconscious

body, checking his pulse. In the corner you could see Christian, as he was being led away, laughing convulsively with blood all over his hands that was staining the blank whiteness of the strait jacket, giving it some color. One of the doctors hovering over Moniz stood up. "He is dead," he declared impassively. The audience roared with cheers, particularly those of the patients.

part II

Chapter 1

After Laura had said those things to her mother that her mother took as lunacy, Laura felt like a part of her that had been stolen was at last restored, and that her mind was becoming what it used to be; depressive, but profound. She started losing things less. During her now almost year long bout of psychosis she had lost everything that was not valuable to her (nothing was valuable to her at this time,) but necessary. She had lost her keys, her wallet several times, her phone, and almost lost her social security card a couple times. It was like she was unconsciously trying to erase herself, and society's version of her identity, which was a series of numbers. She didn't want to be a series of numbers. She hated numbers. She barely even liked words, in spite of being a writer.

And as she was slowly restoring her mind, people were at last beginning to realize that she wasn't stupid. This was always Laura's problem. People, when they first met her, usually thought she was a special needs child. This was due to her obliviousness of anything normal, and her inability to act so, either. And she was incredibly nervous around other people, who she was afraid would be hostile to her, and they usually were, saying things like "are you actually retarded?" And then the people who were nice to her were so because they thought she really was. But in Laura's mind, she had at last discovered there a capability and capacity for genius, as well as the idiocy that goes along with it, which unfortunately, was the only part of this duality that seemed so abnormal but is actually how nature works, when it chooses some unfortunate fool to be a genius, people bothered to look for. A genius is a pitiable thing. A genius is just an idiot without idiocy's bliss. At least that is what other people will always write you off as.

But now that Laura was speaking more, she was becoming less nervous. For the first time in her life, she was unafraid to show people who she actually was. And some people actually found it respectable. This was a previously unknown and unflinching joy for her. She was starting to believe that perhaps she really could make it. Perhaps she really would be an oddball piece of history, an eccentric chattel it could find value in. Before she had thought her desire for literary fame was a fool's errand, but now she realized she was the right fool for it- and all the doctor's would have called it a delusion, but she felt like she was chosen to do this kind of work, by the work itself, and that one day its impassive omniscience would reward her for her obedience to it. It sounds crazy, but if you want to make it as an artist this is the mentality you have to have. You have to be sure of it, more sure of it than anything else, if you are even sure of anything else. It is faith for people without God- faith in yourself instead of God.

So Laura started writing again, a novel she had wanted to write for years, but was afraid she wasn't skilled enough to do. She was, though. The name of the novel was *Providentia*, a tale about two luckless messiahs, one male, and the other female. She listened to music as she wrote. She had always worked this way, and it was nice to return to it. George had given her a satellite radio, and she liked to put it on the classical music station when she wrote. It just put her in the right mood. A piece came on, one Laura had never heard, but it struck her hard, making her stop writing for a moment so she could merely listen to it. It was slow and doleful but rich sounding, pleasant in a haunting way, and Laura realized, something perhaps only the mentally ill would understand. Laura went to the satellite radio to look who wrote it. A man named Erich Satie. She gasped and had to steady herself against something. The piece was called "Gymnopedie."

It all made too much sense. She looked it up. Gymnopedie was a Greek word. It was the name for a festival where men and women would dance naked together. *Gymno* means naked. So Gymnopedie used to be a holy word after all. And what an appropriate name that was for a mental hospital, where all the patients are naked, sometimes literally, but always symbolically, as you can see so many of them walking around with gauze on their wrists, barely covering large scars from knives and razors. And really, mentally ill people are always naked. They make themselves transparent, even the ones like Laura and Nijinsky who don't say anything. You don't always know what they're thinking due to their thick silence, but you know from the look in their eyes they can't mask that it is probably death.

Laura continued her research. Erich Satie had also been insane. Of course. This also made too much sense. Someone who wrote a song like that, one that was so impregnated with longing, only an insane person knows longing like that: the longing for antiquity, where it was not a crime to be mad, where it was not a crime to be naked. The longing for, if not sanity, which is not only unrealistic, but oversold (it is not the same thing as happiness, even if it denotes a lack of depression,) then a world where sanity is not worshipped, not like a God, but a Moloch, where all the unusuals are sacrificed for the glorious, but trite name of normalcy. A longing for an ancient ritual of intimacy, one that doesn't make you feel empty afterwards. A longing for a love that doesn't hurt.

Laura understood the longing all too well. She understood the hopelessly insane Erich Satie, who was, out of the lonely cordon of his sickness, able to create the most tender works of art, those painted with the longing, the *himeros* of insanity- the most plaintive, acute longing in the world. And as I mentioned, it is not a longing for sanity, for the insane know there's not much value in that, but for a different world that can satisfy the values of the worlds that they carry in their heads, which are so different from the values of the actual world, being made more of the phantoms of ideals than materials. It was strange. Laura liked this song, but it hurt, and the fact that it hurt made her like it even more. That's when a piece of art is at its best, when it causes an ambivalently pleasant but desperate pain.

Laura fell in love with this song, in spite of the fact that it was the namesake for the things she feared most.

And she was starting to make new friends. There was a girl who lived in her apartment building, Mary, a gorgeous, soft spoken red head who would have Laura over to her apartment to drink coffee and hash out the problems they were having with their boyfriends, both of whom were unfaithful. And Mary introduced her to her friends, as well, and they were an intelligent, but kind and mild mannered group. One of them Laura was particularly taken with. No one knew his name, but everyone called him Don Giovanni. He was a particularly skilled pianist and composer. Laura liked being around him because he knew who Erich Satie was, and could play Gymnopedie on the piano from memory. He would play it for Laura often and she would go into raptures over it. Oddly, it was keeping her out of the other Gymnopedie. And Don had offered to teach her how to play the piano, as well, an offer that she took almost greedily. She'd always wanted to learn the piano, but she was a little bit musically challenged. Luckily, though, Don was very patient, and told her that her work ethic would make up for it in the end. It always did.

But, in spite of all this progress, Laura would have to go back to Gymnopedie. Two more times. And things between her and George were souring rapidly, as George was envious of the enthusiasm or *enthusiasmos*, possession by a God who was just as deranged as she was, that had taken hold of her. He could not match her passion, and really passion disturbed him. He had never had it himself. He didn't want her to have these new friends, and learn to play the piano, and write novels, and what was the biggest blow to him, the fact that she was beginning to draw, as well. That was supposed to be the thing that he was good at. He was supposed to be the talented and interesting one in the relationship, not Laura, who was meant to merely provide background music and not say anything. But she had gotten tired of that. She was tired of pretending to be an idiot. She had at last realized she wasn't.

And the day she had at last, after a year hiatus, to start the novel, it was like being resurrected. She had felt her heart beat for the first time in almost three hundred and sixty days that it had been sleeping. It was the most exhilarating feeling in the world. Laura supposed it gave her the satisfaction most people could only find in sex, though it was not erotic, merely intellectual. But intellectualism had always been a form of spirituality to Laura, so writing was naturally more satisfying than sex, for the subtle, modest salvation that it implied .She wished often that she was normal, and engaged in simple pleasures instead of striving towards passionate and lofty, high minded ideals, but this was the way she was born, she understood. Something as regular, even routine, and ubiquitous as sex would never thrill her as much as when the words would flow so naturally, without her even having to think about them, as if there was another mind in her, a better mind than the one she used to speak to people, which had suddenly taken over and guided her hand with tender patience, and what was even more, clarity. Her thoughts never felt so clear like this, only during the thirty minutes a day that she would write. And it was like a breath of fresh air to someone who had already drowned, but was still working their way up to the surface for air even after death, that still kept going, instinctively, after they had already expired. It was the will power of a ghost, which is actually quite formidable and inexhaustible. She was back from the dead, and ready to explain what it was like, to at last elucidate the great mystery, the thing itself.

Chapter 11

Lilith was with Mel again. They were quickly becoming friends, and, in spite of their philosophical differences, even beginning to understand one another. This was a great joy for Lilith, who was rarely understood, and typically only by those who don't speak or are dead. She had often hoped that she could find a way to resurrect her favorite writers, temporarily, of course, so she could have someone to talk to. They understood what it was like to be alone around other people. Or maybe everyone knew what that was like, but only a special few were able to admit it to themselves. Really we are all alone all day and through the night which can be even longer. We are all separate from each other, though few of us are individuals, but the individuals feel the pain of this separateness the most, because they cannot, like normal people, find something feckless to enjoy with other people, all of them wanting to be consumed by something that doesn't make them think. Lilith thought Mel perhaps understood this, too. He was a fairly serious minded individual, but not one who was prone to depression. This was where he fell short of genius. But Lilith liked him. Not everyone can be a genius, or the whole world would be in pain, like it already is. Maybe everyone is a genius, then, but most people choose to resign themselves to the destructive aspects of it over the creative ones. But a genius is someone who wants to help the world, (for they know that is the only way they can help themselves,) not destroy it. But they often end up doing both. This makes sense, because only a lunatic would ever want to be a genius, and only a lunatic can really create and really destroy.

Lilith thought of this and became depressed again. It was so easy for her to feel down, but it took a great effort for her to feel up, and then it didn't feel genuine, because she had practically forced it. But she was lucky in one way. The days that she felt genuinely good were so few that she was able to hold onto them. They didn't just pass by like a long parade of farce until the end of her life, where it soon realized it had been wasted. Lilith felt strange. She desperately yearned for the unity or *henosis* of humankind, but she also wanted to be alone.

"What happened to Christian?" she asked Mel, trying to distract herself.

"He's in confinement."

"Did he go to jail?"

"No."

"He's never going to get out of here, is he?" she said through the same never-ending sigh.

"No, probably not."

Neither of them said anything for a moment until Mel smiled at her warmly, trying to make her feel less sad, and less alone, though she wanted to be alone and didn't at the same time. I sometimes think there are two of us in all of us, both with conflicting desires. Kurt Koffka actually said, "the whole is *other* than the sum of its parts." *Je est un autre.*

"You really care about the other patients, don't you?" Mel asked with fondness.

Lilith shrugged. "I've always liked crazy people. Crazy people are the nicest people. We've all been trained to hate ourselves since childhood and it's made us humble."

Mel didn't know whether to laugh or cry, so he decided to laugh because it was more defensive than vulnerable. And no one wants to be vulnerable except crazy people, who get a kind of masochistic adrenaline rush from it. Or maybe they're just honest. The church bells started ringing. Suddenly a scream.

Lilith and Mel ran from Lilith's room across the hospital's grounds, but they had already seen it from the window. The church bells were ringing non -stop, but with a ferocity they had never shown before, as if there was a heavier weight pulling on them now. DING! DING! DING AN SICH! Lilith wanted to scream as well, but she kept it to herself. She grew tired of running and stood still a moment, paralyzed. Mel grabbed her by the hand, but didn't force her to keep going. They were close enough. They were right at the midpoint between the butcher's shop and the chapel, staring numbly at the stark white crucifixes erect in the ground without any names on them. A new grave had been dug, waiting. At last Lilith had the strength to look at the chapel with the furious din of its bells, playing its usual dirge, but this time with frantic anger, the sound of schizophrenia.

The bells were moving sluggishly, encumbered by the weight of Andrei's lifeless body where he had hanged himself off the clapper. His body swung with the bells like a piece of debris that had been attached to them, violently, a puppet being jerked all too rapidly across a small stage with a large audience, as all the patients and employees of Gymnopedie were staring at the sight slack jawed and impotent, not entirely sure what they were looking at. DING! DING! DING AN SICH! The thing itself.

Finally Lilith began to weep. Mel had almost forgotten that he was outside, in front of all the people at Gymnopedie, without a mask on. He hoped he could masquerade as a patient, or one of Lilith's family visiting, as, with an incredible spell of courage that he had never really been known for previously, he held Lilith in his thin, shaking arms and let her weep on his chest. No one cut Andrei down off the bell for a while. It was a long walk up to the belfry, so the bells kept on with their violent, pendulous cry of all hopes lost, and nothing left to do but to pray to God that there is a God, one that will not let lost souls like Andrei be mute in death like they were in life. But Lilith supposed he wasn't mute right now. He kept saying DING! DING! DING AN SICH!

…ding an sich. …ding an sich.

Chapter III

Her mother showed up at her door, knocking frantically. Laura answered sleepily. She had kicked her mother out of her house about a week ago. They had gotten into an argument and her mother had called her a cunt. That was the last straw for her. "Go try to get power of attorney over someone else!" she had screamed, and shoved her out of the door, locking it behind her. On her way out her mother had thrown her phone down the stairs and broken it to get the last word. But Laura had learned the best way to deal with her family was to pretend she had amnesia, and act like she had forgotten about the offense two days later when her mother or father half-heartedly apologized, if they apologized at all. So her mother was already at the door.

"Laura," she said in her same mock calm, mock worry, but fully condescending voice. "You're wearing the same clothes you wore yesterday and you're late for work."

"Yea, cuz I'm twenty two and have a drinking problem."

"You need to go back to the hospital."

"No, I need to go to work. As you said, I'm late. Please leave so I can get ready," and she slammed the door in her mother's face once again.

Only a few minutes later a female cop show up at her door. "For fuck's sake," Laura grumbled, but let her in anyway.

"Your mother called us. She's worried."

"Is that what she told you?"

The cop ignored her. "So, you've been to Gymnopedie four times?"

"Yes, but I'm feeling better."

"Do you have hallucinations?"

"Sometimes, but not right now. And I really need to be getting to work."

"You work at Roland's Pizza, right?"

"Yes."

"I'll give you a ride there." Then she looked around at Laura's tiny apartment. She noticed it was, for the most part, clean, but there was strange art all over the walls. She looked at the book shelves. "You read a lot?" she asked.

"Yes." Laura picked up the book that was sitting on her coffee table. "This is the one I'm reading right now. It's called 'One Flew Over the Cuckoo's Nest.' I feel like I *wrote* this one."

The officer laughed, then gave her a ride to work.

As soon as Laura got there, Jacob, the boss had called. "I'm sorry, Laura, but I'm gonna have to let you go. This is getting too…"

"Well do you want me to finish out the day? I'm here now."

"Oh, you're at work?"

"Yes."

"Oh. Shit. Never mind, carry on." Laura felt stressed about get bombarded by her mother and then a police officer first thing in the morning, but she was happy she had abated what felt like hordes of people who wanted her to go back to Gymnopedie for a reason she couldn't understand. She really was feeling better. She had just woken up late that day.

But the day would slowly unravel her, as it often did. Laura could feel the weight of her work more than usual that day, feeling over aware of how demoralizing it actually was, how demoralizing all work is if it isn't creative. She went into the bathroom to escape. She washed her hands with manic fervor then reluctantly looked into her face. Her eyes were dull and glazed over, all her features impassive, her mouth small and resolutely closed. She looked very dull. The work had done its job. It had robbed her of herself again. She tried to smirk or scoff but not a single line on her face would divert from its stoic, empty mold. So she washed her hands again, trying to get the stain of her looks at least off of her hands. 'One only has to look at themselves to be looking into the void,' she thought mechanically, 'a catoptric lifelessness.'

Time shifted again. The rest of the work day flashed before her eyes like a brief, but uneventful seizure, a moment of useless lightning when it's not raining. She was glad, but the reason it went by so quickly was because she was in a daze, something that resembled the stupor of drugs. And her eyes went all empty and far away again. Her co -worker Darcy was afraid. She knew that look in Laura's eyes all too well, and she knew they had again become the dull, tired looking gates to hell, the entrance to her mind that would close off the rest of the world when it became too sensitive and too ugly inside. Laura had always thought she fell to Earth from some distant star, but now she realized she fell to Earth from Hell, she fell *upwards*, and found little discernible difference between this new world she inhabited from the old one, that they reflected each other like a dual mirror that distorted reality into reality, a catoptric deathlessness in torment. And she could hear that ancient voice again, the low, humming vacuum sound, the *trismos*.

"I am a sick man, a wicked man," she whispered to herself, snakelike.

"What?" Darcy asked.

Laura wouldn't repeat it. 'Oh fuck,' Darcy thought. 'She's going quiet again.'

And Darcy was right to worry. After work she had insisted that Laura go to the bank with her. The bank wasn't very far from Roland's, and Laura neither said yes or no, she just nodded because she wasn't really able to decipher the question that had just been asked her. While they were at the bank Laura tried to throw herself in front of a moving car.

Darcy restrained her, and in her arms Laura kept screaming: "Let me go!" Everyone at the bank had seen it. The whole town of Astrum knew she was off her medication again. Later Laura would not even be able to remember trying to kill herself this way, but it couldn't have been an accident, like it wasn't the first time with the pills or the second time with the pills and the razor. She may not have been aware of what she was doing, but she knew why she was doing it, each time. Because life had never lost anything, because it never had anything to begin with.

Darcy took her home. "Are you gonna be okay by yourself?" but Laura had already walked out of her car without answering, or even listening.

She knew she wasn't feeling well away again, so at last she took the medicine, and decided to lay down for a bit, hoping she could sleep it off. As she lay in bed, staring listlessly at her walls with the strange art work, and the hand drawn version of the *sefirot* hanging above her head, she began to hear the voices in her head again. It was her friends and neighbors, telling her they wanted her to get the hell out of the city of Astrum.

"I'll get out soon," she promised them, but more in the tone of begging. "I'll leave tomorrow. First just please let me get some sleep."

She heard a knock on the door, but feeling unable to be certain if it was only in her mind or not, she didn't answer it. Then she heard another voice. "Paramedics."

She answered the door in a frenzy. "What do you want?" she asked angrily.

"Your mother called, she's worried."

"Is that what she told you?"

"Have you taken your medication today, Laura?"

"I just did, and now if you'll excuse me, I'm trying to take a nap."

She tried to slam the door in the paramedics face, but he stopped the door. "Well, listen, your mother told us…"

"My mother is also insane," she almost screamed. "Listen: My name is Laura Vance. My birthday is July 20th 1991, the president of the United States is Barack Obama…"

"Alright, alright…"

"Listen: I've had an extremely stressful day, and I have just taken my medication, and now I need a bloody nap!"

"Are you sure you're alright?"

"YES! God what I wouldn't give to not be asked that question every day, as if I'm some kind of invalid…"

"Okay, okay. I'll leave you alone," and the paramedic walked back down the stairs with angry, thunderous footfalls. Laura was proud of herself. Again she had abated the menace that wanted her to return to Gymnopedie. She tried to lay down for a nap again, but still the voices.

'The medicine must not have kicked in yet, she thought tiredly, so she decided to watch a movie. She had just ordered a copy of The Sorrow and the Pity online. Woody Allen was always talking about it, and she had grown curious, wanting to see it herself. She put it in. It was perhaps not the wisest movie to watch during a manic psychotic episode.

She watched the whole thing in one sitting, and after it was done she was convinced World War II was happening again, with America acting as Germany in this farcical re run of the most shameful years of history, and she also somehow got it in her head, that instead of the French Resistance, she was the head of the American Resistance. She got on her phone and started dispatching confused, worthless orders to her friends who all knew it meant nothing, that she was probably off her medicine again. It was so disappointing that she actually had taken it that day, but it was too late when she did. The illness or whatever it was that liked to slowly build up and then reappear in her head had already taken hold, and there was no Earthly medicine that could stop it. Her friends politely ignored her.

This just made her feel more alone, giving her that old feeling, a small shed of rationality in this madness, the lonely realization that most people did not care about the world the way she did, and that it was actually *because* she was insane that she did. It is strange to care so much about something you hate. But is it really crazy to care about what happens to the people who are ruined by history? But of course if you're insane, you're one of them, so this is where the understanding and concern comes from, the knowledge that it could happen to you too. Otherwise, if you are completely safe, untouched by any worldly menace, it doesn't bother you. This is the saddest fact of human behavior. In some ways, I'm glad I'm so ill, if it at least has taught me mercy.

No answers, and Laura felt helpless. She thought the Nazis would win this time, if no one cared. Lucky for her, it was a delusion, but delusions always base themselves in the facts of reality we otherwise ignore. If it really were happening, would they care? Did they the first time? And would it happen again? We have to stop letting history repeat itself, and this will be impossible unless we stop it from happening at all. That would be a good day for Laura and I. We could both stop writing and become normal people with normal jobs.

Suddenly she got in her narcissistic, deranged head that she was the second coming, and of course no one would believe her because she was female. She sent another mass text to her friends saying she would be crucified that night. She got some messages in return telling her she needed to go back to the hospital. That was a nicer way of saying she had to return to Gymnopedie.

She stayed up all night, and was surprised when dawn began to break that she hadn't bled to death yet. She was convinced she was going to, and had accepted it with what she thought was grace, but really her mind was just trying to satisfy her death wish, only to reveal by morning that it had tricked her again, that she would have to keep going, that she could be Christ like if she wanted to, but a Christ that would not be satiated by death. And come to think of it, she didn't really want to die for anyone's sins. She thought sin was just part of growing up. All she wanted to do was stop people from committing their crimes against themselves, which she thought was different than sin. Sin is practically blameless.

It's violence that is worse than sin and which people need to stop dying for.

She went to work again.

Lilith sat up with Mel. The hour was late, and he was about to go home, but he wanted to check up on her.

"How are you doing, since…" but he didn't want to say it. Since Andrei died.

"I'm fine," she said. "I'm a little bit depressed, but I'm depressed for no reason…"

"No reason?"

"Well, there's never a reason. And yet there's always a reason."

Mel didn't say anything, running through his head what she had just said, trying to make sense of it, for he felt there was sense to it, but even the simplest things Lilith said were convoluted. He liked that about her. He liked that she was hard to understand, but not so abstract and delirious that the hard to understand things she said were complete nonsense, but were in fact weighted with meaning, though the meaning was always obscure. The meaning is always obscure. There's never a reason, and yet there's always a reason. Grief is not necessarily senseless, though it results from a lifetime of senseless experience.

Mel patted her gently on the leg, then put his mask on and began to leave.

"Wait!" Lilith called.

He turned around, the mask still on. It was unnerving to Lilith. She hadn't seen him like that in a long time, and now he looked nightmarish and intimidating, having completely disguised his gentleness with this macabre face. The face of a doctor, a plague doctor. She thought about the rats, the way they had bitten her all over her body, and how Mel had been the one to prescribe her that torment. And to think that otherwise he was a fairly normal, mild mannered man! It didn't make sense. Nothing made sense, especially when the masks were on.

"Stay with me," she suddenly begged.

Mel lifted the mask off, and Lilith audibly sighed with relief. "I can stay a few minutes more, but then I have to go home."

"No, that's not what I meant. Stay the night."

"Lilith, I could get in a lot of trouble for that…"

"I don't want to have sex. I just want to sleep next to someone. It's been so long since I've slept next to someone."

"You know I have a wife, right?"

Lilith's heart sank. "You…you do?"

"Yes."

"Just for a night, Mel, please. You won't be unfaithful to your wife."

"There's no way we could get away with it."

Lilith didn't say anything, but let her head sink against her breast, gazing at Mel distantly. He sighed. "Just this one time."

He crawled in the bed next to her. Lilith fell asleep almost instantly, feeling comfortable for the first time in years. Mel looked at her as she breathed heavily next to him, an image of peace he had never seen in her before. 'She is pretty,' he thought to himself reluctantly. 'If I weren't married, and we were in a different situation…' He tried to banish these thoughts, though, and turned away from her. He went to sleep, as well, but his sleep was troubled.

So was Lilith's. She went to sleep and almost immediately started dreaming. This was a night terror, as we know today. And as she dreamed these nightmare visions Mel also dreamed, the exact same ones.

Both of them in the secret, troubled world that rested beneath their eyelids first saw an image of Andrei's purple, swollen face hanging from the belfry. This image faded slowly, holding onto the mind for far too long. Then pan to another scene in the mind's eye. A mental hospital in Poland, somewhere in the distant, but yet alarmingly close future. A group of Nazis were storming the hospital, grabbing patients at random and forcing them into train cars. No one protested, not even the patients, who knew how helpless they were. Then pan to another scene. The same group of patients the Nazis had loaded like animals into the train, all standing together naked in a group, *Gymnopedie*, under several shower heads. Suddenly, the dream became like a film, one with a split screen, where both Lilith and Mel could see the patients from the Polish mental hospital in the gas chamber, and right next to that an image of Lilith herself in the showers at Gymnopedie being half drowned by the nurses forcing the ice cold water down her throat and nostrils. This scene played out for a while, also for too long an interval of a time, like Andrei's death. The Polish mental patients slowly start to lose their posture, slumping towards the ground, clawing against the cement wall and gasping for air, dying, while Lilith is gasping for air right next to them, though she is luckier than they are. She is not dying, not yet. Then all the naked bodies fall over each other in a silent but agonized hoard. Fifty or so patients, all dead. The sonderkommando come in to remove the bodies, while on the other side of the image Lilith is being escorted by orderlies out of the shower. 'How could this be,' Lilith thought to herself almost lucidly through the dream. 'The future is supposed to be better than the past.' *But chaos increases with time.* But time doesn't really increase, so chaos is always the same: the past, the present, and the future, all chaos, so there is no "better time" to escape to. Diachrony is synchrony.

You see, the year Lilith was in Gymnopedie State Mental Hospital was about 1869. Many of the things she experienced at the hospital did exist in the present, but many of the other things were in the past, and others in the future. For example, mental hospitals had stopped participating in Sideshow a long time ago, about a couple centuries ago. Sylvia Plath and Anne Sexton weren't born yet, and weren't held in a psychiatric hospital till the sixties, a long way away from Lilith's time. Dr. Egas Moniz had yet to bring the world of madness his miracle lobotomy, and had yet to be murdered. Lilith had hallucinated these things, but they had been real.

As soon as you enter Gymnopedie State Mental Hospital time ceases to appear rational, and presents itself to you for what it is: a landscape of simultaneous events, a circle; *a serpentine mind, always eating itself.* Time is an anachronism. It should have never taken place at all. Patients at Gymnopedie know this, for time to them does not progress, but spins out of control and overwhelms the mind with its actual senselessness. It is terrifying, to experience time as it really is, for it doesn't really exist, and can only be hallucinated. But the hallucinations are real, only reality doesn't exist either. Nothing does.

The worst part, Lilith felt, as she could still see in her dream the shower at the concentration camp and the shower at Gymnopedie, was when the past, present, and future all looked similar, even indistinguishable. Or when the future was just like the present but with added horrors. She woke up and began weeping softly. Mel woke up, too. "Why do they do this to us?" Lilith asked, but Mel was lost for words. He had seen the same thing she had, and he knew in his heart that naturally wanted to deny it that it was true. Suddenly Lilith started screaming, unceasingly. Mel didn't try to stop her.

He realized now she had every right to.

Chapter IV

When Laura got to work she was the only one there. She began making the dough, and of course fucked it up as she always did, even though she had been doing this job for years. 'Maybe people are right', she thought. 'Maybe I am retarded. But I know I'm not stupid.' She sighed as she tried to rectify her mistake. She was not stupid, but she was incapable of doing normal things, the things others were able to do with ease; practical things, common sense things. She could only do extraordinary things, and only when other people weren't looking. Otherwise, when people were around, she was so shy she appeared imbecilic. "I am a sick ma-no, stop. Stop, please. Shut up Laura." And she bent down and felt the unbearable isolation again, the *entfremdung* of being born a person who is made only for the few.

Suddenly as she looked into the menacing machine, the mixing bowl that made the dough, she heard a horrible scream, and there was blood in the bowl, mixing with the dough. Bright red blood, with some glitter in it, and still the screaming. She thought one of her friends must have been in trouble. She turned off the mixing bowl, grabbed her bicycle, the ever reliable Bucephalus, to ride out of Roland's pizza to Mary's house. Her co -worker David had showed up as she was leaving.

"Where the hell do you think you're going?" he asked angrily.

"Something's happened."

"What?"

"I'm not sure yet," and she rode off. She got to Mary's house quickly and knocked on the door with desperation. No one answered, but she heard something. She thought she heard the weak protest, "No," and then a loud banging noise, like someone had been hit over the head. She quickly called the police.

The police couldn't make sense of what she way saying, and Laura grew frustrated, because of course she thought she was making perfect sense. "I think my friend is being raped by her boyfriend!" she screamed again.

"Okay. What's the boyfriend's name?"

"Keith Alvarez."

"Is he Hispanic?"

Laura fumed. "No!" she yelled. "He's white! They're both white! And why the hell does it matter anyway?!"

"And what's your name?"

"Laura."

"Laura what?"

"Laura Olmsted."

"What?"

Laura gulped back tears. "Laura Vance, I mean. Vance."

She was also recently under the delusion that William, the man she had once naively thought she loved, was back in town, and had come to marry her. Of course, this created imaginary complications with George. She thought George and William had taken over the apartment across the hall from her, where they would spend their days trying to stab one another or fucking. Laura didn't mind when they fucked, though. That's what boys do. But really it was an extremely narcissistic delusion, considering neither William or George cared enough about her to fight over her.

She went to leave the apartment complex, but couldn't find her bicycle anywhere. She didn't assume it was stolen, though. She tried never to assume that, especially since she knew how easily she lost things. She walked back to Roland's. It wasn't very far from where her and Mary lived. When she got back to the pizza place she found her bicycle sitting by the back door. She had never taken it with her to begin with. Her phone rang, it was the police. She answered.

"Astrum police."

"Yes?"

"This is Laura…Vance?"

"Yes."

"We talked to your friend Mary. She says you have hallucinations, so we believe what you reported was a hallucination, as well."

"Oh. Well, good."

"Take care, Laura. Take your medicine, get some help…" and on and on.

She went back inside and David yelled at her. She ignored him and tried to get through the day. Luckily it was only a half day; luckily she didn't have to spend ten to twelve hours making the same damn dough over and over again.

"You know, if you don't get your shit together they're gonna lock you up for good," David said with an odd mixture of concern and rage.

"They don't do that anymore."

"Are you taking your fucking medicine?"

"I'm trying to. It doesn't always work."

"I'll give you a ride home when we're done. At this rate you're gonna get fired."

"I know," Laura said without any disappointment. "Honestly, I think that might be good for me."

David paused for a moment, and dropped his tough love mien to be honest with her. "Yea, really you should be on disabilities."

Laura didn't say anything, but she knew he was right. She had never been able to do normal work, and really the thought of getting paid to do things she felt no passion towards, only a sense of inculcated, forced, and begrudging obligation, repulsed her. It wasn't really living, it was just surviving, and Laura had never really cared for surviving. It was an instinct she didn't have. And she was tired of working. She just wanted to go home to beat herself.

When she did get home her mother was there again, leafing through an address book, trying to find a number. Laura knew she was trying to call Gymnopedie.

"Please leave," she said. "I have to get some sleep."

"I'm just going to make myself a cup of tea."

"Alright, but after that I want you to go."

"Laura, you're pushing everyone away again!"

"Because you all want to see me locked up in a mental hospital!"

"Sweetheart, you're ill."

"Piss off," and she climbed in her bed, defeated, waiting for the paramedics to show up again.

Across the hall she heard William and George fighting. "Please, both of you, shut up," she whispered through bared teeth, so her mother couldn't hear her. "The computer is going into sleep mode."

"You have to choose between one of us!" she heard George shouting. "Please pick me." Then she imagined he grabbed a razor and started picking off his skin with it, saying "pick me, pick me," repeatedly.

She sank into the bed. "I pick you,' she said numbly, but tears were falling out of her eyes. If this were actually real, and she did have to make a choice between George and William, she actually would have chosen William. It was obvious to her that he was the better man, though, truthfully, neither of them were that good. But George had already hurt her too many times now. She still heard him through the wall, slicing at himself manipulatively, and the hollow, insistent "pick me, pick me." She pulled the blankets over her ears and kept humming drily, without feeling "yes, I pick you. Yes, I pick you."

"Are you alright, Laura?" her mother called from the other room.

"Yes, I'm fine. Please go now."

"Honey, I've been hearing some strange things about you. This morning you told everyone you and William were married…"

"No. I'm still with George." She cried some more, silently.

"Ok. Good."

"Please go," Laura begged. "I want to be alone."

"That's part of the illness, sweetheart…"

"GO!"

It took her another long five minutes, but she left. "Why are you doing this to yourself?" she heard William ask through the walls. "You know you don't love him."

"I do, though. I really do."

"Why? He barely lets you say a word."

Laura sighed, continuing her conversation with this romantic *tulpa* of hers, her favorite imaginary friend. "It's hard to explain, and honestly I hope you never understand."

"I won't. I'll find a normal girlfriend to do normal things with, and we'll be happy. I'm not gonna love someone who drives me to Gymnopedie every other month."

"I'm sorry," she groaned.

"It's not your fault. It would be too easy to blame you, but this is not the kind of love anyone wants to be in, Laura. Tell him to fuck off, for God's sake."

"I'M GONNA FUCKING KILL YOU!" George screamed and lunged for William's throat. Everyone knew he was right.

A few hours passed, and of course Laura didn't get any sleep. The whole time lying in bed was spent trying to mediate the imaginary violence of two men who didn't care about her, but who she had grown masochistically attached to. There is no reward in unrequited love, but it does seem to hold some charm for the mentally ill, who cannot really imagine, in spite of their fantastical delusions, someone being in love with them. Once Laura found that she could not control George and William, not in real life, and not even in her own head, she just started masturbating over the sound of their discordant approach to romance, which was really her discordant approach to romance, because she had found love mirrored time, the way it would fade but first become blindly chaotic, impulsive and panicked. And the way she fucked herself was also in a panic, as if someone were forcing her to do it. It always felt this way. It felt this way all the times she tried to kill herself, as well. She didn't really want to fuck and die, but there was something in her that made her do it, something that wasn't of her own invention, that had been inside her before she had even been born, a need she did not want that outdated her. And love was a need she did not want, as well. So was living, so was dying, so was fucking, but if Laura would have been allowed to use her own rationale instead of the primordial rationale of her *gattungswesen,* she would have written them all off as too expensive, as things she couldn't afford.

The worst though was when that thing inside of her that wanted to die, the thing that was not her, but some eerie voice from the past, a ghost in her mind, became so persuasive that she agreed with it. Then she would become one with the death instinct, no longer a human but an intense longing for death with a counter intuitive heartbeat. She briefly thought about suicide, but then someone turned the lock of her door with a shaky key and walked in. Her mother again. Laura didn't have the strength to fight it anymore. Deep inside her she knew she would be going back to Gymnopedie tonight. The sane had beaten her again, as they always did, for they were always better armed. No one lets insane people have weapons, or even any defenses, so when they came at her in armies telling her she was mad, she had no choice but to agree with them.

She sat in the living room with her mother. They turned on the TV. Still in the back of her head she heard William's passionate but logical arguments against her staying with George. "You're not as callous as he is, you're really not. I think sometimes you'd like to be, but you're not."

Laura didn't have any alcohol, so she was drinking iced coffee, as quickly and with the same fervor as she would have been drinking wine, like she normally did, but she was trying to quit drinking for George. She was trying to do anything to make him actually love her, but, sadly enough, it only made him resent her. And she was tired of this, her whole life, which seemed like an ironic, tragic moral play about narcissism, featuring a romance that was much more like a screwball comedy than a romance. She wished she had alcohol.

Her and her mother watched PBS. For some reason Laura felt William would be coming any minute now to tell her mother and George and everyone to fuck off and just let her be whoever she wanted to be, crazy or not, but she failed to realize that George was not this kind of hero, and no man ever would be for her, because she was much more brave than they were. She always ended up having to be her own knight in shining armor, which was always disappointing, as she was growing to realize more and more every day that men were not really courageous anymore, and maybe they never had been. She drank the iced coffee and stared numbly at the TV screen.

"Mom," she said wearily.

"Yes, sweetheart?"

"You know that picture in my room with the hands drawing each other?" It was M.C. Esher's "Drawing Hands."

"Yes, dear."

"Please stop moving it. That really bothers me when you move it."

"Move what?"

Laura sighed. "Nevermind. Just please don't move anything in my house."

Her mother didn't say anything for a moment. "I got you something today." And then she pulled out a zigzagged metal wire. "You could wear this to hold up your bra."

Laura ignored this comment and put it on her fourth finger like a ring, and waited expectantly for when William would come and rescue her from herself and the people around her who were making her more insane. But they never saw it this way. They refused to admit her mental illness might not be of her invention, but theirs. Laura thought about the gifts her mother had given her in recent months. A wire to hold up her bra, and a perfume called "La Vida Loca," which she would bring to Laura every time she was in Gymnopedie, although she never requested it. How was that not making fun of her? And then she thought of George. He had laughed about it, too. But, no: that didn't make her crazy, it wasn't them. It was something she was doing to herself, as if it were merely a lifestyle choice. They wouldn't even own up to the fact that, though perhaps they had not caused it, they were making it worse. People are mind boggling. They can commit any evil that briefly strikes their fancy and afterwards forget about it, so they can still say with firm conviction they are innocent, and really believe it, too. They think they're faultless just because they've been lucky enough to have never had a large group of doctors and contemporaries in masks tell them something is wrong with them. To be so lucky. To be so easily accepted for being blissfully unaware of the weight of your guilt, for being blind to the darker nature of humanity even as you take part in it. Laura could only ever dream of being such a comfortable coward.

The rest of the conversation I can't remember. By that point the psychosis had completely taken over. It's a terrible misunderstanding when people think you are your illness, when really it is the exact opposite. Having an illness like this is having someone else inside you, someone completely alien to you, and yet who isn't anyone else. It's the other that really everyone has inside them, but which most people are able to repress with the ease of routine and normalcy. It is the *zweifle*, the doubt of not only your own existence, but existence in general. It's the part of you that wants to hurt yourself to make sure you are still temporal and made of flesh, that you haven't died already and now are just continuing to live life begrudgingly in the small remainder of consciousness you have left, that it isn't just in your head. Unfortunately, none of these things can be proven, your own existence or existence in general. The proof won't even be in the pain. Even that's in your head, but for people like Laura, nothing feels more real than what is in the imagination. Nothing seems more legitimate than a nightmare or a ghost, especially when your mind is like a museum, haunted by aging muses, by dead worlds and their dead languages, old and forgotten words composing themselves in a very old mind that is forced to pretend to be modern. When it feels like you are from both the past and the future, but never the present.

When Laura's mother finally called the cops twenty of them came in and surrounded her. She wigged out immediately and ran across the hallway, hoping William or George would end this nightmare for her, but neither of them had ever been able to do this, even though in passing moments, when they at last realized how alone she was, they had perhaps wanted to. Through years Laura came to terms with the fact that some minds, the ones like hers, are not able to be healed or even put at ease by love, because their critical agitation is actually what makes them able to live. William and George, even if they had loved her, would not have been able to help her.

Still, it was too nice an ideal to give up entirely. She got down on one knee in front of her neighbor's door, where she thought

William was, and held out her hand with the wire ring on it. The police thought it was a weapon, and tased her. The incredible volts of electricity conducted through the wire ring, sending an odd, electric pulse through her hand as she convulsed wildly on the floor of her hallway. The police then put her in hand cuffs and took her outside, slamming her roughly against their squad vehicle before they shoved her in it by the head.

And the whole time she was twitching from the taser and singing at the top of her lungs, "HOWEVER FAR AWAY, I WILL ALWAYS LOOOVEE YOOUU," But at this point she didn't know who she was singing it for anymore.

It was just a nice idea.

Chapter V

Since Andrei's death and that horrible dream, Lilith wasn't the same anymore. She was actually insane now.

She walked around chewing her hands and staring at nothing with a wild frenzy in her eyes, as if in everything she looked at she saw God, and God was ugly. And Mel started avoiding her, too. He didn't want to think about that horrible dream with its damning truth, the awful things that were in store for the world, as he also had now got that feeling, the feeling the mad had, that time doesn't heal but creates new wounds, scarring its own face with its chaotic nonsense, its blind senselessness. He tried his best not to think about it, and that meant avoiding Lilith, who needed him now more than ever. He tried to calm himself down, thinking that by the time this happened, these gas chambers, he would already be long dead, but this only made him feel selfish. He wanted to warn people, but he wasn't sure he knew how to put it into words-he wasn't sure anyone could put it into words, because it was too insane even for the insane to understand, and he realized if he ever spoke about it he would be labelled as one of them. And what was worse than that, the fact that people never heed warnings. Sometimes he thought if he warned people it would just make it happen sooner, the way people, with unconscious self-destruction, make prophecies come to life instead of trying to prevent their foretold happenings. It's strange. The disbelief in prophecies of doom is almost what makes them certain, and denying inevitability is perhaps what creates inevitability.

But Mel couldn't believe something like that was ever meant to be inevitable. He couldn't believe it was pre- destined, for surely even God is not that cruel, but His creations are. They are mirrored in His image, His sadistic, arbitrary image. For the first time in his life, Mel was clinically depressed, no different from his patients, who he now felt he had to wear the mask around, otherwise they would see it in his eyes, and start screaming "Physician, heal thyself!," though he wasn't sure if he could heal anything.

So Lilith no longer had anyone to talk to, except Nijinsky, ever the true friend, but one who would not respond to her grief with words. She began to talk to Adam again, which only made her feel worse. He didn't even begin to understand. She was starting to realize how incredibly stupid he was, because no one had ever hated him without reason. She was just grateful that he didn't rape her again, though he never apologized for it, and they didn't talk about it at all. She tried to explain certain things to him.

"You see, enlightenment is chemical," she would drone on to these unresponsive ears that had never wanted to listen to what was, if not truth, at least a deranged semblance of it. "That's why it's temporary. Anything that is chemical fades, and the whole universe is made out of chemicals. That's why everything fades."

Suddenly Zeir and Arich Anpin walked in. They were permanent residents at Gymnopedie. No one, not even any of the staff, knew how long they had been there, but Lilith got the feeling they were still temporary even though they were older than everyone else. Arich Anpin never said anything, and Zeir did all of the talking. "We agree with you," he said in a mirthful voice, his smile sardonic and his eyes twinkling. They both made Lilith uncomfortable, they always had. She tried not to look at them and turned back to Adam, who she really didn't want to look at either, for she knew he symbolized the way men are so weak, but still dominant over society because they feel a self -entitled right to it.

And Adam reaffirmed this thought immediately. "You should stop reading so much," he said. "It's making you crazier."

Lilith suddenly thought of the French word for gallows. It was "potence," deriving from Latin "potentiae," meaning power. And power is being one of the select few who are allowed to murder. It's being someone who can fake omnipotence without the condemnation of blasphemy, an omnipotence through violence, leaving the victims of power limp and lifeless, hanging with a bag over their heads and broken necks, completely stripped of identity before death. *Omnipotence.* "All gallows." All left to hang. That's God's message to the world, or destiny.

And she remembered the way Adam had punched her against the head, then did whatever he wanted with her, just because he didn't want her on top; because he would rather see her dead than her show even the mildest semblance of power. That's *potence,* the gallows. It's supposed to be the power to punish criminals, but it is mostly exercised as the power to punish whoever the hell you might fancy to, or whoever threatens this position of power. And no, that was not something she had wanted to learn, and it *was* making her crazier, but she had no choice. It was something women have experienced from the beginning of time and still do even to this day, for the world really has not changed much for them.

"That's the part of being crazy I like," she said, trying to sound proud but feeling unable to. "If I were crazy and stupid I'd really be helpless." She thought of the word potence still, and how it really means anything that's powerful can kill you, including knowledge. But it didn't matter. It was worth dying that way. This was the only thing she felt sure of, and she wouldn't let a man take it from her, though they would try to her whole life. It was the only thing she had over them.

Then a voice in her head, asking the same question she had been asked over and over again.

"Why do you hate God?"

"Because He's a man," she hissed.

Nijinsky was sitting quietly in the other room watching the whole exchange. If Adam made any sudden movements he decided he was going to kill him after all. Maybe artists have the right to kill certain thing, too, he decided, or at least try to. It is sometimes hard to get your message through with art, though. Most people are made uncomfortable by it. But people like Nijinsky, and Lilith, and also Laura, there is no other way they can communicate.

He listened to every word Adam said, and with each of them he was made to hate him even more.

"You should stop reading so much. It's making you crazier."

At this Nijinsky wanted to scream, but he had left his vocal chords in abeyance for so long now he forgot how to. 'How cruel the stupid can be,' he thought to himself instead, 'trying to take away all our small comforts just because they are strange to them.'

For a brief moment he wished he could speak. That was what people didn't understand. It wasn't that he didn't want to speak, it was that he *couldn't*. But it was true that he hadn't missed it much, until now, when he wished he could share these thoughts with Lilith. But he had always felt the best way to speak was to dance, to speak kinetically, and he still danced. At least that hadn't left him yet, but it was only a matter of time before it did, once Gymnopedie had broken him completely. He never told anyone, though sometimes he wished he could tell Lilith, but he knew what the word Gymnopedie meant. He was perhaps the only person in the hospital who did. He knew about the festival where men and women danced naked together, a pleasure he had often dreamed of, this freedom of expression that modernity had turned into a prison whose aim was to make people express themselves much less.

He wanted to take his clothes off and dance right now, but he remembered the last time he had danced for Lilith and he had been on fire. He was still on fire. He wondered if the people in hell, danced, too. Probably. The devil is sure to be a great dancer. He looked to Adam with disgust, then to Lilith, and realized how different they were. 'God watches over people with normal values,' he thought bitterly. 'But for those of us that see with new eyes, it is the devil who takes care of us.' That was the difference between Lilith and Adam. God would never let anything bad happen to Adam, because he was a normal white man, but He would damn Lilith, and only Satan would know how to comfort her through the rest of her life that would be luckless.

Finally Nijinsky's moment came. Adam moved to put an arm around Lilith, but before the arm could reach her shoulders

Nijinsky was dragging a knife across it.

The whole ward screamed. Nijinsky was quickly retrained by three harsh orderlies who beat him before they put the strait jacket on him, then they shot him up with sedatives. Lilith wanted to cry but recently had become too crazy to weep, so she just stared on in detached awe. "Let Vaslav go," she said weakly, but she knew it was no use. She had screwed over another one of her friends. She wondered what they would do to him, something like they had done to Andrei and Christian. She shuddered.

A nurse quickly attended to Adam's wound. Lilith was sad. People like Adam would always be protected, even though they were not good. But people like Nijinsky, people who would do anything for a friend, God only knows what horrible things happen to them.

Mel was watching the whole time, as well, but Lilith didn't recognize him because he was in *Il medico della peste* mask again. He drew in closely behind her.

"Lil," he said with the familiarity he had recently resigned. "Is there something you're not telling me?"

When Laura got to Gymnopedie they took her to a wing of the hospital she had never been to before.

"Where are you taking me?" she all but screamed from the stretcher.

None of the medics would answer her, but she knew where she was going. She had been reading One Flew over the Cuckoo's Nest before all this awfulness transpired. They were taking her to the "acute ward," the ward for patients that were considered a danger to themselves or others, or both. At Gymnopedie they had tried to dull the name of this wing, so it didn't seem like the patients were going somewhere that might scare them, calling it "the observation unit." Laura knew better, though. She knew she should be frightened.

This hallway was not like the rest of Gymnopedie. It was very narrow and short, only a few rooms in it, and all of them under surveillance. The nurses sat at their stations behind a wall of bulletproof glass. The chairs were made out of plastic, and it was incredibly dark.

Before they even got her off the stretcher they injected her with a drug called Halidol, and also some Ativan. Laura would quickly learn to hate these drugs. She didn't quite understand why she was here, besides the fact that she was crazy, but she didn't know yet that when her mother had called the cops on her, she had "pink slipped" her, or in other words, forced her into mental hospitalization because she was a "danger to herself and others." All the cops had wrote on their report that when she was down on her knees with the wire ring on her hand that she was trying to attack them with it, that she was using it as a weapon. Her mother had testified to this. An imaginary wedding ring was now a weapon.

She got into her room and fell asleep almost immediately, but first she met her roommate. She was an elderly black woman who was crazed in the eyes but thoughtful and gentle. She looked at Laura one time and clasped her hands desperately.

"Oh, baby. You poor child," she groaned, then she took the golden crucifix necklace off her neck and handed it to Laura. "Take this," she whispered frantically. "You'll need it."

Laura made no objections. Maybe she did need it.

She had trouble putting it on her neck in the dark, so the woman helped her put it on. A nurse walked by.

"What are you two doing?" he asked.

"I'm helping her with her necklace," the woman said.

"You guys aren't allowed jewelry, hand it over."

"No," the old woman said, trembling. "It's mine. I need it." She was begging now, and Laura felt sad. The hospital network that owned Gymnopedie was extremely religious, and yet they wouldn't let a kindly old woman keep an innocuous piece of religious jewelry.

"You guys also aren't allowed to exchange possessions, either. Carla, you can keep your necklace, but take it off Laura's neck."

The two complied numbly, not wanting their situations to get any worse. Laura took off the necklace with some struggle and then gave it back to her roommate. Her roommate looked her in the eyes, with a wild but sad look. "I'm sorry," she whispered to her.

"Don't be. It's not your fault." Laura didn't have the heart to tell her it probably wouldn't have made any difference, not to her anyway. All she saw in Christ's suffering was suffering. No salvation, and Christ himself had said "I am not here to bring peace on Earth." And He could not bring peace to Laura, either. She found something worthwhile in her own suffering.

But she did sometimes feel she was possessed. She had learned something in her readings of cabbala, the different kinds of spiritual possession. The two main ones were *dybbuk* and *Ibbur.* The dybbuk was a malignant spirit, but the ibbur, which literally means "impregnation of soul," was meant to help whoever it takes hold in, to bring them peace and direct them towards ways they can overcome suffering and help to restore the world, as the Jews believe is their sacred duty. Laura believed it was everyone's duty, and was even more so the responsibility of intellectuals, of whom she wanted to be one.

She thought she had both in her, the dybbuk and the ibbur, the ibbur being the instinct in her that wanted to write to help people in the only way she knew how to, to ease loneliness in others the same way her favorite writers had eased her own, but the dybbuk in her was the part of her that sometimes became too loud to ignore, which wanted to abandon all suffering, her own and the planet's, by dying- the urge in her to commit suicide.

And she was starting to realize she couldn't get rid of this dybbuk, she would simply have to find balance between it and the ibbur.

But she didn't have to think about that right now. The drugs took hold and everything span for a second, like a timid, silent ballerina, dancing to the tune of Gymnopedie. After that she fell asleep for a good fourteen hours.

Chapter VI

Nijinsky was put in confinement, later to receive "rigorous moral treatment." A revolutionary doctor had come on the scene, and man named Dr. Sakel. His treatments would be the precursor to electric shock therapy.

What he did to patients was induce them into a temporary coma. But of course it wasn't always temporary. It was like the fever that Mel had induced in Lilith with the rat bites. It didn't really help, it just made one more physically sick than mentally sick for a moment, but patients at Gymnopedie couldn't really tell the difference between the two anymore, and how could they, when the doctors couldn't either? To think that Lilith was insane because of an infection that had spread from her colon, now *that* was insanity, and Lilith, who had never been a modern girl, was one of the few people who could discern it as such. But what could she do? She had never been able to save herself, and now how could she save her truest friend?

She started to be absorbed into herself, into her illness. Her previous intelligence had just become a shell that held trapped within it what was once a woman until her dignity had been stolen, she was confined within a confinement. She had given into the learned helplessness of illness and imprisonment. She had almost thrown the typewriter Mel had given her out the window. And she was withdrawing more and more from him every day, and even Nijinsky, who could not voice his concern, who hid behind the mask of silence, the fetters of shyness, even though it was naturally born. She herself barely spoke anymore, either. And the silence between her and Nijinsky was no longer comfortable, but a mutual helplessness, a shared condemnation, one they could not even talk about. The days she didn't see him when he was held in confinement she didn't even miss him. She didn't miss Mel, either. She didn't even miss herself.

The next sideshow was a presentation of Dr. Sakel's temporary coma, with Nijinsky as the lab rat. First Andrei, now Nijinsky. They were picking off the foreigners. They were intellectuals, and back then intellectuals were just a bunch of eugenicists, a bunch of Nazis. Lilith was highly disappointed. They should have known better than that. She almost wanted to have a child now to spite them, but they had made that impossible. And now what experiment would they perform on her best friend, what right would they steal from him with medicine?

Dr. Sakel took up the platform to explain his procedure. Lilith only half listened to him, but she heard him say "we're going to induce a coma in this man. I'm going to give him 227 shots of insulin."

At last Lilith screamed. "ARE YOU INSANE?!" she bellowed. "THAT WILL KILL HIM!" Everyone ignored her except an orderly that proceeded to sit behind her in case she caused any trouble. She tried to get up, to kill Dr. Sakel. The orderly restrained her, and made her watch.

Nijinsky of course didn't say anything as Sakel injected him over and over again, for a period that lasted about an hour. The orderly held Lilith down by the arms, and she kept struggling until he said "I will tranquilize you and put you in confinement." She went completely still and sobbed silently instead.

Nijinsky tried to say something. He opened his mouth several times, and then closed it as he started to get weaker and weaker. He fell into a coma, and Lilith wept while the orderly held her arms behind her back.

"There," Dr. Sakel said. "We have induced the coma."

"IS HE ALIVE?!" Lilith yelled once again in her desperate frenzy. She looked for Benjy, she looked for Mel, but neither of them were here. She even looked for Adam, but he had quit after Nijinsky had cut him. She should have been relieved, but she wasn't. And then she looked to Nijinsky, who was completely comatose, his head hanging limply on his chest.

"Don't be alarmed," Dr. Sakel said. "He's still alive, and when he wakes up he'll feel much better." Lilith looked at the pin point holes in Nijinsky's arms from the needles, then looked at her own body that still had the fading scars of rat bites. This barbarism was evolving, from rat bites to needles and soon to electric shock, but it was still barbarism in any form.

Later that night Nijinsky's kidney's failed and he died. Lilith was told by Mel.

"I'm very sorry," he had whispered. "I knew how close you two were."

Lilith screamed and tore at her clothing. The orderlies quickly surrounded her as she erupted and then fell to her knees in angry tears.

"YOU BASTARDS!" she shouted through no longer stifled sobs. "YOU KILLED VASLAV NIJINSKY!!"

An orderly quickly injected her with a sedative, even though she hadn't been violent. They were becoming afraid of her. Sometimes the grief of the insane can be terrifying. I think this novel is a testament to that, but still it should never be stifled. It should never be sedated and thrown in a cage, for it is actually the grief of all of us.

In spite of the sedative Lilith still blasted her strident but lachrymose dirge. "YOU KILLED VASLAV NIJINSKY! YOU KILLED VASLAV NIJINSKY!" But eventually her voice became softer as the sobs became louder, and the sedative started to take hold.

"You killed Vaslav Nijinsky," she whispered, holding her hands over her eyes in horror as the tears spilled through the cracks in her fingers, like she was an old vase that was cracking and unable to hold within it what it had always kept secret any longer.

She slowly passed out and the orderlies took her away, into confinement and also into the Uttica Crib. When Lilith awoke she was hanging from the ceiling in that strange device, her arms and legs tied together, slowly rocking back and forth mid- air. In spite of the confinement, every ward on Gymnopedie could hear her sobs that night which went into the early hours of the morning, until she had at last sobbed herself to sleep.

The observation unit was very strange. There was a man who kept trying to kiss Laura, and no one, none of the nurses or social workers or therapists tried to stop him. Laura just had to turn him down as politely as she could, and he would say, "I'm sorry. This medicine makes me so horny."

Laura would then sigh. "Yea," she conceded. "They'll do that."

And the patients in the observation unit weren't allowed to eat in the cafeteria with everyone else. Their food was brought to them in the small room with the plastic chairs, the only room in the ward besides the patient's personal rooms.

Social workers came and went, trying to make sense of Laura's story. They told her at last her mother had said the wire ring wasn't meant to hurt anybody. They told her she wouldn't lose her job, but she almost did, until the owner of Roland's Pizza, who was fond of Laura, intercepted the order to have her fired. Laura didn't know if she was relieved or not. She often felt maybe she would be less crazy if she didn't work there, with David and Darcy always fighting, and that horrible hum of the machines that went on all day until her ears started to ring and any other sound became muted in comparison, even the sound of music, which they would often have to blast over her auditory hallucinations.

She wouldn't let George visit her this time. She had finally called him out on his infidelity, and he had passively neither confirmed nor denied it, which was the same as confirming it. And now he was afraid he was going to lose her to this William fellow, so he tenaciously grasped onto her, making the weakest, most impotent attempts to still try to make her believe he loved her. She knew better by now, though. She decided she would forgive him for sleeping around, but she didn't want to see him right now. And, sadly enough, the psychosis, in spite of all the Halidol, had not completely faded yet, and she still had the crazy notion in her crazy head that William was coming any minute now, and she would not have to be with George anymore. And the only reason she felt she loved William more at this moment was because, in spite of his good looks, he had never been good with women, and had only slept with two of them in his whole life. He wasn't the type who would cheat. He wasn't a smooth talker, therefore he wasn't a liar. He didn't tell people he loved them unless he did.

And she thought about Anna, also. Why had she ruined their relationship? Perhaps it was getting boring, but now she realized that was the most obvious sign that it was working. And the whole time she had been with George, little over a year now, she had missed Anna, had missed having a lover that was also a close friend.

Her parents came to visit her and they fought the whole time. Laura wanted them to bring her some books, but her mother had hypothesized that the books were making her "more ill."

"That's ridiculous, Lucille," her father protested, and Laura firmly agreed with him. "You can't be the Stasi that decides which books are okay for your daughter to read."

"I've looked through some of her books!" her mother riposted. "They don't make any sense!"

"Just because you don't understand something doesn't mean it doesn't make sense," Laura said weakly, but neither her mother nor father heard her. "I hope to write books like that someday."

And Laura was distraught that she was back in Gymnopedie, mostly because it halted production on the novel she was working on. She would often scream to the staff, "How do you expect me to get better if I. Can't. Fucking. Write?" And they would ignore her, too. Eventually, once she was back on the main ward, they would give her a notebook and an extremely blunt pencil, so she couldn't stab herself or anyone else with it, and Laura would wonder to herself how the staff at Gymnopedie could help people they were so obviously afraid of. Lots of people were afraid of Laura, though she had never hurt anyone physically in her life. Oddly enough, the only people who weren't afraid of her were children. And really they know best when it comes to judging character. People forget that. They'd like to think there's some virtue of authority in adulthood, but there isn't. Adulthood is just blind confusion and bills.

What made Laura the most happy of all, though, was the autotelic life, a life that has inherent purpose in itself, and a purpose which comes from within, not without. Of course, this is not a life society has ever been able to understand, and which it has weakly condemned for feeling threatened by it. All this pressure to go back to school, to work, to have a car, but Laura felt so much happier when she taught herself, when the work was creative, and she had the freedom to walk everywhere. This was how she never missed a single detail. And if it weren't for other people, who were secretly motivated by envy when they told her she wasn't good enough, she would have never questioned this lifestyle, would have never felt like there was something wrong with it. In fact, she would never have felt there was something wrong with *her* if only people hadn't constantly told her there was.

But, in spite of their disapproval, the way they wrote her off as a "loser," she would live this autotelic life because one day she would come to realize it was the only way she *could* live, that the normal life full of its chaos masquerading as order would only ever make her insane, that work, school, driving, success… none of these would make her actually happy. So she would have to take the lectures, the disapproval, and the blank looks void of understanding when she told them "failure is unique triumph," or "losing is much more difficult and takes more courage than winning." And she wished more than anything that they understood this life, this loser autotelic life, was not a choice, either. If she ever would have been offered a practical mind, one that fit in like an indistinguishable jigsaw piece with the puzzle of western values, she would have taken it greedily, but this dream, this idea that she could fit into something she had always loathed, and which loathed her in return, was much more unrealistic than the idea that she could at least be a famous author someday. And only she knew this. So she would stay away from schools, from jobs, and even from relationships, from any sign of the hollow "success," people vainly chased after these days, so she could just write the novels. That was all she really wanted to do. She had always known deep in her heart that *success de estime* was much more valuable than average success. And she would never, in the end, be able to claim her life was exciting, but she would be able to say it was fulfilling.

And people wouldn't understand her attachment to writing, either. They wouldn't understand that it was the thin line between her and a razor dragged slowly against the inside of her wrist. Everyone knew, though, *everyone*, that she was "fucked up," as they said it, that there was an incredible darkness within her, a *loud* darkness, one that refused to be ignored, and which her art was a testament to, *provided by*, but what they would often fail to understand was that her various modes of creation were the only way she could explore this strident darkness without getting lost in it, without ending up in Gymnopedie, waiting for men who would never come. And she would learn to fill the hole in her life that was the all devouring loneliness, the absence of kinship even when she was in love, with the stupid words, which she knew she didn't even write that well, but were still all that made the lack in human affection bearable, at least until the end of the night. The end of the night would still always be hard.

Laura had felt lonely all her life, starting in childhood, dragging on endlessly in adolescence, and now having settled almost for death in adulthood. She wondered sometimes if she would be just as lonely while she was dying as she was now, which, sadly, seemed a likely possibility to her. Twenty three years and the loneliness still had not given up its unshakeable claim to her, so why would it in old age? But the thought of dying as lonely as she had lived- she knew it would make death horrifying. So she tried her best to love in the rare moments when it came her way, never staying for very long, always telling her in the end that she was too difficult. This of course made that horrible *dybbuk* in her, who wasn't really that horrible, who just wanted, like everyone else, to be loved in spite of the fact that it was dark and ugly, want to die even more. And the only way she would be able to fight it off was with the writing. But still love would not come, and when it did it was wearing a mask, while underneath its face was just the brief, trite face of desire and death. The writing would have to be enough. Love never fulfilled its promises.

And that was why she needed her creepy books. But sadly, she didn't know how to explain this without writing it down, and even then it might not have been understood.

Luckily, her dad won, as men always win in the end, and she was able to read whatever the hell she liked. He brought her a compendium of The Hitchhiker's Guide to the Galaxy, and it did cheer her up, as often during the night she was unable to sleep, so she roamed the narrow hall of the observation unit at two o' clock in the morning pacing and reading at the same time, until, of course, the nurses would say she was causing a disturbance and inject her with Halidol and Ativan again until she was knocked out. Laura began to refer to these drugs as her "shut the fuck up medicine," as she noticed they were given to her whenever she seemed even slightly rebellious.

She had to stay in the observation unit, or "acute ward," as she called it, for a week before they finally transferred her to the main ward, which she liked better because it had a much bigger hallway for her to pace in. Of course, this annoyed everyone, even the other patients. It always had. Laura could never understand it. She had always thought people's quirks were the most adorable and interesting things about them, but her own quirks were never tolerated. She made friends with an older Hispanic lady, who she liked to discuss Gabriel Garcia Marquez with, and this woman grew fond of her, but even she would complain that Laura had too much energy. It was the mania, though, in spite of the medication. It was something she had little to no control over, as none of us have any control over our quirks in a world where lovers and even friends are no longer tolerant.

It was odd, though. She was starting to talk again, and still many of the things she said didn't make much sense, but people were starting to like her again. The other stays at Gymnopedie were spent in solitude and silence, no company except for books. This time she was making friends, though, and what was crazy, not even with just the patients, but the *staff,* too. By now she knew everyone on a first name basis. There was one male nurse who took a liking to her, Marcus. Laura liked Marcus, too, and if it had been a different situation, *any other* situation, she fancied they would have been good for each other, as lovers, not friends. But she would always sigh as she would quickly see in her mind George covered in long razor marks, torn to ribbons, begging "pick me, pick me." And what was worse, she did still love him, very much, even during her anger, but it was slowly starting to dawn on her that the time to see other people would probably be soon. This broke her heart, and in order not to appear heartbroken she would casually flirt. That almost made her look like a happy, normal girl.

She flirted with many men in Gymnopedie, and women as well. She had finally come to terms with her bisexuality, she had finally "come out of the closet." This honesty in her would be belligerently ignored, and misunderstood by her mother, who, though much more tolerant of it than her father, would often say "I don't care if you're a lesbian, but I can't deal with this 'both' shit." But Laura didn't care anymore. She realized that bisexuality was nothing like it was portrayed in movies. It was not a desperate, lonely, and blind, depraved hedonism. It was a beautiful expression of love for all mankind, of being able to deeply care about anyone, despite what reproductive organs they had. In spite of all the pressure, she realized gratefully that the decision between men and women was not a decision she had to make. She could love them both.

This of course made George uncomfortable. Now he was not only threatened by other men, men like William, but women as well. It is odd how the philanderer becomes the jealous one in the end. Laura wouldn't have ever dreamed of cheating on George, not even with women. But it was a great threat to him, because now he realized the reason she would stand up for Anna. She actually *had* loved her. She had loved someone other than him, two people, he now understood. So, to make him more comfortable, Laura would speak unkindly of both of them, though deep in her heart she knew she didn't mean a word of it, that in spite of the fact they had seemed morally ambiguous at times, due to the drugs, they had actually always been kinder than George. And so was she.

She shivered as she remembered the things she had imagined William said. *"You're not as callous as him..."* It was true. She appeared callous because schizophrenia makes appropriate emotional response almost impossible. That was why she barely spoke. But in most schizophrenics, past the impassive faces and they eyes that can't look at anyone for long, there is an incredible emotional sensitivity, which is all the more damned because it can't be expressed. George always assumed Laura didn't love him because she never told him she did, which is a fair assumption, but really she loved him *too* much to say it. She could not completely abandon her isolation at the time, which was far from being comfortable, but was the only thing she wasn't afraid of. And really, George didn't want her to abandon her isolation, for it was convenient for him. She never bothered him when he was at work.

But she was finally abandoning her isolation. The instinct of self -preservation, after being many months in abeyance, had kicked in again. She realized that as much as she hated showing it, she did need other people, and she could not be alone and silent all the time, not anymore. She started rekindling old friendships, her friends that had, until now, thought she was completely lost. But they weren't bad friends. They were relieved when they found they were wrong. They were relieved when she reached out to them again, as they thought the connection between her and not only them, but *all* people, was dead. And they were right. But she was resurrecting it, and thereby herself, as well.

Even her connection with George, which was sadly, the first to die, was reaching a slow renascence. Why this had made George uncomfortable rather than happy Laura would never understand. Perhaps he just didn't want to be happy. Perhaps he secretly felt the same way she did, that he could spend the rest of his life with this crazy woman, (as she really was starting to become a woman, no longer a girl,) and that scared him. Even the thought that she was becoming a woman was intimidating to him. Every day she got less and less easy to control.

But he was an idiot to abandon her when he did. Laura knew if he would have stuck around only a moment longer she could have made him incredibly happy, but, unfortunately, misery was the most comfortable to him. She tried not to hate him for this, for she did understand it, but it was hard. She would have done anything for him, yet he wouldn't even step out of his comfort zone for her. But he was getting old, aging more noticeably every day, and instead of being turned off, this only made Laura want him all the more, the thought that she could at least try to make his waning years comfortable, and maybe, even better than the years that had preceded them. But he wouldn't let her. He would never let her.

So she would flirt in Gymnopedie, a very strange place to flirt, but you do what you have to in order to make your situation more bearable. The situation of being locked up in a mental hospital, and the situation of being on the verge of losing someone she loved to the point of mad desperation. Her friends at Gymnopedie made fun of her.

"You wear the pants in the relationship, don't you?"

"Damn right. But unfortunately, he makes me wear the skirt as well."

"Is that why you're mad at him?"

"I'm mad at him for a lot of things."

"Poor guy is probably terrified."

Laura threw her head back and laughed at this. "God, I hope so."

Her friends in the ward called her "the joker," due to the long purple coat she wore and the green hat that complimented it. They all told her she should be a female comedian. One day she was stalking the ward late at night, unable to sleep as usual, looking for a deck of cards that she could play solitaire with. She couldn't find any cards anywhere, except for one, which of course was the joker. She laughed to herself.

"Everybody plays the fool," she said, "but I'm exceptionally good at it." So she decided to become a female comedian, in her own way. Her novels were a very long, very sad joke, and people did laugh at them. She wanted to rip the Joker card up, but she wouldn't. She could only laugh at this divine, cosmic jest which she was the butt of. Humor can often be cruel and sad, and that was how she viewed life, cruel and sad, and though she laughed all the time, deep down inside she didn't think any of it was funny. When you are an adult you learn to laugh at everything, though truthfully it doesn't amuse you, it disturbs you, but with aging it becomes very hard to cry, and there is no other alternative. Her weird laugh was really a dirge, the ringing of church bells at a funeral. A very long, very sad joke, the inability to cry at a wake.

Chapter VII

Lilith was kept in confinement, in a strait jacket, for a week. Gymnopedie was doing everything in its power to push her off the fragile edge between barely surviving and the eternity of madness that was its alternative. And it was working. The institution was more powerful than her. She thought about these doctors and intellectuals. Most of them prescribed to the theory of Social Darwinism. To be so lucky. To be "the fittest," of the elite few who are not infirm, and who for some reason don't feel they have any responsibility to the people who are. I suppose that does make it easier to evolve without compassion. But that's actually devolving.

No one would recognize it, but Lilith was an intellectual, too. No one would recognize it because she was a patient in Gymnopedie State Mental Hospital. No one would recognize it because she was not fortunate or healthy enough to be a eugenicist. What idiots, she thought. No genius has ever existed without mental illness. This bright future of only the fittest would be just that, only the fittest, not the most intelligent, not the artistic geniuses, in fact, no genius at all. It would be a world without any Vaslav Nijinsky's, but then again, this world was now robbed of him, too. It would be a culture starved of the only thing culture really needs, invention, therefore it would be a weak culture, and it wouldn't last long. History would not remember it all, and if it did, only for its cruelty, for its systematized murder of the majority who are not healthy white men. If only the Nazis understood this, but Lilith supposed they were a long way off. This didn't make her feel any better. Time heals all wounds except history.

There was nothing in this room of confinement except her, the strait jacket, and a large portrait of Phillipe Pinel. Lilith looked at it with disgust. "This is your legacy!" she screamed to his impassive, painted face, shaking herself and trying to point the strait jacket towards him, but she could barely move in it. Pinel was praised for his compassion towards the mentally ill when he created the asylum, but it was a prison like any other: the same stripping of identity, of helplessness, of the Pirandellian way the patients would learn that they were nothing else but insane, how all their talents were forgotten in this world. She slid herself across the cement floor to get closer to the portrait. Then she started tearing at it with her teeth.

Mel walked in. "Oh…Lilith," he said helplessly as he watched her drag her teeth across the painting, tearing little bits of Pinel's face with them. "What have they done to you?"

"Odd time for you to start giving a shit," she returned, but there was no anger in her voice, only the despair of a lifelong defeat.

"I'm sorry I've been avoiding you."

"It's fine."

"And I'm sorry about Nijinsky."

She shrugged. She wanted to cry again, but she was already too used up.

"I'm here to get you out of confinement," and he slowly, almost tenderly, took the strait jacket off of her.

"I've been in Gymnopedie almost seven years now," she said placidly, almost with sanity, "and I've never felt so crazy in my life as I do now."

"I know," Mel answered, but there was no confidence in his voice. "After this, all this, what they've done to you and your friends…I don't want to work here anymore. I don't want to be a psychiatrist at all anymore."

"So, what are you going to do?"

"I don't know yet. It's so sad. I thought I was going into one of the noblest professions in the world. I thought I was going to be a healer, that I was going to help people, but I've only, as you said, made them more crazy. I've only hurt them."

"The world has a way of corrupting ideals," Lilith said solemnly. "It's not your fault. You're not a bad man. You're just a little too obedient. Nothing is more dangerous than doing as you're told."

"And I think to other people more than to me. I don't understand this. How do we even choose who is insane and who is not? It seems almost arbitrary now, who is the patient and who is the doctor. Who is the torturer and who is the victim. It makes no sense how we become either."

Lilith got off the ground, grabbed Mel by the face and kissed him.

"Lilith, I'm married," he said abashedly.

"I don't care anymore. I'd do anything to make you feel better."

"That won't make me feel better."

Lilith sighed. "No," she said doggedly. "It won't make me feel better either."

"Do you love me?"

"I think so…yes"

"I'm terribly sorry, Lilith…"

"It's okay."

He grabbed her hands while shaking and gave her an extremely rapid, awkward kiss on the cheek. "I can't work here anymore," he declaimed. "And you should get out of here, too. Lie to the doctors as much as you have to, *pretend* to be sane, but please, get the hell out of here. You don't really want to be buried in that coffin."

"You're leaving?"

"I told you. I can't do this anymore."

"But you're my last friend. Olmsted got released because he's rich, they won't let me see Benjy because I kissed him, and Nijinsky…" but she couldn't say it. "You're the last one."

"Friends you meet in a mental hospital are not friends you can keep forever, Lilith. Don't you have any friends on the outside?"

"No, not really."

"Is that why you stay here, because you're not lonely here?"

"I'm still lonely. I always have been and I always will be. But at least here there are other people to be lonely with."

Mel sighed and let go of her hands. "You won't be lonely forever, Lilith," he said this, and he really did believe it. "Friendship and love are supposed to be a lot more than sharing loneliness. They're supposed to eradicate it."

"But they never do."

"You're still young. You have plenty of time. You won't be lonely forever, as long as you get out of this hospital."

Lilith didn't say anything, but bit back tears as she stared absently at the portrait of Pinel. "I've never destroyed a work of art before," she said. "I feel bad."

"Loneliness makes us do stupid things, things we would otherwise never do because we find them morally reprehensible."

"Yes," she agreed numbly. "That's what allowed me to attempt suicide."

"I have to go, Lilith. Please live a happy life, if not for yourself, for me."

"Please don't go."

Mel chuckled, but not unkindly, as he placed his pale, thin fingers gently across her cheek. "Oh, Lilith," he said sadly. "We both know we can't ask that of people."

Laura grew sick of the Haildol, so she requested she be given Melatonin instead. Melatonin is an over the counter, natural supplement, and doesn't make you feel like your head is full of gas and air when you take it, like Halidol does. Halidol is an anti-psychotic, so it was strange that they were giving it to her when she couldn't sleep. Maybe they thought her insomnia was part of the psychosis, but Halidol really knocked Laura out, and she supposed that's why they were giving it to her. It was bullshit. She wasn't disturbing anybody when she was awake late at night *reading*, for Christ's sake. So she requested the Melatonin. First the doctors had to approve it. Laura had taken Melatonin when she was a kid, for she'd had this sleeping problem for most of her life, switching frequently between sleeping twelve hours a day or not sleeping for three days. When she had taken the over the counter, natural supplement she had had a vivid dream, which all sleeping medicine gives you vivid dreams. Even the drugs she was already approved to take gave her vivid dreams. But when she had told her mother about this vivid dream, she thought it was a hallucination, and wouldn't let her take it anymore. Laura trying to get on it again was, (besides the fact that she thought Halidol was the worst drug in the world,) in a way, her trying to rebel against her mother, who she felt had oppressed her these recent months, telling the staff at Gymnopedie she was a dependent, when really her mother was dependent on her at the time, trying to get power of attorney over her, and following her everywhere to make she wasn't smoking the evil marijuana (which was clearly the cause of all psychosis. It can't be a genetic inheritance) - it was all getting to be a bit too much.

And psychosis had only made her more passive, made her more subservient and even easier to beat down than she already had been. George and her mother could pretend to care as much as they wanted, but Laura knew secretly that this silent docility of hers they were both exploiting, perhaps without even realizing it, because this is just the way people are. They can fall very easily into evil, and Laura probably could have too if she wasn't so crazy.

Her mother of course found out about the Melatonin and raised hell. She went running to the nurse's station immediately and Laura followed her. She was relieved. The nurse was Marcus, and Marcus, though he never said it, knew she wasn't crazy.

"She can't take Melatonin!" her mother practically screamed. "It gives her hallucinations."

"Yea, I highly doubt that…" Marcus replied quietly, but her mother either didn't hear him or chose to ignore him.

"It didn't give me hallucinations, I just had a vivid dreams. Listen, Mom. I had a dream about my friend Brittany…"

"No, sweetheart," her mother said in that sickeningly sweet voice one patronizingly uses when they think they're talking to a moron. "You don't remember. You saw rabbits. And the hill covered with blood…"

Laura burst out laughing, while at the same time her hands were shaking with rage. She looked to Marcus. "That's the plot of a book called Watership Down."

"No, sweetheart," her mother still said in her patronizing mock pity. "You don't remember…"

"Yea, I have no idea what goes on in my own brain."

Now Marcus burst out laughing. Laura was glad he was on her side, but she knew in the end that he wouldn't be able to do much. Still, it was nice to have someone believe her, for once. The authorities usually always believed her mother, because she was good at lying. And poor Laura was only good at telling the truth to people who don't give a damn about it, people who refused to believe her because she was insane. Insane is not the same thing as stupid, though. Insane is not the same thing as dishonest.

But the next night when she couldn't sleep she requested Melatonin and they said they couldn't give it to her, doctor's orders. They gave her more Halidol and Ativan instead, even though she wasn't psychotic and she wasn't having a panic attack. Before she went to sleep for fifteen hours of dreamless, heavy sleep, she thought to herself, 'I can't believe these educated motherfuckers haven't read Watership Down.'

Chapter VIII

Lilith never saw Mel again. He left the hospital grounds as soon as he freed Lilith and then he never came back. He didn't even bother to put in a formal resignation. Lilith missed him dearly, for she was, as she had said, friendless now, but she was actually proud of him. She'd never seen him do anything that rebellious before. Rebellion is usually left to the insane, or at least they call rebels insane to discourage people who only want to appear normal from ever making a scene. And Mel was perfectly sane. Lilith had only ever heard rationality come from his mouth, and that was why she needed him so desperately, and, she thought, this discontinuation of his work for Gymnopedie was the final, indelible proof of this sanity. How long could a sane person continue to throw diseased rats on a living body? Mel's days as *Il medico della peste* at Gymnopedie had always been numbered, because he was too smart for this, too educated to continue to suffer and take part in the crimes of the educated, which were quite barbarous back then. Maybe they still are, but, like I said, barbarism keeps evolving. That's all social Darwinism is, evolving atavism, not evolving humanity. Now that Mel had proved that he really was different from the run of the mill intellectuals who secretly don't believe a damn word they say, Lilith only loved him more.

And she thought, if only the situation were different, she really would have been right for him. She wasn't the run of the mill intellectual, either. She was a real intellectual, one who would never believe she was superior for her mind, because she knew that though the value of a brilliant mind in society is theoretically high, in the universe it is only more nothingness. Besides, she had never been in the position in her life to feel better than anyone. She only knew how to feel worse. She was a writer, not just one who reads, therefore she was always in greater pain. She was no *ubermensch*. She was insane and infirm just like Nietzsche, and her work would perhaps be bastardized by the Nazis the same way his was. Or it would be burned by them, as she would be burned by them if she was forced to live through that era. No one knows the value in the insane except the insane themselves, and this is what makes them more intelligent. The world would never dare to admit it, because perhaps it doesn't even know yet, but it cannot survive without them. It cannot survive without the Jews, either. That's why they continue to survive against all odds. It is an act of Martyrdom, the martyrdom of continuing to live rather than dying. That's the only reason I don't kill myself, for the sake of my own idealized masochism. I want to help this world at the expense of my own pain. That's the only way I can make this pain valuable. This is the only way the dybbuk can achieve *Olam tikkun*, the world restored.

So Lilith decided to take Mel's advice, as if it were his dying wish, though he was much more alive in her mind at this time than he had ever been in real life. She would feign sanity, until she could no longer separate herself from the role she was playing, until she actually became sane. A Pirandellian sanity, but all aspects of this life have become Pirandellian with time and its constant bastardization of reality. She thought about *Il medico della peste's* and their masks. By now the masks were who they were. When they got home they were still doctors, prescribing absurd remedies to their families, always attacking the sites of infection, the areas that took on the appearance of mania. But her, she would not be a patient forever. And insanity isn't a mask. It is the true face of God, and all people are afraid of God, even sometimes, people like Lilith, who don't even believe in Him. She thought about a strange piece of artwork she had done during her stay at Gymnopedie. It was a painting of a woman who had just gotten done hanging herself, and had been cut down. As the woman lay naked, her chest bare as well as her neck with the garish rope burns, her dead mouth was half open, and her eyes, though closed, looked like they were rolling around in rapture. She was having an orgasm.

That was how Lilith had tried to commit suicide. She had attempted to hang herself, but her boyfriend at the time, walked in just before she was about to kick the chair. She couldn't even hope to pretend. "Yes," she had conceded naturally with the disturbingly hollow, listless monotone only a true schizophrenic can pull off. "I am trying to kill myself." Immediately her boyfriend had dumped her off at Gymnopedie and never spoke to her again. She wasn't sad.

And she still wanted to hang herself. That was her death of choice. But she didn't want to hang herself also. At the same time she wanted to die she also weakly agreed to live. So that was why she had painted that erotic corpse. It got the image of her own dead body out of her head. She painted many people hanging themselves, over and over again, and it was all that kept her from actually doing it. This was hard for the staff at the hospital to comprehend.

"This scares everyone, Lilith," they would often say.

"Yes," she would agree. "Honestly it scares me out, too." Lilith was God, and she was afraid of herself. All people are God and they are afraid of themselves. They should be, too. That's why they put on the masks. It isn't so other people won't look at them, it's so they themselves don't have to.

Lilith would often go to visit Nijinsky's grave. Of course, since all the graves were unmarked, she didn't know which one exactly was his, so she visited a different grave every day, until she'd visited every unmarked grave on the hospital grounds. She put flowers on each of them, different flowers, because they were all different people, and thereby tried to give some identity back to each person who had died in this prison. She tried to figure out intuitively which grave was Nijinsky's, but it didn't work, so she would often ask the impassive mounds of dirt, "where are you?" but dirt doesn't speak, nor do the people who are hidden under it. She looked hopelessly for Andrei, too. She even put flowers on the mass grave she herself had been interred in, a massive amount of roses for a massive amount of dead.

But before the flowers themselves got the chance to die, the staff at Gymnopedie took all of them off the graves. "Fear of the insane is a fear of compassion," she wrote that day, and continued to put different flowers on each of the same graves even knowing they would be taken away. She was starting to feel human again.

Laura was let out of Gymnopedie for the fifth time, and she

swore to herself she would never come back. Each time she had to come crawling back she felt more and more ashamed, of what, though, she wasn't sure. Ashamed of her insanity, I suppose, but through time she learned it was nothing to be ashamed of. She almost began to take pride in it, for after a while, she realized that it gave her that almost superhuman insight that kept her depressed but also in many ways kept her going. Nurtured by loneliness, she felt she could perhaps make a future of this mess of her mind, if the world would ever let her. But it was hard to be a writer in a world where even intelligent people don't read anymore. But what does it mean for modern civilization? It means, just like the hypothetical civilization of "the fittest," it will not be remembered. The internet will crash and burn some day and there will be no record that we were even here. We will be gone like a ghost, one that was never alive in the first place.

Laura thought of the Latin word for insanity. It was "vesanias." A beautiful word. A holy word. And she realized that even once she did achieve sanity no one would recognize it in her, because no amount of medication could stop her from being so out of place. She would always be considered insane, because she did not fit into any time period. In essence, she was timeless, though she herself was not eternal, but the spirit within her was, both the *dybbuk* and the *ibbur,* so she did not fit into the modern world, because nothing that is timeless ever has. Even the great poets of Greek antiquity probably didn't fit into ancient times, either, due to their marked timelessness. Maybe this is what vesanias really means, when you are something eternal being martyred in a temporal body.

Laura's insanity may have been inconvenient, for herself and her friends and family, but she slowly came to realize, it was where all her more noble qualities stemmed from, where her timelessness was born, though it had never been born, and perhaps had existed even before time. It is a very sad state to be a timeless thing trapped in the confines of time, but, (and though the world often fails to recognize this fact,) there is an element of necessity in this kind of being. Laura was beginning to discover this, and it kept her from the glorious suicide she had dreamed of since she was a girl.

She was let out of Gymnopedie, and she forgave George. They had a few more nice moments before the end. She started going out again. Not very often, for she had never liked going out a lot. That had been the big difference between her and Anna, who always liked to party, while Laura only wanted to do it when she was exceptionally sad, and it usually only worsened the condition. It was frustrating. Laura sometimes felt like the only emotion she was capable of was sorrow, and even then she wasn't very good at communicating it, certainly not through simple conversation. But she would go out with Mary, and it actually felt good. Going out had never felt good before.

They were going to meet Don Giovanni in the city of Dis, the nearest city to Astrum, to go to an event held every year there called "Sideshow." It was a small festival of local artists and musicians, a harmless affair, but for some reason the name of it sent a chill up Laura's spine, like the timid yet not gentle grip of a memory too distant too recall, but not gone long enough to forget completely. She kept her misgivings to herself, though. She wanted to learn how to have fun. She was still so young in spite of feeling old, and though she didn't feel like she was wasting her life being buried in books, every now and then she did want to have a direct experience.

Anna was there, of course. Anna's band was getting famous around Dis, so she was always at the big events. Laura was grateful to see her.

"You look so much better!" Anna beamed.

"I feel a lot better."

"And you're talking again!"

Laura giggled. "I'm never going back to that mental hospital again." Of course, she was wrong, though.

"Here, take a free copy of our LP."

Laura took it and smiled at her. "I'll listen to it tomorrow."

Suddenly Anna embraced her enthusiastically, with relief. "I'm so glad you're not sick anymore. It's been a long time now."

Laura returned the embrace and sighed. "Yes," she said faintly. "I have been sick for a very long time."

But of course it wasn't over, and for a person like her, it probably never would be. She would just have to make it manageable, "high functioning." A high functioning schizophrenic. She was lucky she wasn't homeless. She was lucky she wasn't dead, but she felt that was fool's luck. But she would always be strange, and she would always be depressed. She would always be misunderstood, and though people would observe her right to do the work she loved, no one else would actually enjoy it. She would not be able to share it with a nation of people who don't give a damn, as intellectualism these days is no longer an act of self-sacrificing compassion, and perhaps it never was. Now it is marked by how well you can use a computer. Laura would probably never become famous, but die in the poverty she had grown used to. And no one would read her damn books, because honesty has never been in fashion. She would get as better as she possibly could, which took an incredible amount of courage that would of course fade through the years, but she would never fully recover from this long year. She would never recover from George or her mother and father. She would never recover from herself, either, who was only strong enough to weep because she didn't know how to do anything else…And only in private, of course.

Chapter IX

George and Laura were walking together. A long walk, because they both liked long walks. Their long, elegant strides matched each other perfectly, and for a moment they were completely silent, for the first time, not uncomfortably so. In this moment Laura felt they actually did understand one another, and maybe even belonged together. But George either failed to recognize this, or Laura had merely hallucinated it. She had probably hallucinated it. She was bogged down with delusions of love, unable to see clearly past his eyes. They were going to his friend's house. As they walked and talked a little bit Laura didn't even think about Anna and William. They had both been replaced by an icon, and she was an idolater, at last converted to a strange pagan monotheism, the ancient, occult religion of love with someone you know well, and who is also a stranger to you. *Enkekalymmenos.* A fallacy love.

She wanted to hold his hand as they walked together. They used to do that, but not anymore. They barely touched each other at all now. Still, she felt at ease with him for the first time in almost a year. They reached their destination, George's friend Mark's house. Mark opened the door eagerly, because he was fond of both of them, even Laura, who was actually easier to relate to than George sometimes. She wasn't afraid, in spite of her intelligence, creativity, and insanity, to relate to common men. George, on the other hand, was a bit more of a snob, and Mark knew this, but they had been friends for almost ten years now, and Mark really did love him, though George would often say when he wasn't around "if I ever do get famous I probably won't take him with me."

Laura would smile at this and say, "That's okay. I'll take him with me when I get famous instead."

Mark let them in. He had just fixed the God awful plumbing at Laura's house and she gave him ten dollars for it. They went inside. Mark's daughter, Caylee was standing in the hallway. Laura almost screamed when she looked at her. She had long blond hair and light brown eyes. She was wearing an almost identical pair of glasses to the ones George wore, and a pair of Eeyore pajamas Laura herself would have worn. Laura looked at her once and looked away. She couldn't make eye contact with the girl, she was too similar to herself and the man who had impregnated her.

Caylee, with the intuition only children have, wouldn't look at Laura, either. This could have been shyness, but Laura got the eerie feeling that she knew, that she knew someone who was just like her had died inside this older woman who looked so similar to her. Laura looked to George. "Hi, Caylee," he said with trepidation.

"Hi," she said back, and ran away. Laura, who actually enjoyed spending time with children on less psychologically warping situations, was relieved she was gone.

"Kids," Mark half groaned and half laughed. "Don't have 'em, guys. Stick to dogs and cats."

As he said this Laura noticed George stiffened and his face

twitched subtly. This only made her feel worse. 'It's fucking with him, too,' she thought, which was strange, because he had so vehemently declared to her religious parents when she was pregnant that she *had* to get an abortion. Laura hated to think that now suddenly he had changed his mind. They didn't speak of the miscarriage. Both of them had to pretend it never happened, but Laura had never realized this before. She thought it was just her who had to bury herself in work to not think about it. She never knew that George was the same, that, though, like Laura, he never wanted to have kids, he also kept hidden deep inside him that he would have loved that child if it had lived. And of course Laura felt the same. She had felt it as soon as she had lost it, first the feeling of relief, then the feeling of incredible religious guilt immediately followed by the heartbreaking afterthought of, 'but I would have loved it.' She would have loved the child because it would have been George's, and it had just dawned on her, that even though his feelings for her were waning, George would have loved the child too because it was hers.

She wanted to reach out to him now more than ever. She wanted to grab him by the hand desperately, and she should have. Maybe it would have fixed everything while they both could have still retained their silence. But Laura was too shy. She wasn't even able to bring it up. George was an asshole, but Laura came to realize with time and great regret, she was partially responsible for the ruin of their relationship, not because she had gotten pregnant, but because after the fact she never tried to find a way that she could comfort him. She had never known that perhaps he was just as broken and traumatized from this as she was. She bit back tears as Caylee walked back into the room, noticing George couldn't look at her now either.

Laura went outside to smoke. She couldn't take it anymore, that girl. She smoked two cigarettes in a row, trembling, trying not to think about it anymore. Then George came outside and told her it was time to leave. Mark was taking them home, but George wouldn't stay with her. He asked to be dropped off at the bus stop to go back home. Laura was angry. She needed him now more than ever, and thought perhaps he needed her too, if he would ever lose the masculine pride to admit it. Still, when Mark dropped her off she kissed him passionately goodbye, even in her anger. And he returned the kiss with equal fervor, something he hadn't done in a long time. She knew he loved her again, but, sadly, he didn't.

She got back home and started drawing, a picture of George with the little girl on his knee. She looked at it after she had finished it. She had drawn George well, which made sense because she had looked at him so many times, always when she hoped he wasn't looking and wouldn't notice. She looked at him, the dour face with the glasses hiding soft eyes. She looked at him and knew this was all she was going to be able to hold onto of him, this picture. The relationship itself was damned, and had been for a very long time. It officially died when that damn impertinent fetus did. It was almost over, and though this brought Laura an incomparable sadness, (for truthfully, she had never loved someone like this before, almost to a point of naïve obsession,) it was probably a good thing. But the obsession was getting a little less naïve. She was starting to see George for who he really was- philautic, cold, and obdurate, and she loved him still- she loved him still even though he frustrated her endlessly now. And she frustrated him endlessly, too, but because he was a man, he didn't understand that this meant he loved her -as she was, not as what he had previously mythologized her to be. All the love illusions were breaking now.

They had been together long enough for this to happen, and while Laura was willing to stay with him in spite of the flaws she ignored before but now seemed obvious, he was not. He had decided a long time ago that he wanted to spend his life alone. That was the most infuriating flaw of all, his cowardice.

Laura despised cowardice, particularly in men. It was a moot detestation, though, for now, looking back, Laura had been a coward most of her life, particularly around George. Still, like any hypocrite, all her time spent with him now was her silent daring for him to be brave, and he came to resent her for this, feeling as if she was asking too much of him. Maybe she was. He was too old to change, but she was too young to give up with him. It is hard to have dreams and a man at the same time. George would leave Laura soon, but, in a way, it was partially her choice, as well, though she didn't realize it. She had chosen the writing over love.

It left her empty for many years, feeling as if an essential part of her would always be missing, that it had run away from her, but she would compensate for this emptiness with her often inept words, and that would have to be enough. It was, in the end, a heartbreaking good decision.

They are few, but some things are more important than love.

Chapter X

"I want to be good so badly," she wrote onto the impassive but noisy typewriter. "But I always fall short. The majority of the population are too spiritually impotent to be either good or evil. I don't even think these doctors, with all their horrible experiments, are evil, but they are not good, either. That's what allows them to do these things. I don't want to be like that. I don't want to be someone who can complacently, almost numbly follow a group like the Nazis of tomorrow. We have three choices. Be good, be evil, or be nothing. Most of us are nothing. But it's not really a choice. We are born or evil or good or nothing, and most of us are born nothing, which is only natural. Most people cannot be extraordinary. I probably can't be. That's why I always fall short of being good. I am not extraordinary like I used to think I was because I was insane.

"But I have one saving grace, and that's the insanity. If I live through the reign of the Nazis they will throw me into the gas chamber, as well, so I have no choice but to hate them. I'm glad of that. I do not want to be on the side of the winners, because it is mixed with incredible evil and incredible nothing. I will always want to be on the side of the victims, even if that means I have to be a victim myself. This is a noble thought I'm not sure I can live up to. I will try, though. I might decide to be that ancient prophet of doom nobody has ever wanted, and tell them about the dream. Sometimes you have to say the things you know no one will listen to, even if you scream them, because at least they will no longer be on your conscience. This is a selfish motivation for doing what I perceive to be the right thing, but it is sufficient. I will probably be kept in Gymnopedie for several more years for it, if not the rest of my life, so at least there is an element of self- sacrifice in it.

"The martyr personality is supposedly delusional and masochistic. So it will be an insane person who saves the world. I don't think it will be me. Actually, I *know* it won't be me. I am crazy enough, but I am not pure enough. In my heart I sometimes try to be, but in my mind it is impossible. Maybe I'm lucky for that. 'Nothing is more difficult than to be simple.' I am complicit and odd. I am full of phobias, neuroses, louche tastes, and lurid fantasies. I am not a *soteria*. All I can do is try. Depression has stolen from me my right and duty to try, now I am taking it back. I am still depressed, but no longer to the extent I have been for years, to the point where I wasn't human. We all, sane and insane alike, are obligated to *try* to save the world. It is the only obligation that's real, the only one that's truly compulsory, and the only one that actually means something.

"And are we always doomed to fail in carrying out this obligation? I honestly don't think so. The only reason we have failed so far is not enough people have accepted the obligation, due to that damned learned helplessness which is the biggest load of bullshit white men have ever come up with to keep people compliant. Don't listen to that hopeless bilge. It's a lie.

"I think of some of my favorite musicians. Rachmaninoff, Bartok, Erik Satie. I used to listen to them mostly when I was depressed, and even though it wasn't my own work, even though *I* wasn't the one who wrote the music, it still felt like I was engaging in some kind of creative sublimation. It felt like I could write something like that. And, though it didn't totally erase the sorrow, it eased it like an opiate. I listened to this music and felt like I had comrades, that this suffering of mine, though rare, wasn't implicitly unique, therefore, I wasn't as alone as I felt. Great artists can do that. They can help you even after they're dead, and in that way they're still alive. Sometimes they were dead before you were even born and they can still help you. These people who never met me and can have no idea that I've ever existed sometimes know me better than anyone. For people of a certain sad but dream like disposition, the dead can actually help more than the living. And I am of that disposition. But it isn't enough anymore to just listen to this music and read these books. I have to make some of my own. These dead people I cannot help the way they helped me, their struggle is over, they have nothing left but the beauty of their own work. But maybe I can help others in the same way. Maybe I can be that dead person who gets some weirdo with a similar and proscribed disposition to mine through the week. To leave an impact like that, one that can outlast you, it's all I want to do. All I want to do is help people even after I'm dead. That's the only graceful immortality, the only one that isn't agonizing."

Lilith removed herself from the typewriter. For a moment she felt like it and she had become indistinguishable, that she was attached to it to the point that it had become another limb, and she would not be able to extricate herself from it. It wasn't a bad feeling.

She knew by now that even as the psychosis was waning, she would still wake up depressed every day. If she didn't sit down at the typewriter and get even the most exiguous amount of writing done, the day would be unbearable. This way, getting the words down first thing in the morning, would make it possible to endure. But if she didn't, if she succumbed to that hopeless thing in her mind that wanted her to be nothing, it wouldn't be. She had to write every day now, before doing anything else, before even going outside, because each morning it was what prepared her for the world, defended her against it.

Like Laura, she was also the unfortunate energumen of two equal but opposite forces. Everyone is. The writing was what made her able to make sense of both of them, and even to appease them. She could speak openly and freely about her desire to die, and that made it go away for a little while. It was no different than talking to a therapist, but one that wasn't wearing a mask. She could even speak about her more secret desire to live, and it reaffirmed this wish that she was often afraid to speak of, because it was so fleeting. She was frightened if she talked about it it would leave for good. One day it probably would, but she hoped it wouldn't be until she was old enough to die anyway.

But maybe she would get lucky. Maybe she would never get tired of writing and this would make her always want to live *sotto voce*, subliminally, underneath the more obvious threshold of her mind that wanted to die. It is always a contradiction when a person like Lilith, who upon first sight always appears dead, picks up an enduring passion. It is an act of a person who was born without faith having to suddenly act *sole fide*, on faith alone, and *sans peur*, without fear, this person who is neurotically afraid of everything.

But everything is a paradox, because everything is within the delimitations of time, which is also a paradox. Walking paradoxes, all trying to make sense of themselves, to reify themselves, to become whole in a body that is operated by a mind that splits everything in two. It's maddening, but that is the quest of being a human.

The staff wouldn't let her walk on the grounds anymore, because of the flowers, but she would often sneak out at night to do it anyway. Until that time she would just have to make daylight and the ward interesting, something she was surprisingly good at. She suddenly found a way to make everything interesting, as she had discovered at last, everything *is* interesting. She was suddenly in the grips of an incredible, all devouring curiosity. She read rabidly. She was curious about everything, whereas before she had only been curious about nothing. This curiosity for nothing of course would not go away, but when you see nothing in everything, it is easy to satiate it without death.

Even the staff at Gymnopedie thought she was doing a lot better, and it was rumored that she would be able to go home soon. Of course, Lilith didn't have a home to go to. She was living with that man who had found her trying to put a rope around her neck then abandoned her. I've never understood it, but people find it particularly easy to abandon the hopeless. I think they're afraid of them, afraid of people like Lilith and Laura, and even me, though we all three are essentially harmless. I wonder why. They are frightened of us when we do have hope, as well, perhaps even more so then.

But the staff were trying to help her find a place to live if they did set her loose. A halfway house type of deal. It was better than nothing, and truthfully, it was probably better than living with a boyfriend, as well. Lilith was trying not to think of Mel, which was difficult considering he gave her the typewriter. But she was forcing herself to fall out of love with him. She realized, if she was going to get better, she would have to be alone to do it. Some people that is the only way they can grow sane again. Besides, it's not particularly healthy to fall in love with your psychiatrist. She wanted a healthy, normal romance, which was hard to achieve because even if she did become healthy, she would still never be normal. And it was odd. She really didn't like sex at all. Yet she was a nymphomaniac.

It is maddening to want something you don't even really desire, and to want it all the time, even while knowing that if you get it, it will not satisfy you. You will only need more of it. It is filling yourself with emptiness, and knowingly, too. It was making sex, an act of creation, an act of self- destruction. This is an easy thing to do, particularly when sex isn't your preferred method of creation. And now this aspect of it, of creation, the aspect that had always made her uneasy, was forbidden her. She could *not* create that way anymore. She almost wanted to thank *Il medico della peste* that had sterilized her. It was a choice she would have made herself, if she were allowed to make choices.

But she couldn't help but wonder, what if? What if one day she got lonely enough to want a child? She tried not to think about it. She just wanted to get to the point where she wasn't so lonely that she always craved sex with people she didn't even like. Maybe that was the only reason she had fallen in love with Mel. Maybe he was just a good friend, but since she knew no other way to get close to someone, and particularly a man, she wanted to have sex with him. She should have known better. Maybe she would feel close to someone while she was fucking them, but as soon as it was over she felt like she inhabited a different planet entirely from the world they lived in: The real world, supposedly, the world of the sane. The only way she knew how to abate loneliness made her feel lonelier.

Thank God for the typewriter. This would make it easier. She could convert it into a sexual object, into an animal need, and then not feel that lonely anymore, so lonely to fall drunk into the arms of a stranger. This typewriter, it would be her id, her ego, and her superego all at once, as it carried within it forbidden memories of a man who she honestly had loved. It wasn't just the urge to feel close to nothing. Not that time.

She knew this, but she didn't want to admit it out loud, or even on paper, her ascribed place to admit things she was too cowardly to say to the people who had inspired them. She had told Mel that she loved him, though. At least she had done that. But she was too late when she had met him, and at the time he was wearing a mask. She probably was, too. She was probably playing the role of the sexy disturbed girl whose insanity made her a vixen in bed. That wasn't who she really was, that was what men had made her, though really she didn't want to be that person at all. She wanted to relax and be as bad in bed as she pleased. She didn't want to have to put on a show, even while she was making love. And in the end it never mattered, anyway. They still left you, once they tired of the persona they themselves made you put on.

She went to the dining room to get a cup of coffee. She felt exhausted, and she had only just woken up. The poor girl. She knew the planet she inhabited was in crisis, but she didn't know how to help. She had the instinct to be good, but not the skill. The only way she knew how to comfort other people was the only way she knew how to comfort herself, with the stupid words on paper, but it always fell short. It only ever helped her. It didn't help anyone else, who didn't even want to read it. This was the only way she knew how to assist the needs of a dying planet, and it wasn't enough.

Laura was doing well until one day she of course she woke up psychotic, in spite of the fact that she really was trying to stay on the medication, and had even found a routine to balance her life with the productivity she now found she needed, as long as it was autotelic, as long as it wasn't the obligations other people forced upon her, but the ones that actually mattered to her. She woke up every day at seven o clock in the morning, to drink coffee and watch the BBC World News. She didn't know why, but it comforted her. It shouldn't have, though. The news of the world is always bad news, but she found it felt good to do something even moderately intellectual when she woke up, so she could remind herself who she was in case she had forgotten in her sleep. Sometimes she really did.

She was having bad dreams again. Nightmares were something she had dealt with her entire life, but it was better than auditory hallucinations. She could deal with it. She did wish there was a medicine you could take to stop it, but she realized that life was a game of compromises, of having to be loyal to the lesser evil, if you're lucky enough to find one. Nightmares were better than hallucinations. It was a trade off her mind had made without her, but she realized it was doing it for its own good, thereby, her own good as well. Still she woke up one day not sure who she was, if she was anybody, and even with having a nightmare only minutes before, it had followed her into the daytime, in the form of schizophrenia.

She still tried. She watched the BBC news and today it seemed horrifying. Perhaps she was too awake. She went to work and thought several people shouted the word "fag" to her on the way, but she ignored them. She kept walking to work even though as she was walking she felt like she was going to topple over. She was wearing sunglasses even though it wasn't that bright outside, because even a little bit of sunlight she thought might make her blind forever. She felt like she wasn't walking, but was being dragged by invisible forces through hell.

When she got to work it was only her and David that day. For some reason she felt frightened of David, who was actually a good friend. She had always been a little frightened of men, though, and the psychosis exacerbated that fear, as it did all fears. That's where it takes root in your brain and starts to derange you, in whatever part of the mind feels fear. Then it makes you afraid of everything, particularly other people, and even the ones you know well. This is why schizophrenics withdraw so heavily. Maybe it is paranoid mistrust, but mostly it is a social panic. Laura thought David wanted to murder her.

She wouldn't walk near him as he was holding the knife to cut the large mounds of dough. She kept inching towards the phone in case she had to call the police. Oddly enough, she didn't feel afraid. She felt like she could outsmart him, that she could outsmart all men. This, of course, was something they would never forgive her for.

"You're acting a little strange today," David said. "Are you taking your medication?"

"Yes," she said hollowly. She wasn't lying this time. Sometimes the chemicals in the pills that counteracted with the chemicals in her head, the privation of dopamine, were too late. When her mind decided to revolt against itself there was nothing to stop it, no amount of love, or writing, or medicine could save her at that point. She cut the dough stoically, keeping her eyes on David and the phone.

Eventually David got fed up. "You're not taking your fucking medication!" he roared.

"Yes, I am," she protested weakly.

"Go home!" he yelled. "Don't come back until you've sorted yourself out. You have to get out of this funk."

Laura barely repressed the urge to roll her eyes. This is the least helpful thing you can say to a person who's going crazy, "you have to get out of this funk." It doesn't offer ways you can do this or even a *reason* to. She went home as David instructed, and she was relieved. She had already worked too many days through schizophrenia, and it had visibly worn her down to nothing else but a mere schizophrenic, a mere lunatic, someone who couldn't really hold a job because work like that was intimidating and impossible to feel devotion towards.

David wouldn't let Laura walk home by herself, though. He was sometimes rough in the way he spoke to her, and he was prone to bouts of anger, but he did care about the girl. It wasn't his fault he didn't say the right things. Really, no one did, because no one had even the slightest idea of what was happening inside her, though they could see visibly it was terrifying, but they knew even less to help her than she, in her illogical state, knew how to help herself. And Laura was tired of tough love. It didn't seem like love at all anymore.

Roland, the owner of Roland's pizza, took her home. He was Anna's grandfather, and sometimes Laura would call him grandpa herself, because he knew she and his granddaughter had been lovers and he didn't care, unlike her actual grandfather, the priest, whom if she told would probably disavow her. Not like he talked to her much anyway. As Roland dropped her off she could see the concern in his face. Genuine concern, the kind of concern you only feel for a member of your family. She hugged him and called him grandpa as she left.

When she got home it was unbearable to be alone, but she didn't even notice. She was alone so often, and had gotten so used to it that she didn't realize when the time came to try to be with other people. She turned on PBS. The pope was on. The narrator was speaking of the pattern of child molestation in the Vatican, and how shocked the pope was to find this out. He was blessing thousands of priests, all of them gay. He was declaring that homosexuality was no longer a sin.

Laura didn't know what else to do. She fell to her knees and started weeping. It was the kind of weeping you engage in when suddenly a great burden you weren't even consciously aware of has been lifted off your mind that is exhausted from repressing it for so long. It took her so long to admit to herself she was bisexual, and even longer to admit it to other people. She realized now it was because of the religious element in her family, the grandfather who was a priest. She had been raised her whole life to believe the person she was born as naturally is an unforgiveable sin. She didn't believe in God, but it is hard to get rid of the lies they tell you about yourself when you're a child. Laura wept because this was all over now. She could tell her father and grandfather that she was no longer a sinner, that if there was a God, He didn't hate her for having loved a woman. She wept with joy, relief, and gratitude.

She hadn't felt this happy in a long time. Never in her life, actually. She watched the gay priests getting blessed by the Pope, and as the aspergillum shook small drops of water on each of their heads, they were weeping as well, the same tears of incredible relief, at having lived to see a day that was foretold to never come. Laura had never felt this way before. She felt like praying.

Then it was all over. PBS didn't seem to know the magnitude of what it had just shown. Maybe the pope didn't either. The only people who did were probably gay people themselves. PBS then skipped over to a segment about Putin trying to steal a work of art. Immediately Laura's bliss faded, as she remembered there were still tyrants in this world. She remembered that in Putin's Russia, it was a crime to be gay. She remembered that Hitler had stolen works of art, as well. She remembered both Hitler and Putin wanted to kill the gay men who had just been blessed by the pope. She cried more, no longer of overwhelming relief, but now of overwhelming dismay. In the 60s the pope had also said that Jews were no longer to be held responsible for the death of Jesus, but still people declaimed vehemently that they were. The Vatican does a good thing once every fifty years or so, and religious people all over the world ignore it. They didn't observe that the Jews hadn't killed Jesus and now they probably wouldn't observe that being gay is no longer a sin. People like Putin certainly wouldn't. Her father wouldn't either.

Laura kept watching, though. Learning was difficult, because the things you learn are so cruel and deranged, but she still liked it for what she thought might be a noble reason, though there was still an element of masochism in it, like there was in almost everything she did. Her high school history teacher told her "history is happening every day." At the time she heard that she found it exciting, but now she found it horrifying. "History is repeating itself every day," was what he had meant to say.

The television showed a close up of the painting Putin was trying to steal. It was a Michelangelo, or a Davinci, I'm not sure which, though. It was a painting of a woman. Laura winced when she felt the woman looked like her. "Is this my fate?" she asked herself. "To be filched by a tyrant?" She didn't even feel the thrill one is supposed to feel when they realize there are elements of themselves that are a work of art. What happens to works of art? They get corrupted by time and opinions in spite of their God like immortality.

The thoughts were running so dangerously fast through her head that it was hard to make sense of what was happening on the television screen. Perhaps she was imagining the whole thing. They started talking about Marc Chagall. Laura tried to pay attention. She liked Marc Chagall. He was a Jewish painter, and one of his paintings, "The Fiddler," was the inspiration for Fiddler on the Roof. Putin was trying to steal his work, too. As if Marc Chagall hadn't been through enough. During World War II his paintings were banned for their appreciation of the Jewish culture. As if it is a crime to appreciate your own culture. Laura had been born in Germany, then came to the United States. Neither of these cultures did she feel any pride in. Their histories were too ignominious.

She thought her fate was being played before her eyes on the television screen, that even though she was no longer a sinner it wouldn't offer her any protection from elements of the world that have always wanted to destroy her, and so far were successful. The documentary on Putin and the artwork ended quickly. Time was going too fast again. Now a baseball game was on PBS, and Laura thought everyone at the game would be able to see her through the TV. She ran to the kitchen and hid behind the refrigerator. Que William's voice: "See how humble my wife is," he said.

Laura whimpered behind the refrigerator. "Go away," she said. "I don't love you anymore. I never loved you. I love George."

"Oh, sweetheart, you don't love him either."

"I only wish that were true," she spat back.

"Don't hide behind the refrigerator," William responded coaxingly. "No one's watching you. Just me." Then a knock on the door. It was Laura's father. She didn't want to talk to him right now. She thought he was one of the Nazis that were after her.

"You can't come in!" she screamed from behind the refrigerator.

"Why not?"

"I just want to be left alone!"

Her father then marched down the stairs angrily. It sounded like goose stepping. She crawled out from behind the fridge once she heard his car leave. She was out of cigarettes, but she was too frightened to leave the house to get more. It was sad. It was a beautiful day, but she couldn't leave the apartment again. She just smoked all the butts in the ashtray, and turned off the TV so no strangers could see her through it. She put on music instead, loud music. This calmed her down for a moment until her entire family came back and started knocking on the door.

"Please. For the love of God. Leave me alone."

"We're worried about you, Laura," her mother yelled through the door. "You only push people away like this when you're sick!"

"Bullshit," Laura muttered to herself. "I push people away all the time."

"Let us in!"

"GO THE HELL AWAY!"

Suddenly she heard her younger brother's voice. "Laura, can I come in?" he asked with trepidation.

She paused. "Yes."

Jason, her younger brother walked in. "What's going on?"

"Mom and Dad are Nazis and they're trying to kill us!" she screamed.

"Laura, I think you need to go back to the hospital."

"Are mom and dad making you say that?'

"NO! YOU REALLY ARE CRAZY!"

Laura pushed him out the door and slammed it behind him. "GO THE FUCK AWAY! ALL OF YOU!"

They goose stepped down the stairs again, but they didn't leave. They just stood outside of her apartment building and discussed what to do next. Laura waited for about half an hour and they still wouldn't leave, so Laura opened the window and started shouting at them.

"GET THE FUCK AWAY FROM MY HOUSE! I WANT TO BE FUCKING LEFT ALONE!"

"My God!" Laura's mother shouted. "She's going to jump out of the window!"

Laura groaned and sat back down on her couch, away from the window she actually had no plans to jump out of, and smoked another butt. Still her family would not leave. She went back to the window, though she shouldn't have. A large group of police were there now, walking towards her. She opened the window to point at her family in the corner, trying to tell them to get rid of them, but the policeman instead held an intimidating finger up to her. Then a knock on the door. This time Laura answered, because she realized she had no choice.

Twelve police officers came in, including the female officer who had tased her. Laura sat down. "You have to come with us," one of the officers said.

"Where are you going to take me?"

"The hospital."

"No, please." Her lip quivered and tears fell rapidly down her eyes.

"Come with me," the officer said again.

"Please don't tase me."

"We won't if you come peacefully."

Laura nodded her head, continuing to cry, as she followed the officer out. She came to the door of her apartment, where the other eleven cops were standing. Laura looked at the woman who had tased her. "You go first," she said. All the officers made to grab for their guns, but the head officer, the one who had talked to Laura, motioned to them to listen to her, to leave out of the door first. They collectively groaned as if they were disappointed, but followed orders, the only thing they knew how to do, and that is why they're so violent. After they left Laura exited with the head officer, who was holding her hand as if she were a child who might easily get lost.

Once they got to the police car he patted her down gently, to make sure she was carrying no weapons, and then told her to get in the back seat, behind the bars. This time at least they didn't handcuff her. Before she got in she looked at her family. Her father and brother looked anxious, while her mother was wailing in overly dramatic tears.

She flipped them off before she got into the police car.

At the general hospital they told her she would have to go back to Gymnopedie.

"Please," Laura begged. "Take me anywhere else. I'll go to rehab or something, anything but Gymnopedie, please."

"You have no choice," the nurse droned on. "You've been pink slipped again."

"Please," Laura said again, on the verge of tears for the second time of the day. "I've already been there five times, each time against my will."

"You have no choice," the nurse said again and left.

Laura didn't bother to hold it back anymore. She sobbed at an incredible volume, until the nurse came flying back in.

"Please, keep it down, Laura!" she said. "You're disturbing the other patients!"

"Then don't force me to go back to Gymnopedie!"

"Doctor!" the nurse yelled. The doctor came in with a syringe full of Halidol.

Laura squirmed so they couldn't inject it in her arm, meanwhile screaming, "NO! NOT HALIDOL, PLEASE!"

"You have no choice," the doctor said, and he violently grabbed her IV and pumped the drug through it.

"I'M JUST GOING TO SOB EVEN LOUDER!" she screamed. "YOU CAN'T FUCKING SILENCE ME EVERY TIME I BECOME AN INCONVENIENCE!"

The doctor left, ignoring Laura, but on his way out she heard him whisper to the nurse, "if she continues to make a scene, just give her more Halidol."

Once they loaded her up in the ambulance, Laura had ceased to cry. She was exhausted of crying and resigned without dignity to her fate again, as she had been doing the entire year. She looked out of the window of the ambulance. It was a gorgeous day, and she had spent all of it inside cowering, hiding from something, though she herself didn't know any longer what she was hiding from. She was starting to realize it wasn't worth it, though, this hiding. It seemed to bring her more directly to the thing she feared.

The EMT assaulted her with her usual slew of questions about her health and history. Laura looked at her and noticed she was actually quite pretty. It had been so long since she'd been with a woman, she was beginning to miss it. She tried to get the EMT to feel some sympathy for her, and thereby even like her.

"It's such a beautiful day out," she half moaned, half spoke, and half histrionically. "I just wanted to go outside today."

The beautiful EMT paused. "Then why didn't you?"

People are particularly hostile to you when you're insane.

Chapter Xl

A knock on the door. To Lilith's great surprise and relief it was Benjy. They embraced rapidly but with warmth, hoping no one saw them as Lilith quickly snuck him into her room.

"I hear you're going home in a month," Benjy said with a solemn, but appreciative sorrow. It was obvious he was happy for her.

"Yes."

"I just wanted to say goodbye. If we get caught we'll surely be put in confinement, but I had to say goodbye. You're the most interesting person on this ward, besides maybe Nijinsky."

Lilith hung her head. "Yes. He didn't even speak and still he was so interesting."

"I think it was actually *because* he didn't speak," Benjy said, laughing softly.

"Yea."

"Do you miss him?"

"Very much. He was the truest friend I ever had."

"Do you miss me?"

Lilith smiled. "Yes, Benjy," she said. "You were the truest *lover* I ever had."

"But which one matters more, in the end."

Lilith paused, hoping not to hurt Benjy's feelings when she said softly through bared teeth, but with conviction, "the friend."

Benjy laughed again. He didn't mind. "You're right," he said. "Friendship lasts a lot longer. That's why I'm glad you and I were always friends first."

Lilith smiled and gave Benjy a quick kiss on the cheek. "We're young, though," she said gravely. "And when you're young everyone in your life is transitory, friends and lovers alike. That's the worst part of youth. Nothing stays consistent."

"But isn't that the thrill of it?" Benjy said with a wry smile.

Lilith shrugged. "I don't know. I was born old, so I've always craved consistency. Being young has never made sense to me."

Benjy smiled still and put his arms around her. "Poor girl," she said. "I can understand that. Being a woman has never made sense to me."

"How do we get born in the wrong time and in the wrong bodies? Why does nature let that happen?"

"Maybe nature is just as confused as everyone else."

"Or blind."

Benjy chuckled and removed his arms from her, giving her a grin of affection. "Who knows?" he said. "Maybe God is blind."

Now Lilith laughed. "Yes, that would make sense."

"It does make sense," Benjy said stoically. "That's why you and me are locked up in this hell hole, because people are afraid we actually make *too much sense.*"

Lilith paused and thought about this. "Yes," she said. "Maybe we're not mad enough, and that's why they call us mad. I know you're not mad, anyway. Some people really do get born in the wrong body."

Benjy smiled. "And I know you're not mad, either, because you say things like that." He gestured broadly to the walls of Gymnopedie State Mental hospital. "It's this place that's mad. I'm glad you're getting out of it. You don't belong here. You're smarter than all of us."

"No I'm not."

"Yes, you are. You know you are, too. No need to try to be humble about it."

Lilith laughed. "Okay. I'm glad I'm getting out, too, but I'm nervous, as well. I'll be living alone. I've never lived alone before."

"I have," Benjy said reassuringly. "It's good for crazy people, I think."

"I could see that."

A nurse knocked on the door, and Benjy quickly hid under the bed. "Come in," Lilith said waveringly.

The nurse walked in. "Were you talking to someone?"

"No," she said. "I wrote a play, and I was reading the lines aloud to myself, see how they sounded." Lilith was impressed with herself for the lie.

"That's good," the nurse said. "I do hope when you get out you publish."

"Me too."

"Well, I was just checking on you. Carry on." The nurse left and Benjy crawled out from under the bed.

"That was close," he said. "I better go, but it was good to talk to you again. I missed you. You and Nijinsky, out of everyone on the ward, were always the kindest to me." He paused. "I'm sorry about what happened to him."

Lilith sighed. "Yea, me too. I want to be like Christian and kill a doctor."

"You'll never get out of here if you do."

Laura was wheeled into the Observation Unit, or "The Acute Ward," as she kept calling it, and she groaned when she saw the narrow hallways, plastic chairs, windowless rooms, and the nurses station behind bullet proof glass. She didn't understand why she was here again. She didn't understand why she had been there the first time, either. She hadn't hurt anyone either time, not even herself. She got the feeling that these social workers and doctors and police officers got kind of a power thrill off being able to throw people in here. It's odd, the way people seem to get a pleasant adrenaline rush from condemning someone. And to be condemned for insanity is so stupid, because really most of the time it means nobody any harm. The insane people who do want to hurt you hold political office, Laura thought.

They took her off the gurney and sat her on one of the plastic chairs. A social worker came in. "This is the sixth time you've been in here, Laura," she said, almost admonishingly.

"I was informed that I have no choice."

The social worker softened a little bit. "What happened?"

"I had another bad day at work. They sent me home and I still wasn't feeling that great, but my family came and bombarded me, and that just made it worse."

"They said you were going to jump out of the window."

Laura groaned. "I wasn't going to jump out of the fucking window. I don't want to kill myself anymore, I really don't."

"Have you ever tried to kill yourself?"

"Yes," she admitted, and an incredible swell of relief came over her, not quite the relief she felt when it seemed like the pope had blessed her, but it was the next best thing. This was the first time she had owned up to the fact that she had tried to take her life, three times now. She felt clean for the first time in years.

"Once?"

"Three times."

"How did you try to do it all three times?"

"First I overdosed on alcohol and pills. Then I overdosed on pills and tried to slit my wrists. The third time I tried to throw myself in front of a car."

"Yes," the social worker agreed tiredly. "It says here you had two antipsychotic overdoses, but that you denied you were trying to kill yourself each time."

"Did you guys really believe me?"

The social worker laughed. "No, Laura."

"Have you ever read The Idiot?" Laura suddenly asked.

"No. I've heard of it."

"I've read it twice. I really like it. I wrote a poem about it."

"What did your poem say?"

"You get to see the idiot burn…"

"Is that how you feel? Like you're burning?"

"Yes, and that everyone is watching me do it. They're watching me, but they're not trying to help me out of the fire."

"Your family does want to see you better…"

"I know they do, but they're still watching me burn. They're not getting me out of the fire. I think they probably must feel just as helpless as I do. No one's going to help me. I'll have to get out of the damn thing myself. "

"We will try to help you. Now, speaking of your writing, last time you stayed here you wrote a short story that was very dark…"

"Most of the stories in the bible are dark, too. Everyone forgets that. Everyone forgets that religion is actually very dark."

"Are you religious?"

"In my own way."

"The doctor kept the story in your file for observation. He said it was a little bit concerning."

"I don't know," Laura shrugged. "It made me feel better. It was about me and my boyfriend."

Laura remembered the story. It was Dystopian Sci Fi, like most of her stories. It was about two people who worked for population control, with orders to murder random people officially, a kind of law enforcement agency. Then, two of these workers fell in love with one another. Then they got orders to kill each other, and they ignored the order for as long as they could, but there were chips in their head that forced them to follow orders. It ends with them shooting each other simultaneously.

"It was a very dark story," the social worker said again.

"Honestly, my relationship *is* pretty dark," she said. This was another thing she knew to be true that she hadn't spoken out loud yet. This relationship of hers, it was just like a suicide attempt.

"How is your relationship dark?"

"It's hard to explain. We love each other to the point of madness and then we don't give a damn about each other at the same time. We have no emotional interest in one another, but somehow we're still in love."

"That does sound hard. I have other patients to talk to, but I'll see you again soon. I'm building your case file. Goodbye, Laura."

"Goodbye."

The social worker left and Laura went to her room. She didn't have any books with her, so she drew. It felt good. This felt good no matter where she was. George couldn't take that away from her. She wouldn't let him. She had let him take her sanity almost willingly, then gave him her will to live, until now, when she realized she needed them more than not only George, but any lover at all. She could still love him without having to sacrifice all that she was. You do have to sacrifice a lot for love when you want it to endure, but if you sacrifice your own soul for it, you yourself will die. She realized this now. George had almost killed her. Love had almost killed her, and in spite of what the poets say, that is not a nice way to die.

Lilith put the flowers on the graves. No one tried to stop her now. It was raining and the church bell was going off with the same fury it did when Andre had hanged himself off it, howling with the same menacing velocity, as large drops of rain fell off it like beads of sweat. The bells were in hell, too. Every hell has a church.

Lilith liked the rain. It made her feel clean and dirty at the same time, as if she was some kind of sacred sinner, and nature had made her that way because it was the most natural thing in the world. Maybe we are all sacred sinners. Maybe we are both guilty and innocent, and that's the most natural thing in the world. Maybe that's just what being self –aware does to you- it makes you know you're guilty but in that recognition you also become innocent, sanctifying yourself. It's hell and heaven at the same time.

Lilith was going home in three weeks. She would live in a

house on the grounds, so she could still go to Nijinsky's grave, whichever one it was, whenever she liked. She wasn't going to try to find him ,though, and she wasn't going to try to find Mel, either. They had both cared about her, but she knew they were happier where they were, Mel with his wife, and Nijinsky with the worms. It had been nice of them to stay as long as they did. But everyone has to leave eventually. No one can stay in the same place forever. Even the people who die in Gymnopedie leave for the ground. No one asks to come into this world, the non- existent know better than that. The existent don't.

And it's strange. I see no discernible difference between reason and unreason. Both are self- aware, but only just so. It's like how they say we can't travel backwards in time because there would be too many paradoxes, but I think there are just as many paradoxes moving forward in time, as well, just different paradoxes, paradoxes that are easier to adjust to. That's the real madness.

Laura again made friends at Gymnopedie. One man about her age who she could her screaming all night because he still had nightmares about his Girlfriend's death. A girl who had dissociative identity disorder, who was bisexual also and loved Iggy Pop as much as she did. She was fun to flirt with. A boy who was the top chef at a Chinese restaurant, who really seemed pretty normal. He flirted with her. And really none of them seemed insane to Laura. Maybe because she was insane herself, but she felt the only crime any of them had committed was being unlike other people. And that shouldn't be a crime, but it is. It gets you locked up for anywhere from two weeks to ninety days in Gymnopedie. They tried to keep Laura in there for ninety days this time, for three months, but they decided she was stabilizing faster than they thought she would. Again she promised to herself that this would be the last time she would be in this hell hole, even though it was nice being around nice people to flirt with who were like her, being unlike other people.

And she realized what people really hate about the insane, which gave her a one up on them, because they don't even know themselves. People are threatened by the insane because they realize we have something they don't, and something important, too. We are real people living lives of our own instead of actors stiffly playing either tragic or comic roles. Most people pretend to be happy, a few pretend to be sad, but the vast majority of people are neither. The insane are a little bit of both, and *genuinely* so. It's not something we have to practice. It seems to come out before we ourselves are even aware of it.

And Laura was coming to the sad truth about George. He was a character without an author, too. He was pretending to be sad. He was pretending to be in love. He was something out of his own comic books, and though he invented himself, he was still not real. He was just like any other man.

And still she loved him. She had loved him for so long now it had become another self- destructive habit. It was no different than drinking or smoking, she wanted to do it until it killed her. The only difference was that she didn't have deep feelings for the cigarette or the glass of wine. This only made it worse, more addictive and more deleterious, and harder to come down from.

But it was almost over. She could have herself back soon, just probably without any of her old emotions.

In a week she was let out of the observation unit. They hadn't given her much Halidol this time, which was nice. Laura had lost her job, though, and she felt anxious about this, not knowing how she was going to pay for her apartment or food or anything one needs to stay alive. It's a terrible choice they leave you with. You must choose between either sanity or food. Still, she was glad she hadn't ended up staying in that damn place forever like she almost thought she would. She was too young to stay always in one place like that already. This was probably why her and George were disintegrating, as well, although they had initially wanted to stick with each other until the end, but that was the most comfortably unrealistic idea they'd ever come up with together. Laura was too young for it, and George was too much of a *puer aeternus*.

He came to visit her, though, a final, but mute and ineffectual goodbye, in a way. He could have visited her in the observation unit, but her parents were too embarrassed by it, and had told him she wasn't allowed to have visitors there. Laura's birthday was coming up, and she was trying to get out before that. She didn't want to spend her twenty third birthday in a mental hospital. She wanted to spend it with George. She wanted this final, but mute and ineffectual goodbye to last for as long as she could make it last. It's strange how we tend to idealize things that we know deep in our hearts shouldn't be idealized - how if we didn't wrongly ascribe a sense of poetry to them, we would see they're actually horrifying, and that there is nothing poetic about them. Laura tried to think that this couldn't be broadly attributed to love itself, but it certainly described the love she had earned for herself, that she had worked so hard to keep together even as it was always ripping at the seams. She could tell George felt a bit put out when he had seen her.

That night one of her friends was shipped off to the observation unit. Apparently she had tried to strangle herself. She did it because they were sending her home tomorrow, and at home there was nothing, no one, not even a damn cat, just an empty house filled with neuroses, a boring and daily death. At least at Gymnopedie there were people to talk to you, the only people she had ever met in her life that would listen to her without judgment.

Laura at last realized, that though times for her were dark and difficult right now, she was incredibly lucky to have the luxury to hate Gymnopedie.

The next day she went on trial, in the hospital. Apparently if you are involuntarily hospitalized two times in a month you have to go to trial, as if you've committed a crime. In Lilith's time, beings insane was immoral, today it is a crime if you do it too much.

First a psychologist talked to her. Lilith made sure to speak articulately and clearly, proving at least that if she was insane, at least she wasn't stupid. The psychologist told her he felt she was stable enough to leave the hospital right now. Then a lawyer came into her room and talked to her. He said at this point if she disregarded the hospital's treatment method she would go to jail. If she left the hospital now, as the psychologist thought she was well enough to do, she would go to jail. See, in modern mental hospitals they tell you if you're an adult you can leave whenever you want, but it's not true. They make you sign a consent to treatment form, which basically means you're at their mercy, and they say signing this form is voluntary, but it's not either. They force you to sign that, as well, while attempting to make you believe you still have free will. Mental hospitals have progressed amazingly through the years! In Lilith's day, the patients were treated like prisoners, and today they are treated like children!

Then they took her into "the activity room" with a group of lawyers and doctors who talked about Laura's case like she wasn't sitting in the room with them. It was very quick. The lawyers rapidly spit out some legal jargon Laura could only half understand, then someone banged a rubber gavel and it was all over.

"What just happened?" Laura asked her social worker after she half- heartedly shook the lawyer's and doctor's hands in a daze.

"You're fine," was all the social worker said. "You're not going to jail because you followed the treatment plan…"

"But that doctor said he thought I was fine."

"Still, you can't leave."

"Can I get out of here before my birthday?"

"I'll try to get that done for you. Now, later today you have that meeting with your parents. We can't let you go until we've done that."

"Fine," Laura said, "but just so you know that's going to be more like going on trial than this ever was."

Laura patiently waited in her room for the social worker and her parents. The girl she had attached herself to had given her a fake cigarette that she could imagine she was smoking to deal with what she knew would be an absurd *batrachomyomachia,* and she kept pounding on the nicotine patch on her arm so it might kick in. She drew as she waited for them. She was drawing a picture for the girl who had given her the fake cigarette, as a thank you gift. As her parents and the social worker walked in she continued to draw and pretended to smoke, almost ignoring them.

"Hello, Laura," her mother said.

"Hello," Laura said back stiffly, and all of them sat around her like some ridiculous Last Supper, where she was not Christ but all of them were Judas.

The social worker gathered up her papers. "So," the social worker said. "You didn't plan on jumping out of the window?"

"No."

"But you have tried to kill yourself before," she asseverated calmly and Laura noticed her father barely stifle a sob. She was amazed. It is all too easy to forget that your parents love you. And she realized now, at last, that even her father did, although there was that large part of her, her bisexuality, that he refused to understand and quietly condemned, he still loved her. And her mother probably loved her, too, almost effusively, it was just a shame that the way she showed it was more often than not controlling and officious. Still, she loved her, she just enjoyed the idea of her being in a mental hospital because it meant she wasn't the only insane person in the family. Suddenly her mother interrupted.

"Honey, what's that in your mouth?"

"A fake cigarette."

Laura's mother looked to the social worker. "Don't you think that's a little delusional?"

The social worker shrugged. "She knows it's fake. Lots of people in here smoke plastic cigarettes, it's really not that uncommon. Now, anyway, what happened to you that day?"

Laura took a drag of pure air off the delusional cigarette and continued. "I got sent home from work because I was acting funny, so when I went home I watched PBS…"

"Yes?"

"And, I don't know, it was all documentaries, so technically I wasn't struggling between fantasy and reality, because it was real…"

"What were the documentaries about?"

"Putin was stealing art, like Hitler used to."

The social worker nodded. "I could see how that upset you. You're an artist."

Laura smiled and finally admitted it. "Yes," she said. "I am."

"But what about her not letting us in the house!" her mother interrupted angrily. "When she gets like this she pushes us away!"

The social worker looked to Laura. "Well," Laura said, "I'll be honest, sometimes you guys stress me out even more. And when you bombard me like that I know it means you're about to send me back here again."

"You need to be here!" her mother interjected.

The social worker stopped her. "She is showing great improvement," she said solemnly. "The first four times she was here she barely said a word, and at least now she's speaking and participating. She wants to get out of here before her Birthday and I think she's ready for that."

"But she won't take her medicine!"

Laura took another long drag off the plastic cigarette.

"She seems to be doing okay to me," her father said.

"Yes, she's stabilized," the social worker said.

"I'll never come back here ever again," Laura proclaimed. "I just won't."

Chapter XII

Laura was sent home two days later, exactly on her Birthday. She hugged all her new friends, and while they said they weren't comfortable enough to keep in contact with her, they would still always be her friends. For this she thanked them, and she understood. She didn't really want to keep in contact with them, either, because it was a reminder of this place, and how sick she had to be to get here six times. Her father came to pick her up and she said goodbye to everyone, last of all Zeir and Arich Anpin, and she even hugged them, whom she had never liked because they'd always frightened her, but now she was coming to terms with them. She had never seen these two leave Gymnopedie, they were permanent residents, but she also got the odd feeling that they weren't just in the hospital, that they were everywhere she went.

Everywhere is a mental hospital.

Lilith grabbed her bags and looked out one last time on the grounds of Gymnopedie State Mental Hospital. It had been seven years now, seven years in a sanatorium away from the real world, as if she were some hapless Hans Castorp, but she couldn't help but think perhaps it wasn't that much different from the real world; it was exactly like the real world but magnified, so you couldn't ignore it. It was just like the real world but the madness was no longer subtle. If she could survive seven years of that, she could certainly survive society, which is just the repressed version of the desperation she had already lived through.

She didn't have many people to say goodbye to, as most of her friends had not survived the isolated, unveiled realism of Gymnopedie. And she wasn't able to see Benjy one last time, either, or Mel. She realized she was never going to see either of them again, and that was probably a good thing. They were a reminder that she had once tried to hang herself, and how she had to pay the price for that. The only people she said goodbye to were Zeir and Arich Anpin, and she felt this was an unnecessary goodbye, for she would surely see them again. They were everywhere.

Everywhere is a mental hospital.

Epilogue

I am Laura. I'm sure you've realized this already, as I've made no attempt to disguise it. The majority of the things that happened to Laura in this novel also happened to me, very few of them are made up, although some of the dialogue I've embellished to try to make the experience seem meaningful to a reader, although the experience wasn't meaningful at all, and particularly not the words spoken during, although, it is true, I rarely spoke back then, and when I did it was with great effort that came out as nothing more than a stifled, blunted affect. Many of the things that happened to me and Laura I've left out, because I was so confused at the time that even now, when I'm relatively sane, I am still too disoriented to describe them, or even to make sense of them. And many more things that happened to me during this time I've been lucky enough to forget.

Laura was released from Gymnopedie State Mental hospital for the last time on July 20th 2014, directly on her Birthday. She never had to go back there again, although her struggles with the illness, what was first major depression with psychotic features, then undifferentiated schizophrenia, then finally bipolar disorder with psychotic features (which is the polite way of saying Bipolar Disorder *and* Schizophrenia) would never end. She got out on her Birthday hopeful that she could spend the day with George, the man she stupidly loved in spite of the fact he was interested in nothing, and not her, either, but he ignored her all day. Shortly after that he left her, in the cowardly fashion that seems to befit the modern man, by simply not responding to her anymore until she "got the hint."

Lilith was let out of Gymnopedie after seven years on the same day, only a couple centuries before. Her story was fiction mixed with research. Essentially, this novel has been a work of fictitious non-fiction. But, more to the point, Lilith didn't have to go back to Gymnopedie, either. She moved on with her life, and so did Laura, and though neither of them would ever be wholly divested of their grief, they would learn to live with it, as well as the tenacious memory of Gymnopedie.

They both learned to think it had been nothing more than a very long headache.